PRACTICAL MAGIC

Alice Hoffman

BERKLEY
New York

BERKLEY
An imprint of Penguin Random House LLC

ISBN: 978-1-64385-722-0

Printed in the United States of America

Cover art by Matt Mahurin
Cover design by Joni Friedman

INTRODUCTION

In the world of *Practical Magic*, lilacs bloom overnight, the real and the magical overlap, and the Owens women have been witches for generations. This novel is an attempt to unlock the secrets of the human heart. What price are we willing to pay for love? How do we recognize and understand our truest selves? How does our past affect our present? Many of us know what it's like to try to escape a family legacy of one sort or another, only to discover that in the long run we carry our heritage with us no matter how far we might run. The Owens family is one in which the women will do anything for each other; they may argue, they may disagree, but they are fiercely devoted to one another.

Witches are outsiders, and those among us who have been bullied and ostracized can relate to their plight. Part of our fascination with witches is that they are the only female mythic figures with power. These are women who don't need to be rescued by a prince or a king but, instead, can save themselves—sometimes with the help of a sister. They are wise and fearless women of courage. In short, they are everything little girls wish to grow up to become. In both *Practical Magic* and its prequel, *The Rules of Magic*, girls are always encouraged to choose courage, and Courage Tea is the aunts' most treasured remedy. *Practical Magic* is the mythic reconfiguration of the journey most women must make, whether they are sisters, mothers, daughters, or aunts.

The Owens women practice magic in the modern world. Sally is the steady older sister who yearns for a "normal" life. Gillian is the wild, unpredictable younger sister who searches out danger. Although they are opposites, each is wary of love, for they have seen lovestruck women come to their aunts for potions and remedies. The original Owens ancestor, Maria Owens, after being abandoned by one of the magistrates at the Salem witch trials, called down a curse upon her family to protect them from the troubles of love. Sally and Gillian know that they carry Maria's curse. Both must fight for love in a world that is more dangerous when you open your heart, but which is also more meaningful and joyful once you do. The sisters can't escape magic any more than they can escape love, and in the end they realize this is a blessing rather than a curse.

TWENTY-FIVE years after its publication, I am delighted to say that *Practical Magic* lives on. Just as there are three generations of women in the novel, the book has been embraced by three generations of readers. I've met daughters and mothers and grandmothers who have shared the novel, and nothing brings me more joy than to know that *Practical Magic* is a family affair. This is a book about magic, but more importantly, it's an ode to sisterhood and family, and to the power of love.

Readers have said that when they return to *Practical Magic* for a second or third reading, they experience the novel in a completely different way than they did the first time around. The meaning of the book changes for them depending on the stage of their life. The family dynamics are complex; and as often happens in our own lives, how we view the people close to us, even when they are fictional characters, depends on where we stand in the world at that time.

Over the years, readers have asked for another novel about the Owens women. My interest in personal history led me to go back in time and write a prequel rather than a sequel. *The Rules of Magic* tells the story of the aunts from *Practical Magic*, Franny and Jet, when they are young and first experience their own magical awakenings. I wanted to explore how Franny and Jet became the wise, beloved aunts in *Practical Magic*. The young Franny is a beautiful red-haired girl, fearless and confident in her powers; the young Jet is wounded in love but still willing to open her heart. The aunts are raised—without any knowledge of their magical family history—in the sixties, a magical and revolutionary time in New York, the time and place I had known as a girl. It was a pleasure to go back to the sixties and discover how the aunts had lived their lives, both magically and practically. It was also a pleasure for me to return to Greenwich Village as a researcher and revisit the landscape of my own youth. The novelist can be the last to know what a novel is about, and I'm often surprised by the turns in my own stories and by the choices my characters make. Franny and Jet's brother, Vincent, has a story that neither he nor I would have predicted, one that is at the heart of *The Rules of Magic*.

I start writing a novel with a question I need answered. *Practical Magic* addresses serious questions about the place of women in our society—questions that are as important, or more so, than they were twenty-five years ago. Unfortunately, over the past quarter century, the place of a woman in society has not moved forward as we had wished, then and now. There are still many of the same issues left to address: equal pay, childcare, healthcare, sexual assault. Magic may not be able to right these wrongs, but sisterhood just might. The years have only intensified the importance of telling women's stories, and doing our best to ensure that women who have been forced to be silent can speak and tell their own truths.

Fortunately, the Owens women spoke to me. It was as if they had walked through the door and all I had to do was chart their histories. I loved magic from the start, beginning with the stories my Russian grandmother told me. If "magic" was in the title of a book, I was bound to find it. In the world of fairy tales, the amazing is recounted in a matter-of fact tone, with the practical and the magical living side by side. One day there is a knock at the door, or a rose that blooms through the winter, or a spindle that must be avoided at all costs. It was the melding of the magical and the everyday that was most affecting to me as a reader, for the world I lived in seemed much the same. People you loved could disappear, through death or divorce; they could turn into heroes or beasts. My personal experience and my childhood reading left me longing for a world in which anything could happen, magic or not, on an ordinary day.

More and more readers have come to feel that magical

literature is the original form of storytelling, including fairy tales, folktales, myth, and modern fiction. If I were to write *Practical Magic* today, I would begin in exactly the same way as I did twenty-five years ago.

For more than two hundred years, the Owens women have been blamed for everything that has gone wrong in town.

There are those who have come to the book after watching the film version of *Practical Magi*c, which has become a much loved cult movie and boasts one of the most exceptional casts of women ever gathered: Sandra Bullock, Nicole Kidman, Stockard Channing, Dianne Wiest, Evan Rachel Wood, Camilla Belle, Chloe Webb, and Margo Martindale. It's a rare film that is so chock-full of interesting female characters who argue, form friendships, hurt one another, and support each other. The film is great fun, but it doesn't avoid the darkness in the story: Gillian's history of abuse resonates, as does Sally's emotional journey of love and loss, which leads her to understand that the only chance for happiness is to be true to herself.

At this writing, I am beginning a third magic book about Maria Owens, *Magic Lessons*, going even further back in time, charting the initial history of the Owens family and their magical abilities. I can't wait for readers to discover the origins of the family, and I can't wait to discover it for myself. The story may surprise me, and I expect it will take on a life of its own, but I know that within it I will find that once upon a time, there was a woman or a girl who was different, who was an outcast, who looked for beauty in the world, who was wounded, who fell in love despite the warnings, who would do anything for her sister or her niece or her daughter or her mother, who knew that despite the dangers, we must fall in love whenever we can.

For every evil under the sun,
There is a remedy, or there is none.
If there be one, seek till you find it;
If there be none, never mind it.

MOTHER GOOSE

PRACTICAL MAGIC

Alice Hoffman

SUPERSTITION

For more than two hundred years, the Owens women have been blamed for everything that has gone wrong in town. If a damp spring arrived, if cows in the pasture gave milk that was runny with blood, if a colt died of colic or a baby was born with a red birthmark stamped onto his cheek, everyone believed that fate must have been twisted, at least a little, by those women over on Magnolia Street. It didn't matter what the problem was—lightning, or locusts, or a death by drowning. It didn't matter if the situation could be explained by logic, or science, or plain bad luck. As soon as there was a hint of trouble or the slightest misfortune, people began pointing their fingers and placing blame. Before long they'd convinced themselves that it wasn't safe to walk past the Owens house after dark, and only the most foolish neighbors would dare to peer over the black wrought-iron fence that circled the yard like a snake.

Inside the house there were no clocks and no mirrors and

three locks on each and every door. Mice lived under the floorboards and in the walls and often could be found in the dresser drawers, where they ate the embroidered tablecloths, as well as the lacy edges of the linen placemats. Fifteen different sorts of wood had been used for the window seats and the mantels, including golden oak, silver ash, and a peculiarly fragrant cherrywood that gave off the scent of ripe fruit even in the dead of winter, when every tree outside was nothing more than a leafless black stick. No matter how dusty the rest of the house might be, none of the woodwork ever needed polishing. If you squinted, you could see your reflection right there in the wainscoting in the dining room or the banister you held on to as you ran up the stairs. It was dark in every room, even at noon, and cool all through the heat of July. Anyone who dared to stand on the porch, where the ivy grew wild, could try for hours to look through the windows and never see a thing. It was the same looking out; the green-tinted window glass was so old and so thick that everything on the other side seemed like a dream, including the sky and the trees.

The little girls who lived up in the attic were sisters, only thirteen months apart in age. They were never told to go to bed before midnight or reminded to brush their teeth. No one cared if their clothes were wrinkled or if they spit on the street. All the while these little girls were growing up, they were allowed to sleep with their shoes on and draw funny faces on their bedroom walls with black crayons. They could drink cold Dr Peppers for breakfast, if that was what they craved, or eat marshmallow pies for dinner. They could climb onto the roof and sit perched on the slate peak, leaning back as far as possible, in order to spy the first star. There they would stay on windy March nights or humid August evenings, whispering, arguing over whether it was feasible for even the smallest wish to ever come true.

The girls were being raised by their aunts, who, as much as they might have wanted to, simply couldn't turn their nieces away. The children, after all, were orphans whose careless parents were so much in love they failed to notice smoke emanating from the walls of the bungalow where they'd gone to enjoy a second honeymoon, after leaving the girls home with a babysitter. No wonder the sisters always shared a bed during storms; they were both terrified of thunder and could never speak above a whisper once the sky began to rumble. When they did finally doze off, their arms wrapped around each other, they often had the exact same dreams. There were times when they could complete each other's sentences; certainly each could close her eyes and guess what the other most desired for dessert on any given day.

But in spite of their closeness, the two sisters were entirely different in appearance and temperament. Aside from the beautiful gray eyes the Owens women were known for, no one would have had reason to guess the sisters were related. Gillian was fair and blond, while Sally's hair was as black as the pelts of the ill-mannered cats the aunts allowed to skulk through the garden and claw at the draperies in the parlor. Gillian was lazy and liked to sleep past noon. She saved up her allowance money, then paid Sally to do her math homework and iron her party dresses. She drank bottles of Yoo-Hoo and ate goopy Hershey's bars while sprawled out on the cool basement floor, content to watch as Sally dusted the metal shelves where the aunts kept pickles and preserves. Gillian's favorite thing in the world to do was to lie on the velvet-cushioned window seat, up on the landing, where the drapes were made of damask and a portrait of Maria Owens, who had built the house so long ago, collected dust in a corner. That's where she could be found on summer afternoons, so relaxed and languid that moths would land on her, mistaking her for a cushion, and proceed to make tiny holes in her T-shirts and jeans.

Sally, three hundred ninety-seven days older than her sister, was as conscientious as Gillian was idle. She never believed in anything that could not be proven with facts and figures. When Gillian pointed to a shooting star, it was Sally who reminded her that what was falling to earth was only an old rock, heated by its descent through the atmosphere. Sally was a take-charge sort of person from the start; she didn't like confusion and mess, both of which filled the aunts' old house on Magnolia Street from attic to cellar.

From the time she was in third grade, and Gillian in second, Sally was the one who cooked healthy dinners of meat loaf and fresh green beans and barley soup, using recipes from a copy of *Joy of Cooking* she'd managed to smuggle into the house. She fixed their lunchboxes each morning, packing up turkey-and-tomato sandwiches on whole-wheat bread, adding carrot sticks and iced oatmeal cookies, all of which Gillian tossed in the trash the instant after Sally had deposited her in her classroom, since she preferred the sloppy joes and brownies sold in the school cafeteria, and she often had swiped enough quarters and dimes from the aunts' coat pockets to buy herself whatever she liked.

Night and Day, the aunts called them, and although neither girl laughed at this little joke or found it amusing in the least, they recognized the truth in it, and were able to understand, earlier than most sisters, that the moon is always jealous of the heat of the day, just as the sun always longs for something dark and deep. They kept each other's secrets well; they crossed their hearts and hoped to die if they should ever slip and tell, even if the secret was only a cat's tail pulled or some foxglove stolen from the aunts' garden.

The sisters might have sniped at each other because of their differences, they might have grown nasty, then grown apart, if they'd been able to have any friends, but the other children in town avoided them. No one would dare to play with the sisters, and most girls and boys crossed their fingers when Sally and Gillian drew near, as if that sort of thing was any protection. The bravest and wildest boys followed the sisters to school, at just the right distance behind, which allowed them to turn and run if need be. These boys liked to pitch winter apples or stones at the girls, but even the best athletes, the ones who were the stars of their Little League teams, could never get a hit when they took aim at the Owens girls. Every stone, each apple, always landed at the sisters' feet.

For Sally and Gillian the days were filled with little mortifications: No child would use a pencil or a crayon directly after it had been touched by an Owens girl. No one would sit next to them in the cafeteria or during assemblies, and some girls actually shrieked when they wandered into the girls' room, to pee or gossip or brush their hair, and found they'd stumbled upon one of the sisters. Sally and Gillian were never chosen for teams during sports, even though Gillian was the fastest runner in town and could hit a baseball over the roof of the school, onto Endicott Street. They were never invited to parties or Girl

Scout meetings, or asked to join in and play hopscotch or climb a tree.

"Fuck them all," Gillian would say, her beautiful little nose in the air as the boys made spooky goblin noises when the sisters passed them in the hallways at school, on the way to music or art. "Let them eat dirt. You wait and see. One day they'll beg us to invite them home, and we'll laugh in their faces."

Sometimes, when she was feeling particularly nasty, Gillian would suddenly turn and shout "Boo," and some boy always pissed in his pants and was far more humiliated than Gillian had ever been. But Sally didn't have the heart to fight back. She wore dark clothes and tried not to be noticed. She pretended she wasn't smart and never raised her hand in class. She disguised her own nature so well that after a while she grew uncertain of her own abilities. By then, she was as quiet as a mouse. When she opened her mouth in the classroom she could only squeak out wrong answers; in time she made sure to sit in the back of the room, and to keep her mouth firmly shut.

Still they would not let her be. Someone put an open ant farm in her locker when Sally was in fourth grade, so that for weeks she found squashed ants between the pages of her books. In fifth grade a gang of boys left a dead mouse in her desk. One of the cruelest children had glued a nametag to the mouse's back. *Sali* had been scrawled in crude letters, but Sally took not the slightest pleasure in the misspelling of her name. She had cried over the little curled-up body, with its tiny whiskers and perfect paws, but when her teacher had asked what was wrong, she'd only shrugged, as though she had lost the power of speech.

One beautiful April day, when Sally was in sixth grade, all of the aunts' cats followed her to school. After that, even the teachers would not pass her in an empty hallway and would find an excuse to head in the other direction. As they scurried away, the teachers smiled at her oddly, and perhaps they were afraid not to. Black cats can do that to some people; they make them go all shivery and scared and remind them of dark, wicked nights. The aunts' cats, however, were not particularly frightening. They were spoiled and liked to sleep on the couches and they were all named for birds: There was Cardinal and Crow and Raven and Goose. There was a gawky kitten named Dove, and an ill-tempered tom called Magpie, who hissed at the others and kept them at bay. It would be difficult to believe that such a mangy bunch of creatures had come up with a plan to shame Sally, but that is what seemed to have happened, although they may have followed her on that day simply because she'd fixed a tunafish sandwich for lunch, just for herself, as Gillian was pretending to have strep throat and was home in bed, where she was sure to stay for the best part of a week, reading magazines and eating candy bars with no cares when it came to getting chocolate on the sheets, since Sally was the one who took responsibility for the laundry.

On this morning, Sally didn't even know the cats were behind her, until she sat down at her desk. Some of her classmates were laughing, but three girls had jumped up onto the radiator and were shrieking. Anyone would have thought a gang of demons had entered the room, but it was only those flea-bitten creatures that had followed Sally to school. They paraded past chairs and desks, black as night and howling like banshees. Sally shooed them away, but the cats just came closer. They paced back and forth in front of her, their tails in the air, meowing with voices so horrible the sound could have curdled milk in the cup.

"Scat," Sally whispered when Magpie jumped into her lap and began kneading his claws into her nicest blue dress. "Go away," she begged him.

But even when Miss Mullins came in and smacked her desk with a ruler and used her sternest voice to suggest that Sally had better rid the room of the cats—*tout de suite*—or risk detention, the revolting beasts refused to go. A panic had spread and the more high-strung of Sally's classmates were already whispering witchery. A witch, after all, was often accompanied by a familiar, an animal to do her most evil bidding. The more familiars there were, the nastier the bidding, and here was an entire troop of disgusting creatures. Several children had fainted; some would be phobic about cats for the rest of their lives. The gym teacher was sent for, and he waved a broom around, but still the cats would not leave.

A boy in the rear of the room, who had stolen a pack of matches from his father just that morning, now made use of the chaos in the classroom and took the opportunity to set Magpie's tail on fire. The scent of burning fur quickly filled the room, even before Magpie began to scream. Sally ran to the cat; without stopping to think, she knelt and smothered the flames with her favorite blue dress.

"I hope something awful happens to you," she called to the boy who'd set Magpie afire. Sally stood up, the cat cradled in her arms like a baby, her face and dress dirty with soot. "You'll see what it's like then," she said to the boy. "You'll know how it feels."

Just then the children in the classroom directly overhead began to stomp their feet—out of joy, since it had been revealed their spelling tests had been eaten by their teacher's English bulldog—and an acoustic tile fell onto the horrid boy's head. He collapsed to the floor in a heap, his face ashen in spite of his freckled complexion.

"She did it!" some of the children cried, and the ones who did not speak aloud had their mouths wide open and their eyes even wider.

Sally ran from the room with Magpie in her arms and the other cats following. The cats zigzagged under and around her feet all the way home, down Endicott and Peabody streets, through the front door and up the stairs, and all afternoon they clawed at Sally's bedroom door, even after she'd locked herself inside.

Sally cried for two hours straight. She loved the cats, that was the thing. She sneaked them saucers of milk and carried them to the vet on Endicott Street in a knitting bag when they fought and tore at each other and their scars became infected. She adored those horrible cats, especially Magpie, and yet sitting in her classroom, embarrassed beyond belief, she would have gladly watched each one be drowned in a bucket of icy water or shot with a BB gun. Even though she went out to care for Magpie as soon as she'd collected herself, cleaning his tail and wrapping it in cotton gauze, she knew she'd betrayed him in her heart. From that day on, Sally thought less of herself. She did not ask the aunts for special favors, or even request those small rewards she deserved. Sally could not have had a more intractable and uncompromising judge; she had found herself lacking, in compassion and fortitude, and the punishment was self-denial, from that moment on.

After the cat incident, Sally and Gillian became more feared than ignored. The other girls in school no longer teased; instead, they quickly walked away when the Owens sisters passed by, and they all kept their eyes cast down. Rumors of witchcraft spread in notes passed from desk to desk; accusations were whispered in hallways and bathrooms. Those children who had black cats of their own begged their parents for a different pet, a collie or a guinea pig or even a goldfish. When the football team lost, when a kiln in the art room exploded, everyone looked toward the Owens girls. Even the rowdiest boys did not dare to hit them with dodge balls at recess, or aim spitballs in their direction; not a single one threw apples or stones. At slumber parties and Girl Scout meetings there were those who swore that Sally and Gillian could induce a hypnotic trance that would make you bark like a dog or jump right off a cliff, if they so desired. They could put a spell on you with a single word or a nod of their heads. And if either of the sisters was truly angry, all she needed to do was recite the nine times table backward, and that would be the end of you. The eyes in your head would melt. Flesh and bones would turn into pudding. They'd serve you in the school cafeteria the very next day, and no one would be the wiser.

The children in town could whisper whatever rumors they wished, but the truth was that most of their mothers had gone to see the aunts at least once in their lives. Occasionally, someone might appear who wanted red pepper tea for a persnickety stomach, or butterfly weed for nerves, but every woman in town knew what the aunts' real business was: their specialty was love. The aunts were not invited to potluck suppers or library fund-raisers, but when a woman in town quarreled with her lover, when she found herself pregnant by someone who wasn't her husband, or discovered that the man she'd married was unfaithful as a hound, then there she'd be, at the Owens back door, just after twilight, the hour when the shadows could hide your features so that no one would recognize you as you stood beneath the wisteria, a tangled vine that had grown above the door for longer than anyone in town had been alive.

It didn't matter if a woman was the fifth-grade teacher at the elementary school, or if she was the pastor's wife, or perhaps the longtime girlfriend of the orthodontist on Peabody Street. It didn't matter that people swore black birds dropped from the sky, ready to peck out your eyes when you approached the Owens house from the east. Desire had a way of making a person oddly courageous. In the aunts' opinion, it could sneak up on a grown woman and turn her from a sensible creature into something as foolish as a flea that keeps chasing after the same old dog. Once someone had made the decision to come to the back door, she was more than ready to drink pennyroyal tea, prepared with ingredients that couldn't even be spoken aloud, which would surely bring on bleeding that night. She'd already decided to let one of the aunts prick the third finger of her left hand with a silver needle if that's what it took to get her darling back once more.

The aunts clucked like chickens whenever a woman walked up the bluestone path. They could read desperation from half a mile away. A woman who was head over heels and wanted to make certain her love was returned would be happy to hand over a cameo that had been in her family for generations. One who had been betrayed would pay even more. But those women who wanted someone else's husband, they were the worst. They would do absolutely anything for love. They got all twisted up, like rubber bands, just from the heat of their desire, and they didn't give a damn for convention and good manners. As soon as the aunts saw one of those women walking up the path, they sent the girls straight to the attic, even on December nights, when twilight came well before four-thirty.

On those murky evenings, the sisters never protested that it was too early, or that they weren't yet tired. They tiptoed up the stairs, holding hands. From the landing, beneath the dusty old portrait of Maria Owens, the girls called out their good nights; they went to their rooms, slipped their nightgowns over their heads, then went directly to the back staircase, so they could creep down again, press their ears against the door, and listen in to every word. Sometimes, when it was an extremely dark evening and Gillian was feeling especially brave, she would push the door ajar with her foot, and Sally wouldn't dare to close it again, for fear it might creak and give them away.

"This is so silly," Sally would whisper. "It's utter nonsense," she'd decree.

"Then go to bed," Gillian would whisper right back. "Go on," she'd suggest, knowing that Sally wouldn't dare to miss any of what happened next.

From the angle of the back stairs, the girls could see the old black stove and the table and the hooked rug, where the aunts' customers often paced back and forth. They could see how love might control you, from your head to your toes, not to mention every single part of you in between.

Because of this, Sally and Gillian had learned things most children their age had not: that it was always wise to collect fingernail clippings that had once been the living tissue of your beloved, just in case he should take it into his head to stray; that a woman could want a man so much she might vomit in the kitchen sink or cry so fiercely blood would form in the corners of her eyes.

On evenings when the orange moon was rising in the sky, and some woman was crying in their kitchen, Sally and Gillian would lock pinkies and vow never to be ruled by their passions.

"Yuck," the girls would whisper to each other when a client of their aunts would weep or lift her blouse to show the raw marks where she'd cut the name of her beloved into her skin with a razor.

"Not us," the sisters would swear, locking their fingers even more tightly.

During the winter when Sally was twelve and Gillian almost eleven, they learned that sometimes the most dangerous thing of all in matters of love was to be granted your heart's desire. That was the winter when a young woman who worked in the drugstore came to see the aunts. For days the temperature had been dropping. The engine of the aunts' Ford station wagon sputtered and refused to turn over and the tires were frozen to the concrete floor of the garage. Mice would not venture out from the warmth of the bedroom walls; swans in the park picked at icy weeds and still they went hungry. The season was so cold and the sky so heartless and purple it made young girls shiver just to look upward.

The customer who arrived one dark evening wasn't pretty, but she was known for her kindness and sweet disposition. She delivered holiday meals to the elderly and sang in a choir with a voice like an angel's and always put an extra squirt of syrup in the glass when children ordered vanilla Cokes at the soda fountain. But when she arrived at twilight, this plain, mild girl was in such agony that she curled up on the hand-hooked rug; her fists were so tightly clenched they were like the claws of a cat. She threw her head back and her glossy hair fell over her face like a curtain; she chewed on her lip until her flesh bled. She was being eaten alive by love and had already lost thirty pounds. Because of this the aunts seemed to take pity on her, something they rarely did. Though the girl hadn't much money, they gave her the strongest potion they could, with exact instructions on how to make another woman's husband fall in love with her. Then they warned her that what was done could never be undone, and so she must be sure.

"I'm sure," the girl said, in her calm beautiful voice, and the aunts must have been satisfied, because they gave her the heart of a dove, set on one of their best saucers, the kind with the blue willows and the river of tears.

Sally and Gillian sat on the back stairs in the dark, their knees touching, their feet dirty and bare. They were shivering, but still they grinned at each other and whispered right along with the aunts a charm they knew well enough to recite in their sleep: "My lover's heart will feel this pin, and his devotion I will win. There'll be no way for him to rest nor sleep, until he comes to me to speak. Only when he loves me best will he find peace, and with peace, rest." Gillian made little stabbing motions, which is what the girl was to do to the dove's heart when she repeated these words for seven nights in a row before she went to bed.

"It will never work," Sally whispered afterward, as they felt their way along in the dark, up the stairs and along the hall to their rooms.

"It might work," Gillian whispered back. "Even though she's not pretty, it's still within the realm of possibility."

Sally drew herself up; she was older and taller and always knew best. "We'll just see about that."

For nearly two weeks, Sally and Gillian watched the lovesick girl. Like hired detectives, they sat for hours at the counter in the drugstore and spent all their pocket money on Cokes and french fries so they could keep an eye on her. They trailed after when she went home to the apartment she shared with another girl, who worked at the dry cleaner's. The more they followed her schedule, the more Sally began to feel they were invading the girl's privacy, but the sisters continued to believe they were doing important research, although now and then Gillian was confused as to what their goal really was.

"It's simple," Sally told her. "We need to prove that the aunts have no powers whatsoever."

"If the aunts are full of baloney"—Gillian grinned—"then we'll be just like everyone else."

Sally nodded. She could not begin to express how deeply she felt about this matter, since being like everyone else was her personal heart's desire. At night Sally dreamed of ranch houses and white picket fences, and when she woke in the morning and looked out to see the black metal spikes that surrounded them, tears formed in her eyes. Other girls, she knew, washed with bars of Ivory and sweet-scented Camay, while she and Gillian were forced to use the black soap the aunts made twice a year, on the back burner of their stove. Other girls had mothers and fathers who didn't give a hoot about desire and fate. In no other house on their street or in their town was there a drawer crammed with cameos, given in payment for desires fulfilled.

All Sally could hope for was that perhaps her life was not quite as abnormal as it appeared. If the love charm didn't work for the girl from the drugstore, then perhaps the aunts were only pretending their powers. So the sisters waited and prayed that nothing would happen. And when it seemed certain that nothing would, the principal of their school, Mr. Halliwell, parked his station wagon outside the drugstore girl's apartment, just as the light was fading. He casually walked inside, but Sally noticed that he made sure to look over his shoulder; his eyes were bleary, as though he hadn't slept for seven nights.

That evening the girls did not go home for supper, despite Sally's promise to the aunts that she would fix lamb chops and baked beans. The wind picked up and a freezing rain had begun to fall; still the girls stood across the street from the drugstore girl's apartment. Mr. Halliwell didn't come out until after nine, and he had a strange expression on his face, as if he didn't quite know where he was. He walked right past his own car, not recognizing it, and not until he was halfway home did he remember he'd parked somewhere, and then it took him nearly an hour to locate the forgotten spot. After that, he appeared every evening at the exact same time. Once he had the nerve to come to the drugstore at lunch and order a cheeseburger and a Coke, although he didn't eat a bite and instead stared longingly at the girl who'd put a spell on him. He sat there on the very first stool, so hot and amorous that the linoleum countertop on which he rested his elbows began to bubble. When he finally noticed Sally and Gillian watching him, he demanded that the sisters head back to school, and he reached for his burger, but he still couldn't keep his eyes off the girl. He'd been hit by something, all right; the aunts had gotten to him just as sure as if they'd picked him off with a bow and arrow.

"Coincidence," Sally insisted.

"I don't know about that." Gillian shrugged. Anyone could see that the girl from the drugstore looked all lit up inside as she fixed hot fudge sundaes and rang up prescriptions for antibiotics and cough syrup. "She got what she wanted. However it happened."

But as it turned out, the girl didn't have exactly what she'd wanted. She came back to the aunts, more distraught than ever. Love was one thing, marriage quite another. Mr. Halliwell, it seemed, was not certain he could leave his wife.

"I don't think you want to watch this," Gillian whispered to Sally.

"How do you know?"

The girls were whispering right in each other's ears; they had a scared feeling they didn't usually have when they spied from the safety of the stairs.

"I saw it once." Gillian looked particularly pale; her fair hair stuck out from her head in a cloud.

Sally drew away from her sister. She understood why people said blood could turn to ice. "Without me?"

Gillian often came to the back stairs without her sister to test herself, to see how fearless she could be. "I didn't think you'd want to. Some of the things they do are pretty gross. You won't be able to take it."

After that, Sally had to remain beside her younger sister on the stairs, if only to prove that she could. "We'll just see who can take it and who can't," she whispered.

But Sally never would have stayed, she would have run all the way to her room and locked the door with a deadbolt, had she known that in order to compel a man to marry you when he doesn't wish to, something horrible has to be done. She closed her eyes as soon as they brought the mourning dove in. She covered her ears with her hands so she wouldn't have to listen to it shriek as they held it down on the countertop. She told herself she had cooked lamb chops, she had broiled chicken, and this wasn't so different. All the same, Sally never again ate meat or fowl or even fish after that evening, and she got a shivery feeling whenever a flock of sparrows or wrens perched in the trees startled and took flight. For a long time afterward she would reach for her sister's hand when the sky began to grow dark.

All that winter, Sally and Gillian saw the girl from the drugstore with Mr. Halliwell. In January he left his wife to marry her, and they moved into a small white house on the corner of Third and Endicott. Once they were man and wife, they were rarely apart. Wherever the girl went, to the market or her exercise class, Mr. Halliwell would follow, like a well-trained dog that has no need for a leash. As soon as school let out, he would head for the drugstore; he would show up at odd hours, with a handful of violets or a box of nougat, and sometimes the sisters could hear his new wife snipe at him, in spite of his gifts. Couldn't he let her out of his sight for a minute? That's what she hissed to her beloved. Couldn't he give her a minute of peace?

By the time the wisteria had begun to bloom the following

spring, the girl from the drugstore was back. Sally and Gillian were working in the garden at dusk, gathering spring onions for a vegetable stew. The lemon thyme in the rear of the garden had started to give off its delicious scent, as it always did at this time of year, and the rosemary was less chalky and brittle. The season was so damp that the mosquitoes were out in full force and Gillian was hitting the bugs that had settled on her skin. Sally had to tug on her sleeve to get her to notice who it was coming up the bluestone path.

"Uh-oh," Gillian said. She stopped smacking herself. "She looks awful."

The drugstore girl didn't even look like a girl anymore, she looked old. Her hair wasn't shiny, and her mouth had a funny shape, as though she'd bitten into something sour. She rubbed her hands together; perhaps the skin was chapped, but more likely she was nervous in some terrible way. Sally picked up the wicker basket of onions and watched as their aunts' customer knocked on the back door. No one answered, so she pounded against the wood, frantic and angry. "Open up!" she called out, again and again. She kept right on knocking, and the sound echoed, unanswered.

When the girl noticed the sisters and headed toward the garden, Gillian turned white as a ghost and clung to her sister. Sally stood her ground, since there was, after all, nowhere to go. The aunts had nailed the skull of a horse to the fence, to keep away neighborhood children with a taste for strawberries and mint. Now Sally found herself hoping it would keep away evil spirits as well, because that's what the drugstore girl looked like, that's what she seemed to be as she flew at them, in that garden where lavender and rosemary and Spanish garlic already grew in abundance, while most of their neighbors' yards remained muddy and bare.

"Look what they did to me," the girl from the drugstore cried. "He won't leave me alone for a minute. He's taken all the locks off, even on the bathroom door. I can't sleep or eat, because he's always watching me. He wants to fuck me constantly. I'm sore inside and out."

Sally took two steps backward, nearly stumbling over Gillian, who was clinging to her still. This was not the way people ordinarily spoke to children, but the girl from the drugstore obviously didn't give a damn about what was right or wrong. Sally could see that her eyes were red from crying. Her mouth looked mean, as if only bad words could come from between those lips.

"Where are the witches who did this to me?" said the girl.

The aunts were looking out the window, watching what avarice and stupidity could do to a person. They shook their heads sadly when Sally glanced at the window. They did not wish to be involved any further with the drugstore girl. Some people cannot be warned away from disaster. You can try, you can put up every alert, but they'll still go their own way.

"Our aunts went on vacation," Sally said in a breakable, untrustworthy voice. She had never told a lie before, and it left a black taste in her throat.

"Go get them," the girl shouted. She was no longer the person she used to be. At choir practice she wept during her solos and had to be led into the parking lot so she wouldn't disrupt the entire program. "Do it now, or I'll smack you silly."

"Leave us alone," Gillian said from the safety of her hiding place behind Sally. "If you don't, we'll put a worse curse on you."

The girl from the drugstore snapped when she heard that. She grabbed for Gillian and flung her arm forward. But it was Sally she slapped, and she struck her so hard that Sally lurched backward and trampled the rosemary and the verbena. Behind the window glass, the aunts recited the words they were taught as children to hush the chickens. There had been a whole pen of scrawny brown-and-white specimens, but by the time the aunts got through with them they never screeched again; in fact, it was their silence that allowed for them to be carried off by stray dogs in the middle of the night.

"Oh," Gillian said when she realized what had happened to her sister. A blood-red mark was forming on Sally's cheek, but Gillian was the one who started to cry. "You horrible thing," she said to the drugstore girl. "You're just horrible!"

"Didn't you hear me? Get me your aunts!" Or at least that was what the drugstore girl tried to say, but no one heard a word. Nothing came out of her mouth. Not a shout or a scream and certainly not an apology. She put her hand to her throat, as though someone were strangling her, but really she was choking on all that love she thought she'd needed so badly.

Sally watched the girl, whose face had already grown white with fear. As it turned out, the girl from the drugstore never spoke again, although sometimes she made little cooing noises, like the call of a pigeon or a dove, or, when she was truly furious, a harsh shrieking that was not unlike the panicked sound chickens make when they're chased and then caught for basting and broiling. Her friends in the choir wept at the loss of her beautiful voice, but in time they began to avoid her. Her back had become arched, like the spine of a cat who has stepped onto a burning hot coal. She could not hear a kind word without covering her ears with her hands and stamping her foot like a spoiled child.

For the rest of her life she'd be followed around by a man who loved her too much, and she wouldn't even be able to tell him to go away. Sally knew the aunts would never open the door for this client of theirs, not if she came back a thousand times. This girl had no right to demand anything more. What had she thought, that love was a toy, something easy and sweet, just to play with? Real love was dangerous, it got you from inside and held on tight, and if you didn't let go fast enough you might be willing to do anything for its sake. If the girl from the drugstore had been smart, she would have asked for an antidote, not a charm, in the first place. In the end, she had gotten what she'd wanted, and if she still hadn't learned a lesson from it, there was one person in this garden who had. There was one girl who knew enough to go inside and lock the door three times, and not shed a single tear as she cut up the onions that were so bitter they would have made anyone else cry all night long.

ONCE a year, on midsummer's eve, a sparrow would find its way into the Owens house. No matter how anyone tried to prevent it, the bird always managed to get inside. They could set out saucers of salt on the windowsills and hire a handyman to fix the gutters and the roof, and still the bird would appear. It would enter the house at twilight, the hour of sorrow, and it always came in silence, yet with a strange resolve, which defied both salt and bricks, as though the poor thing had no choice but to perch on the drapes and the dusty chandelier, from which glass drops spilled down like tears.

The aunts kept their brooms ready, in order to chase the bird out the window, but the sparrow flew too high to be trapped. As it circled the dining room, the sisters counted, for they knew that three times around signified trouble, and three times around it always was. Trouble, of course, was nothing new to the Owens sisters, especially as they grew up. The instant the girls began high school, the boys who had avoided them for all those years suddenly couldn't keep away from Gillian. She could go to the market for a can of split pea soup and come back going steady with the boy who stocked the frozen food case. The older she got, the worse it became. Maybe it was the black soap she washed with that made her skin seem illuminated; whatever the reason, she was hot to the touch and impossible to ignore. Boys looked at her and got so dizzy they had to be rushed to the emergency room for a hit of oxygen or a pint of new blood. Men who'd been happily married, and were old enough to be her father, suddenly took it into their heads to propose and offer her the world, or at least their version of it.

When Gillian wore short skirts she caused car accidents on Endicott Street. When she passed by, dogs tied to kennels with thick metal chains forgot to snarl and bite. One blistering Memorial Day, Gillian cut off most of her hair, so that it was as short as a boy's, and nearly every girl in town copied her. But none of them could stop traffic by revealing her pretty neck. Not one of them could use her brilliant smile in order to pass biology and social studies without taking a single exam or ever doing a night's homework. During the summer when Gillian was sixteen, the entire varsity football team spent every single Saturday in the aunts' garden. There they could be found, all in a row, hulking and silent and madly in love, pulling weeds between the rows of nightshade and verbena, careful to avoid the scallions, which were so scorchingly potent they burned the skin right off any boy's fingers if he wasn't paying attention.

Gillian broke hearts the way other people broke kindling for firewood. By the time she was a senior in high school, she was so fast and expert at it that some boys didn't even know what was happening until they were left in one big emotional heap. If you took all the trouble most girls got into as teenagers and boiled it down for twenty-four hours, you'd wind up with something the size of a Snickers candy bar. But if you melted down all the trouble Gillian Owens got herself into, not to mention all the grief she caused, you'd have yourself a sticky mess as tall as the statehouse in Boston.

The aunts didn't worry in the least about Gillian's reputation. They never once thought to give her a curfew or a good talking to. When Sally got her license she used the station wagon to pick up groceries and haul trash to the dump, but as soon as Gillian could drive she took the car every Saturday night and she didn't come home until dawn. The aunts heard Gillian sneak in the front door; they found beer bottles hidden in the glove compartment of the Ford. Girls would be girls, was the way the aunts figured it, which was especially true for an Owens. The only advice the aunts offered was that a baby was easier to prevent than to raise, and even Gillian, as foolhardy as she was, could see the truth in that.

It was Sally the aunts brooded about. Sally, who cooked nutritious dinners every night and washed up afterward, who did the marketing on Tuesdays and hung the laundry out on Thursdays, so the sheets and the towels would smell fresh and sweet. The aunts tried to encourage her not to be so good. Goodness, in their opinion, was not a virtue but merely spinelessness and fear disguised as humility. The aunts believed there were more important things to worry about than dust bunnies under the beds or fallen leaves piling up on the porch. Owens women ignored convention; they were headstrong and willful, and meant to be that way. Those cousins who married had always insisted on keeping their own name, and their daughters were Owenses as well. Gillian and Sally's mother, Regina, had been especially difficult to control. The aunts blinked back tears whenever they thought about how Regina would walk along the porch railing in her stocking feet on evenings when she drank a little too much whiskey, her arms out for balance. She may have been foolish, but Regina knew how to have fun, an ability the Owens women were proud of. Gillian had inherited her mother's wild streak, but Sally wouldn't have known a good time if it sat up and bit her.

"Go out," the aunts urged on Saturday nights, when Sally was curled up on the couch with a library book. "Have fun," they suggested, in their small, scratchy voices that could scare the snails out of their garden but couldn't get Sally off the couch.

The aunts tried to help Sally become more social. They began to collect young gentlemen the way other old ladies collected stray cats. They placed ads in college newspapers and telephoned fraternity houses. Every Sunday they held garden parties with cold beef sandwiches and bottles of dark beer, but Sally just sat on a metal chair, her legs crossed, her mind elsewhere. The aunts bought her tubes of rose-colored lipstick and bath salts from Spain. They mail-ordered party dresses and lace slips and soft suede boots, but Sally gave it all to Gillian, who could put these gifts to use, and she went on reading books on Saturday nights, just as she did the laundry on Thursdays.

This is not to say that Sally didn't try her best to fall in love. She was thoughtful and deep, with amazing powers of concentration, and for a while she accepted offers to go to the movies and dances and take walks around the pond down at the park. Boys who dated Sally in high school were astounded by how long she could concentrate on a single kiss, and they couldn't help but wonder just what else she might be capable of. Twenty years later, many of them were still thinking of her when they shouldn't, but she had never cared for a single one and could never even remember their names. She wouldn't go out with the same boy twice, because in her opinion that wouldn't be fair, and she believed in things like fairness back then, even in matters as strange and unusual as love.

Watching Gillian go through half the town made Sally wonder if perhaps she had only granite in the place where her heart should have been. But by the time the sisters were out of high school, it became clear that although Gillian could fall in love, she couldn't stay there for more than two weeks. Sally began to think they were equally cursed, and given their background and their upbringing, it really was no surprise that the sisters should have such bad luck. The aunts, after all, still kept photographs on their bureaus of the young men they had once loved, brothers who'd had too much pride to take shelter during a stormy picnic. The boys had been struck down by lightning on the town green, which was where they were now buried, beneath a smooth, round stone where mourning doves gathered at dawn and at dusk. Each August, lightning was drawn there again, and lovers dared each other to run across the green whenever black storm clouds appeared. Gillian's boyfriends were the only ones lovesick enough to take the risk of being struck, and two of them had found themselves in the hospital after their runs across the green, their hair forever standing on end, their eyes open wide from that time onward, even while they slept.

When Gillian was eighteen she stayed in love for three months, long enough to decide to run off to Maryland and get married. She had to elope since the aunts had refused to give their blessing. In their estimation Gillian was young and stupid and would get herself pregnant in record time—all the prerequisites for a miserable and ordinary life. As it turned out, the aunts were right only about her stupidity and youth. Gillian didn't have time to get pregnant—two weeks after the wedding, she left her husband for the mechanic who fixed their Toyota. It was the first of many marital disasters, but on the night she eloped anything seemed possible, even happiness. Sally helped to tie a line of white sheets together so that Gillian could escape. Sally considered her little sister greedy and selfish; Gillian thought of Sally as a prig and a prude, but they were still sisters, and now that they were about to be separated, they stood in front of the open window and hugged each other and cried, then vowed they would be apart for only a short while.

"I wish you were coming with us." Gillian's voice had been whispery, the way it was during thunderstorms.

"You don't have to do this," Sally had said. "If you're not sure."

"I've had it with the aunts. I want a real life. I want to go where nobody has ever heard of the Owenses." Gillian was wearing a short white dress that she had to keep pulling down against her thighs. Instead of sobbing, she rummaged through her purse until she found a crumpled pack of cigarettes. Both sisters blinked when she lit the match. They stood in the dark and watched the orange glow of the cigarette each time Gillian inhaled, and Sally didn't even bother to point out that hot ashes were falling onto the floor she had swept earlier that day.

"Promise me you won't stay here," Gillian said. "You'll get all crumpled up like a piece of paper. You'll ruin your life."

Down in the yard, the boy Gillian was about to run off with was nervous. Gillian had been known to back out when it came time to commit; in fact, she was famous for it. This year alone, three college boys had each been convinced that he was the one Gillian meant to marry, and each had brought her a diamond ring. For a while Gillian wore three rings on a gold chain, but in the end she gave them all back, breaking hearts in Princeton, Providence, and Cambridge all in the very same week. The other students in her graduating class took bets on who her date would be for the senior prom, since she'd been accepting and breaking invitations from various suitors for months.

The boy in the yard, who would soon be Gillian's first husband, began to toss stones up on the roof, and the echo sounded exactly like a hailstorm. The sisters threw their arms around each other; they felt as though fate was picking them up, rattling them around, then releasing them into completely alternate futures. It would be years before they'd see each other again. They'd be grown-up women by then, too old to whisper secrets or climb up to the roof in the middle of the night.

"Come with us," Gillian said.

"No," Sally said. "Impossible." Certain facts of love she knew for certain. "Only two people can elope."

There were dozens of stones falling on the roof; there were a thousand stars in the sky.

"I'll miss you too much," Gillian said.

"Go on," Sally said. She'd be the last one in the world to hold her sister back. "Go now."

Gillian hugged Sally one last time, and then she disappeared out the window. They'd fed the aunts barley soup laced with a generous amount of whiskey, so the old women were asleep on the couch. They never heard a thing. But Sally could hear her sister running down the bluestone path, and she wept all that night and imagined she heard footsteps when nothing was moving outside but the garden toads. In the morning, Sally went outside to collect the white sheets Gillian had left in a heap beside the wisteria. Why was Sally the one who always stayed behind to do laundry? Why did she care that there were dirt stains in the fabric that would need extra bleaching? She had never felt more alone or lonely. If only she could believe in love's salvation, but desire had been ruined for her. She saw craving as obsession, fervor as heated preoccupation. She wished she had never sneaked down the back stairs to listen in while the aunts' customers cried and begged and made fools of themselves. All of that had only served to make her love-resistant, and frankly, she thought she'd probably never change.

For the next two years postcards from Gillian would occasionally arrive, with hugs-and-kisses and wish-you-were-heres, but without a forwarding address. During this time Sally had less hope that her life would open up into something other than cooking meals the aunts didn't want and cleaning a house where the woodwork never needed polishing. She was twenty-one; most of the girls her age were finishing up college, or getting a raise at work so they could move into their own apartments, but the most exciting thing Sally did was walk to the hardware store. Sometimes it took close to an hour for her to choose between cleansers.

"What do you think? What's best for a kitchen floor?" she'd ask the clerk, a good-looking young man who was so confused by this question he'd simply point to the Lysol. The clerk was six-foot-four, and Sally could never see the expression on his face as he directed her to the preferred cleaning product. If she had been taller, or had climbed up on the stepladder used for stocking the shelves, Sally would have noticed that whenever the clerk looked at her his mouth was open, as if there were words he wished would spill out of their own accord to convey what he was too shy to speak of.

Walking home from the hardware store, Sally kicked at stones. A band of black birds took to following her, screaming and cawing over what a laughable creature she was, and although she cringed each time the birds flew overhead, Sally agreed with them. Her fate appeared to be set. She would forever be scrubbing the floor and calling the aunts in from the garden on afternoons that were too chilly and damp for them to be down in the dirt on their hands and knees. In fact, the days were seeming more and more similar, interchangeable even; she barely noticed the difference between winter and spring. But summertime in the Owens house had its own delineation—that dreadful bird who invaded their peace—and when the next midsummer's evening arrived, Sally and the aunts were ready for their unwanted guest, as they were every year. They were waiting in the dining room for the sparrow to appear, and nothing happened. Hours passed—they could hear the clock in the parlor—and still, no arrival, no flutter, no feathers. Sally, with her odd fear of birds in flight, had tied a scarf around her head, but now she saw there was no need for it. No bird came in through the window or through the hole in the roof the handyman hadn't managed to find. It did not fly around three times to announce misfortune. It did not even tap at the window with its small sharp beak.

The aunts looked at each other, puzzled. But Sally laughed out loud. She, with her insistence of proof, had just been granted some powerful evidence: Things changed. They shifted. One year was not just like the next and the one after and the one after that. Sally ran from the house and she kept right on running until she got to the front of the hardware store, where she crashed into the man she would marry. As soon as she looked at him, Sally felt dizzy and had to sit on the curb, with her head down so she wouldn't faint, and the clerk who knew so much about washing a kitchen floor sat right beside her, even though his boss yelled for him to get back to work, since a line had already formed at the cash register.

The man Sally fell in love with was named Michael. He was so thoughtful and good-natured that he kissed the aunts the first time he met them and immediately asked if they needed their trash taken out to the curb, which won them over then and there, no questions asked. Sally married him quickly, and they moved into the attic, which suddenly seemed the only place in the world where Sally wished to be.

Let Gillian travel from California to Memphis. Let her marry and divorce three times in a row. Let her kiss every man who crossed her path and break every promise she ever made about coming home for the holidays. Let her pity her sister, cooped up in that old house. Sally did not mind a bit. In Sally's opinion, it was impossible to exist in the world and not be in love with Michael. Even the aunts had begun to listen for the sound of his whistle when he came home from the hardware store in the evenings. In autumn, he turned the garden for the aunts. In winter, he put up the storm windows and filled in the cracks around the foggy old windows with putty. He took the ancient Ford station wagon apart and put it back together, and the aunts were so impressed they gave him the car, as well as their abiding affection. He knew enough to stay out of the kitchen, especially at twilight, and if he noticed the women who came to the back door, he never questioned Sally about them. His kisses were slow and deep and he liked to take off Sally's clothes with the bedside table light turned on and he always made certain to lose when he played gin rummy with one of the aunts.

When Michael moved in, the house itself began to change, and even the bats in the attic knew it and took to nesting out by the garden shed. By the following June, roses had begun to grow up along the porch railing, choking out ragweed, instead of the other way around. In January, the draft in the parlor disappeared and ice would not form on the bluestone path. The house stayed cheery and warm, and when Antonia was born, at home, since a horrid snowstorm was brewing outside, the chandelier with the glass teardrops moved back and forth all on its own. Throughout the night, it sounded as if a river were flowing right through the house; the noise was so beautiful and so real that the mice came out of the walls to make certain the house was still standing and that a meadow hadn't taken its place.

Antonia was given the last name of Owens, at the aunts' insistence, in accordance with family tradition. The aunts set about spoiling the child immediately, adding chocolate syrup to her bottles of formula, allowing her to play with unstrung pearls, taking her into the garden to make mud pies and pick chokeberries as soon as she could crawl. Antonia would have been perfectly happy to be an only child forever, but three and a half years later, at midnight exactly, Kylie was born, and everyone noticed right away how unusual she was. Even the aunts, who could not have loved another child more than Antonia, predicted that Kylie would see what others could not. She tilted her head and listened to the rain before it fell. She pointed to the ceiling moments before a dragonfly appeared in the very same spot. Kylie was such a good baby that people who peeked into her stroller felt peaceful and sleepy just looking at her. Mosquitoes never bit her, and the aunts' black cats wouldn't scratch her, even when she grabbed for their tails. Kylie was a peach of an infant, so sweet and so mild that Antonia grew greedier and more selfish by the day.

"Look at me!" she'd cry, whenever she dressed up in the aunts' old chiffon dresses or when she finished every pea on her plate. Sally and Michael patted her head and went about taking care of the baby, but the aunts knew what Antonia wanted to hear. They took her out to the garden at midnight, an hour too late for a silly infant, and they showed her how nightshade bloomed in the dark, and how, if she listened carefully with her big-girl's ears, which were much more sensitive to sound than her little sister's ever would be, she could hear the earthworms moving through the soil.

To celebrate the baby's arrival, Michael had invited everyone who worked at the hardware store, which he now managed, and all the people on their block to a party. To Sally's surprise they all showed up. Even those guests who'd been afraid to hurry past their front walkway on dark nights seemed eager to come and celebrate. They drank cold beer and ate icebox cake and danced along the bluestone path. Antonia was dressed in organdy and lace, and a circle of admirers applauded when Michael lifted her onto an old picnic table so she could sing "The Old Gray Mare" and "Yankee Doodle."

At first the aunts refused to participate and insisted upon watching the festivities through the kitchen window, like black pieces of paper taped against the glass. They were antisocial old dames who had better things to do with their time, or so they maintained. But even they couldn't resist joining in, and when at last everyone raised a glass of champagne in tribute to the new baby, the aunts shocked them all when they came into the garden for the toast. In the spirit of a good time, they threw their glasses onto the path, not caring that for weeks afterward shards would appear in the earth between the rows of cabbages.

You will not believe how everything has changed, Sally confided to her sister. She wrote to Gillian at least twice a month, on pale blue paper. Sometimes she would misfire completely, sending her letters to St. Louis, for instance, only to discover that her sister had already moved to Texas. *We seem so normal*, Sally wrote. *I think you might faint if you could see us. I really and truly do.*

They had dinner together every night when Michael came home from work, and the aunts no longer shook their heads when they saw the healthy platters of vegetables Sally insisted on serving her daughters. Though they set no store by good manners, they didn't cluck their tongues when Antonia cleared the table. They didn't complain when Sally signed Antonia up for nursery school at the community center, where she was taught to say "Please" and "Thank you" when she wanted cookies and where it was suggested that it might be best not to carry worms in her pockets if she wanted the other little girls to play with her. The aunts did, however, put their foot down about children's parties, since that would mean cheerful, rowdy monsters traipsing through the house, laughing and drinking pink lemonade and leaving piles of jelly beans between the couch cushions.

For birthdays and holidays, Sally took to giving parties in the back room of the hardware store, where there was a gumball machine and a metal pony that would give free rides all afternoon if you knew to kick it in the knees. An invitation to one of these parties was coveted by every child in town. "Don't forget me," the girls in Antonia's class would remind her as the day of her birthday approached. "I'm your best friend," they'd whisper, as Halloween and the Fourth of July drew near. When Sally and Michael took the children for walks, neighbors waved to them instead of quickly crossing the street. Before long, they found themselves invited to potluck suppers and Christmas parties, and one year Sally was actually placed in charge of the pie booth at the Harvest Fair.

It's just what I wanted, Sally wrote. *Every single thing. Come visit us*, she begged, but she knew Gillian would never come back of her own free will. Gillian had confessed that when she even thought the name of their town, she broke out in hives. Just seeing a map of Massachusetts made her sick to her stomach. The past was so wretched she refused to think about it; she still woke in the night remembering what pathetic little orphans they'd been. Forget a visit. Forget any sort of relationship with the aunts, who never understood what it meant for the sisters to be such outsiders. Someone would have to pay Gillian a quarter of a million, cash, to get her to cross back over the Mississippi, no matter how much she would love to see her dear nieces, who were, of course, always in her thoughts.

The lesson Sally had learned so long ago in the kitchen—to be careful what you wish for—was so far and so faded it had turned to yellow dust. But it was the sort of dust that can never be swept up, and instead waits in the corner and blows into the eyes of those you love when a draft moves through your house. Antonia was nearly four, and Kylie was beginning to sleep through the night, and life seemed quite wonderful in every way, when the deathwatch beetle was found beside the chair where Michael most often sat at supper. This insect, which marks off time, clicking like a clock, issues the sound no one ever wants to hear beside her beloved. A man's tenure on earth is limited enough, but once the beetle's ticking begins there's no way to stop it; there's no plug to pull, no pendulum to stop, no switch that will restore the time you once thought you had.

The aunts listened to the ticking for several weeks and finally drew Sally aside to issue a warning, but Sally would pay no attention. "Nonsense," she said, and she laughed out loud. She tolerated the clients who still came to the back door at dusk every now and then, but she would not allow the aunts' foolishness to affect her family. The aunts' practice was rubbish and nothing more, a gruel mixed up to feed the delusions of the desperate. Sally wouldn't hear another word about it. She wouldn't look when the aunts insisted on pointing out that a black dog had taken to sitting out on the sidewalk every evening. She wouldn't listen when they swore that the dog always pointed its face to the sky whenever Michael approached, and that it howled at the sight of him and quickly backed away from his shadow, tail between its legs.

In spite of Sally's admonition, the aunts placed myrtle beneath Michael's pillow and urged him to bathe with holly and a bar of their special black soap. Into his jacket pocket they slipped the foot of a rabbit they had once caught eating their lettuce. They mixed rosemary into his breakfast cereal, lavender into his nightly cup of tea. Still they heard the beetle in the dining room. Finally they said a prayer backward, but of course that had consequences of its own: soon everyone in the house came down with the flu and insomnia and a rash that wouldn't go away for weeks, not even when a mixture of calamine and balm of Gilead was applied to the skin. By the end of the winter, Kylie and Antonia had begun crying whenever their father tried to leave the room. The aunts explained to Sally that no one who was doomed could hear the sound of the deathwatch beetle, and this was why Michael insisted that nothing could possibly go wrong. All the same he must have known something: He stopped wearing a watch and set back all the clocks. Then, when the ticking grew louder, he pulled down all the shades in the house and kept them drawn against the sun and the moon, as if that could stop time. As if anything could.

Sally didn't believe a word the aunts said. Still she grew nervous from all this talk of death. Her skin became blotchy; her hair lost its shine. She stopped eating and sleeping and she hated to let Michael out of her sight. Now whenever he kissed her, she cried and wished she had never fallen in love in the first place. It had made her too helpless, because that's what love did. There was no way around it and no way to fight it. Now if she lost, she lost everything. Not that it would happen just because the aunts said it would. They were know-nothings, as a matter of fact. Sally had gone down to the public library and looked through every entomological reference book. The deathwatch beetle ate wood and nothing more. How did the aunts like that! Furniture and woodwork might be in danger, but flesh and blood were safe, or so Sally then believed.

One rainy afternoon, as she was folding a white tablecloth, Sally thought she heard something. The dining room was empty and no one else was home, but there it was. A click, a clatter, like a heartbeat or a clock. She covered her ears with her hands, allowing the tablecloth to tumble to the floor in a heap of clean linen. She refused to believe in superstition, she wouldn't; yet it was claiming her, and that was when she saw something dart beneath Michael's chair. A shadowy creature, too swift and too artful to ever be caught beneath a boot heel.

That night, at twilight, Sally found the aunts in the kitchen. She dropped to her knees and begged them to help her, just as all those desperate women before her had done. She offered up all that she had of any value: the rings on her fingers, her two daughters, her blood, but the aunts shook their heads sadly.

"I'll do anything," Sally cried. "I'll believe in anything. Just tell me what to do."

But the aunts had already tried their best, and the beetle was still beside Michael's chair. Some fates are guaranteed, no matter who tries to intervene. On a spring evening that was particularly pleasant and mild, Michael stepped off the curb on his way home from the hardware store and was killed by a car full of teenagers who, in celebration of their courage and youth, had had too much to drink.

After that, Sally didn't talk for an entire year. She simply had nothing to say. She could not look at the aunts; they were pitiful charlatans, in her opinion, old women who wielded less power than the flies left to die on the windowsills, trapped behind glass, translucent wings tapping weakly. *Let me out. Let me out.* If she heard the rustle of the aunts' skirts announce their entrance into a room, Sally walked out. If she recognized their footsteps on the stairs, as they came to check on her or wish her good night, she got up from the chair by the window in time to bolt her door, and she never heard them knocking; she just put her hands over her ears.

Whenever Sally went to the drugstore, for toothpaste or diaper rash cream, she'd see the drugstore girl behind the counter and their eyes would lock. Sally understood now what love could do to a person. She understood far too well to ever let it happen to her again. The poor drugstore girl couldn't have been much more than thirty, but she seemed old, her hair had already turned white; if she needed to tell you anything—a price, for instance, or the special ice cream sundae of the week—she'd have to write it out on a pad of paper. Her husband sat on the last stool at the counter nearly all the time, nursing a cup of coffee for hours. But Sally barely noticed him; it was the girl she couldn't take her eyes off; she was looking for that person who had first appeared in the aunts' kitchen, that sweet rosy girl filled with hope.

One Saturday, when Sally was buying vitamin C, the drugstore girl slipped her a piece of white paper along with her change. *Help me*, she had written, in perfect script. But Sally could not even help herself. She couldn't help her children or her husband or the way the world had spun out of control. From then on Sally would not shop at the drugstore. Instead, she had everything they needed delivered by a high school boy, who left their order on the bluestone path—rain, sleet, or snow—refusing to come to their door, even if that meant forfeiting his tip.

During that year, Sally let the aunts take care of Antonia and Kylie. She let bees nest in the rafters in July and allowed snow to pile up along the walkway in January so that the postman, who had always feared that he'd break his neck one way or the other delivering mail to the Owenses, would not venture past their gate. She didn't bother about healthy dinners and mealtimes; she waited until she was starving, then ate canned peas out of the tin as she stood near the sink. Her hair became permanently knotted; there were holes in her socks and her gloves. She rarely went outside now, and when she did, people made sure to avoid her. Children were afraid of the blank look in her eyes. Neighbors who used to invite Sally over for coffee now crossed the street if they saw her coming and quickly murmured a prayer; they preferred to look straight into the sun and be temporarily blinded, rather than see what had happened to her.

Gillian phoned once a week, always on Tuesday nights, at ten o'clock, the only schedule she had kept to in years. Sally would hold the receiver to her ear and she'd listen, but she still wouldn't talk. "You can't fall apart," Gillian would insist in her rich, urgent voice. "That's my job," she'd say.

All the same, it was Sally who wouldn't bathe or eat or play pattycake with her baby. Sally was the one who cried so many tears there were mornings when she couldn't open her eyes. Each evening she searched the dining room for the deathwatch beetle who'd been said to have caused all this grief. Of course she never found it and so she didn't believe in it. But such things hide, in the folds of a widow's black skirts and beneath the white sheets where one person sleeps, restlessly dreaming of everything she'll never have. In time, Sally stopped believing in anything at all, and then the whole world went gray. She could not see orange or red, and certain shades of green—her favorite sweater and the leaves of new daffodils—were completely and utterly lost.

"Wake up," Gillian would say when she called on her appointed night. "What do I have to do to snap you out of it?"

Really, there was nothing Gillian could say, although Sally kept on listening when her sister called. She thought over her sister's words of advice because lately Gillian's voice was the only sound she wanted to hear; it brought a comfort nothing else could, and Sally found herself positioned by the phone on Tuesdays, awaiting her sister's call.

"Life is for the living," Gillian told her. "Life is what you make of it. Come on. Just listen to what I'm saying. Please."

Sally thought long and hard each time she hung up the phone. She thought about the girl in the drugstore and the sound of Antonia's footsteps on the stairs when she went up to bed without a good-night hug. She thought about Michael's life and his death, and about every second they had spent together. She considered each one of his kisses and all the words he had ever said to her. Everything was still gray—the paintings Antonia brought home from school and slipped beneath her door, the flannel pajamas Kylie wore on chilly mornings, the velvet curtains that kept the world at bay. But now Sally began to order things in her mind—grief and joy, dollars and cents, a baby's cry and the look on her face when you blew her a kiss on a windy afternoon. Such things might be worth something, a glance, a peek, a deeper look.

And when a year had passed, to the very day, since the moment when Michael had stepped off the curb, Sally saw green leaves outside her window. It was a delicate vine that had always wound its way up the drainpipe, but on this day Sally noticed how tender each leaf was, how absolutely new, so that the green was nearly yellow, and the yellow rich as butter. Sally spent a good portion of her days in bed, and it was already afternoon. She saw the golden light filtering through the curtains, and the way it spread out in bars across her wall. Quickly, she got out of bed and brushed her long black hair. She put on a dress she hadn't worn since the previous spring, took her coat from the hook by the back door, and went out for a walk.

Again it was spring, and the sky was so blue it could take your breath away. It was blue and she could see it, the color of his eyes, the color of veins beneath the skin, and of hope and of shirts pinned to a laundry line. Sally could make out nearly every shade and hue that had been missing all year, although she still could not see orange, which was too close to the color of the faded stop sign the teenagers never saw on the day Michael was killed, and she never would again. But orange was never a great favorite of Sally's, a small loss, considering all the others.

She walked on, through the center of town, wearing her old wool coat and her high black boots. It was a warm and breezy day, too warm for Sally's heavy clothes, so she draped her coat over her arm. The sun went through the fabric of her dress, a hot hand across flesh and bones. Sally felt as though she'd been dead and now that she was back she was particularly sensitive to the world of the living: the touch of the wind against her skin, the gnats in the air, the scent of mud and new leaves, the sweetness of blues and greens. For the first time in ages, Sally thought how pleasant it would be to speak again, to read bedtime stories to her daughters and recite a poem and name all the flowers that bloomed early in the season, lily of the valley and jack-in-the-pulpit and purple hyacinth. She was thinking about flowers, those white ones shaped like bells, when, for no particular reason, she turned left on Endicott Street and headed for the park.

In this park there was a pond, where a couple of horrid swans ruled, a playground with a slide and swing, and a green field where the older boys held serious soccer matches and baseball games that went on past dusk. Sally could hear the voices of children playing, and she walked into the park eagerly. Her cheeks were pink and her long black hair flew out behind her like a ribbon; amazingly enough, she had discovered that she was still young. Sally planned to take the path down to the pond, but she stopped when she saw the wrought-iron bench. Sitting there, as they did every day, were the aunts. Sally had never thought to ask what they did with the children all day while she stayed in bed, unable to drag herself from beneath the covers until the long afternoon shadows fell across her pillowcase.

On this day's outing, the aunts had brought their knitting along. They were working on a throw for Kylie's crib, made out of the finest black wool, a coverlet so soft that whenever Kylie would sleep beneath it she'd dream of little black lambs and fields of grass. Antonia was beside the aunts, her legs neatly crossed. Kylie had been plopped down on the grass, where she sat motionless. All of them wore black woolen coats, and their complexions seemed sallow in the afternoon light. Antonia's red hair looked especially brilliant, a color so deep and startling it appeared quite unnatural in the sun. The aunts did not speak to each other, and the girls certainly did not play. The aunts saw no point in jumping rope or tossing a ball back and forth. In their opinion, such things were a silly waste of time. Better to observe the world around you. Better to watch the swans, and the blue sky, and the other children, who shouted and laughed during wild games of kickball and tag. Learn to be as quiet as a mouse. Concentrate until you are as silent as the spider in the grass.

A ball was being walloped around by a bunch of unruly boys, and finally it was booted too hard. It flew into the bright blue air, then rolled along the grass, past a quince in bloom. Antonia had been imagining that she was a blue jay, free among the branches of a weeping birch. Now she happily jumped off the bench and scooped up the ball, then ran toward a boy who'd been sent to retrieve it. The boy wasn't more than ten, but he was still as death, pale as paste, when Antonia approached. She held the ball out to him.

"Here you go," Antonia said.

By then all the children in the park had stopped their playing. The swans flapped their big, beautiful wings. More than ten years later, Sally still dreams about those swans, a male and a female who guarded the pond ferociously, as though they were Dobermans. She dreams about the way the aunts clucked their tongues, sadly, since they knew what was about to happen.

Poor Antonia looked at the boy, who had not moved and did not even appear to be breathing. She tilted her head, as though trying to figure whether he was stupid or merely polite.

"Don't you want the ball?" she asked him.

The swans took flight slowly as the boy ran to Antonia, grabbed the ball, then pushed her down. Her black coat flared out behind her; her black shoes flew right off her feet.

"Stop it!" Sally called out. Her first words in a year.

The children on the playground all heard her. They took off running together, as far away as possible from Antonia Owens, who might hex you if you did her wrong, and from her aunts, who might boil up garden toads and slip them into your stew, and from her mother, who was so angry and protective she might just freeze you in time, ensuring that you were forever trapped on the green grass at the age of ten or eleven.

Sally packed their clothes that same night. She loved the aunts and knew they meant well, but what she wanted for her girls was something the aunts could never provide. She wanted a town where no one pointed when her daughters walked down the street. She wanted her own house, where birthday parties could be held in the living room, with streamers and a hired clown and a cake, and a neighborhood where every house was the same and not a single one had a slate roof where squirrels nested, or bats in the garden, or woodwork that never needed polishing.

In the morning, Sally phoned a real-estate broker in New York, then lugged her suitcases out to the porch. The aunts insisted that, no matter what, the past would follow Sally around. She'd wind up like Gillian, a sorry soul that only grew heavier in each new town. She couldn't run away, that's what they told her, but in Sally's opinion, there was no proof of that. No one had driven the old station wagon for over a year, but it started right up and was sputtering like a kettle as Sally got her girls settled into the backseat. The aunts vowed she'd be miserable and they shook their fingers at her. But as soon as Sally took off, the aunts began to shrink, until they were like little black toadstools waving good-bye at the far end of the street where Sally and Gillian used to play hopscotch on hot August days, when they had only each other for company and the asphalt all around them was melting into black pools.

Sally got onto Route 95 and went south, and she didn't stop until Kylie woke, sweaty and confused and extremely overheated beneath the black woolen blanket that smelled of lavender, the scent that always clung to the aunts' clothes. Kylie had been dreaming that she was being chased by a flock of sheep; she called out *"Baa, baa"* in a panicky voice, then climbed over the seat to be closer to her mother. Sally soothed her with a hug and the promise of ice cream, but it was not so easy to deal with Antonia.

Antonia, who loved the aunts and had always been their favorite, refused to be consoled. She was wearing one of the black dresses they'd sewn for her at the dressmaker's on Peabody, and her red hair stuck out from her head in angry wisps. She gave off a sour, lemony odor, which was a mixture of equal parts rage and despair.

"I despise you," she informed Sally as they sat in the cabin of the ferry that took them across Long Island Sound. It was one of those odd and surprising spring days that suddenly turn nearly as hot as summer. Sally and her children had been eating sticky slices of tangerine and drinking the Cokes they'd bought at the snack bar, but now that the waves had grown wilder, their stomachs were lurching. Sally had just finished a postcard she planned to send to Gillian, although she wasn't certain whether her sister was still at her last address. *Have finally done it*, she'd scrawled in handwriting that was looser than anyone would have expected from someone so orderly. *Have tied the sheets together and jumped!*

"I will hate you for the rest of my life," Antonia went on, and her little hands formed into fists.

"That's your prerogative," Sally said brightly, though deep down she was hurt. She waved the postcard in front of her face in order to cool off. Antonia could really get to her, but this time Sally wasn't going to let that happen. "I do think you'll change your mind."

"No," Antonia said. "I won't. I'll never forgive you."

The aunts had adored Antonia because she was beautiful and nasty. They encouraged her to be bossy and self-centered, and during that year when Sally had been too sad and broken to speak to her children, or even take an interest in them, Antonia had been allowed to stay up past midnight and order adults around. She ate Butterfingers for dinner and smacked her baby sister with a rolled-up newspaper for fun. She had been doing just as she pleased for some time, and she was smart enough to know all that had changed as of this very day. She threw her tangerine down on the deck and squashed it beneath her foot, and when that didn't work she cried and pleaded to be taken home.

"Please," she begged her mother. "I want the aunts. Take me back there. I'll be good," she vowed.

By then, Sally was crying too. When she was a girl, the aunts had been the ones to sit up with her all night whenever she'd had an ear infection or the flu; they'd told her stories and fixed her broth and hot tea. They were the ones who'd rocked Gillian when she couldn't fall asleep, especially at the start, when the girls first came to live at the house on Magnolia Street, and Gillian couldn't sleep a wink.

There had been a rainstorm the night that Sally and Gillian were told their parents weren't coming back, and it was their bad fortune that another storm struck when they were in the plane on their way to Massachusetts. Sally was four, but she remembers the lightning they flew through; she can close her eyes and conjure it with no trouble at all. They were right up in the sky alongside those fierce white lines, with no place to hide. Gillian had vomited several times, and when the plane began to land she started to scream. Sally had to hold her hand over her sister's mouth and promise her gumballs and licorice sticks if she'd only be quiet for a few minutes more.

Sally had picked out their best party dresses to wear for the trip. Gillian's was a pale violet, Sally's pink trimmed with ivory lace. They were holding hands as they walked through the airport terminal, listening to the funny sound their crinolines made every time they took a step, when they saw the aunts waiting for them. The aunts stood on tiptoe, the better to see over the barricades; they had balloons tied to their sleeves, so that the children would recognize them. After they hugged the girls and collected their small leather suitcases, the aunts bundled Sally and Gillian into two black wool coats, then reached into their purses and brought out gumballs and red licorice, as if they knew exactly what little girls needed, or, at any rate, exactly what they might want.

Sally was grateful for all the aunts had done, really she was. Still, she had made up her mind. She would get the key at the realtor's for the house she would later buy, then get hold of some furniture. She would have to find a job eventually, but she had a little money from Michael's insurance policy, and frankly she wasn't going to think about the past or the future. She was thinking about the highway in front of her. She was thinking about road signs and right turns, and she just couldn't afford to listen when Antonia started to howl, which set Kylie off as well. Instead, she switched on the radio and sang along and told herself that sometimes the right thing felt all wrong until it was over and done with.

By the time they turned into the driveway of their new house, it was already late in the day. A band of children was playing kickball in the street, and when Sally got out of the car she waved and the children waved back, each and every one of them. A robin was on the front lawn, pulling at the grass and the weeds, and all up and down the street, lights were being turned on and tables were set for dinner. The scent of pot roast and chicken paprikash and lasagna drifted through the mild air. Sally's girls had both fallen asleep in the backseat, their faces streaked with dirt and tears. Sally had bought them ice cream cones and lollipops; she'd told stories for hours and stopped at two toy stores. Still, it would take years before they forgave her. They laughed at the little white fence Sally put up at the edge of their lawn. Antonia asked to paint her bedroom walls black and Kylie begged for a black kittycat. Both of these wishes were denied. Antonia's room was painted yellow, and Kylie was given a goldfish named Sunshine, but that didn't mean the girls had forgotten where they came from or that they didn't long for it still.

Every summer, in August, they would visit the aunts. They would draw in their breath as soon as they turned the corner onto Magnolia and could spy the big old house with its black fence and green-tinted windows. The aunts always made a tipsy chocolate cake and gave Antonia and Kylie far too many presents. There were no bedtimes, of course, and no well-balanced meals. No rules were put forth about drawing on the wallpaper or filling the bathtub so high that bubbles and tepid water sloshed over the sides and dripped down through the ceiling of the parlor. Every year the girls were taller when they arrived for their visit—they knew this because the aunts were seeming smaller all the time—and every year they went wild: they danced through the herb garden and played softball on the front lawn and stayed up past midnight. Sometimes they ate nothing but Snickers and Milky Ways for nearly the whole week, until their stomachs began to ache and they finally called for a salad or a glass of milk.

During their August vacations, Sally insisted on getting the girls out of the house, at least in the afternoons. She took them on day trips, to the beach at Plum Island, to the swan boats in Boston, out into the blue bay in Gloucester on rented sailboats. But the girls always begged to return to the aunts' house. They pouted and made Sally's life miserable, until she gave in. It wasn't the girls' bad temper that convinced Sally to turn back for the house, it was that they were united in something. This was so unusual and so delightful to see that Sally just couldn't say no.

Sally had expected Antonia to be a big sister in the same manner she herself had been, but that wasn't Antonia's style. Antonia felt no responsibility to anyone; she was nobody's caretaker. From the very start she would tease Kylie without mercy and could bring her little sister to tears with a glance. It was only at the aunts' house that the girls became allies, perhaps even friends. Here, where everything was worn and frayed, except for the shining woodwork, the girls spent hours together. They collected lavender and had picnics in the shade of the garden. They sat in the cool parlor late in the day, or sprawled out on the second-floor landing where there were thin bands of lemony sunlight, playing Parcheesi and endless rounds of gin rummy.

Their closeness may have been the result of sharing the attic bedroom, or only because the girls had no choice of playmates, since the children in town still crossed over to the other side of the street when they passed the Owens house. Whatever the reason, it brought Sally great joy to see the girls at the kitchen table, heads bent near enough to touch as they worked a puzzle or made a card to send off to Gillian at her new address in Iowa or New Mexico. Soon enough, they'd be at each other's throats, arguing over petty privileges or some nasty trick of Antonia's—a daddy longlegs left under Kylie's baby blanket, which she continued to be attached to at the age of eleven and even at twelve, or dirt and stones slipped into the bottom of her boots. And so Sally allowed the girls to do as they wished, for that one week in August, even though she knew, in the end, it was not to their benefit.

Each year, as their vacation wore on, the girls always slept later and later in the day; black circles appeared around their eyes. They began to complain about the heat, which made them too tired to even walk to the drugstore for ice cream sundaes and cold bottles of Coke, though they found the old woman who worked there fascinating, since she never said a word and could make a banana split in seconds flat, peeling the banana and pouring out the syrups and marshmallow whip before you could blink your eyes. After a while, Kylie and Antonia were spending most of their time in the garden, where belladonna and digitalis have always grown beside the peppermint, and the cats the aunts love so dearly—including two ratty creatures from Sally's childhood, Magpie and Raven, who have simply refused to die—still dig in the rubbish heap for fish heads and bones.

There is always a time when Sally knows they have to leave. Each August, a night comes when she wakes from a deep sleep, and when she goes to the window she sees that her daughters are out by themselves in the moonlight. There are toads between the cabbages and the zinnias. There are green caterpillars munching at the leaves, preparing to turn into white moths that will fling themselves at screen windows and at the lights that burn brightly beside back doors. There is the same horse's skull nailed to the fence, bleached white now and falling to dust, but still more than enough to keep people away.

Sally always waits until her girls come inside the house before she crawls back into bed. The very next morning, she will make her excuses and take off a day or two earlier than scheduled. She will wake her daughters, and though they gripe about the early hour and the heat, and will surely be sullen all day, they'll pile into the car. Before she leaves, Sally will kiss the aunts and promise to phone often. Sometimes her throat closes up when she notices how the aunts are aging, when she sees all those weeds in the garden and the way the wisteria is drooping, since no one ever thinks to give it water or a bit of mulch. Still, she never feels as though she's made a mistake after she drives down Magnolia Street; she doesn't allow herself a single regret, not even when her daughters cry and complain. She knows where she's going, and what she has to do. She could, after all, find her way to Route 95 South blindfolded. She could do it in the dark, in fair weather or foul; she can do it even when it seems she will run out of gas. It doesn't matter what people tell you. It doesn't matter what they might say. Sometimes you have to leave home. Sometimes, running away means you're headed in the exact right direction.

PREMONITIONS

CROSSED knives set out on the dinner table means there's bound to be a quarrel, but so do two sisters living under the same roof, particularly when one of them is Antonia Owens. At the age of sixteen, Antonia is so beautiful that it's impossible for any stranger seeing her for the first time to even begin to guess how miserable she can make those closest to her. She is nastier now than she was as a little girl, but her hair is a more stunning shade of red and her smile is so glorious that the boys in the high school all want to sit next to her in class, although once they do, these boys freeze up completely, simply because they're so close to her, and they can't help embarrassing themselves by staring at her, all googly-eyed and moon-faced, infatuated beyond belief.

It makes sense that Antonia's little sister, Kylie, who will soon be thirteen, spends hours locked in the bathroom, crying over how ugly she is. Kylie is one inch short of six feet, a giant, in her book. She's as skinny as a stork, with knees that hit against each other when she walks. Her nose and eyes are usually pink as a rabbit's from all the sobbing she's been doing lately, and she's just about given up on her hair, which has frizzed up from the humidity. To have a sister who is perfect, at least from the outside, is bad enough. To have one who can make you feel like a speck of dust with a few well-chosen mean words is almost more than Kylie can take.

Part of the problem is that Kylie can never think of a smart comeback when Antonia sweetly inquires whether she's considered sleeping with a brick on her head or thought about getting herself a wig. She's tried, she's even practiced various mean putdowns with her one and only friend, a thirteen-year-old boy named Gideon Barnes, who is a master at the art of grossing people out, and she still can't do it. Kylie is the sort of tender spirit who cries when someone steps on a spider; in her universe, hurting another creature is an unnatural act. When Antonia teases her, all Kylie can do is open and close her mouth like a fish that has been thrown onto dry land, before locking herself in the bathroom to cry once more. On quiet nights, she curls up on her bed, clutching her old baby blanket, the black wool one that still does not have a single hole, since it somehow seems to repel moths. All up and down the street the neighbors can hear her weeping. They shake their heads and pity her, and some of the women on the block, especially the ones who grew up with older sisters, bring over homemade brownies and chocolate cookies, forgetting what a plateful of sweets can do to a young girl's skin, thinking only of their own relief from the sound of crying, which echoes through hedges and over fences.

These women in the neighborhood respect Sally Owens, and

what's more, they truly like her. She has a serious expression even when she laughs, and long dark hair, and no idea of how pretty she is. Sally is always the first parent listed on the snow chain, since it's best to have someone responsible in charge of letting other parents know when school will be closed in stormy weather, rather than one of those ditsy mothers who are prone to believe life will work itself out just fine, without any intervention from somebody sensible. All over the neighborhood, Sally is well known for both her kindness and her prudent ways. If you really need her, she'll baby-sit for your toddler at a moment's notice on a Saturday afternoon; she'll pick your kids up at the high school or lend you sugar or eggs. She'll sit there with you on your back porch if you should find some woman's phone number written on a slip of paper in your husband's night-table drawer, and she'll be smart enough to listen rather than offer some half-baked advice. More important, she'll never mention your difficulties again or repeat a word you say. When you ask about her own marriage, she gets a dreamy look on her face that is completely unlike her usual expression. "That was ages ago," is all she'll say. "That was another lifetime."

Since leaving Massachusetts, Sally has worked as an assistant to the vice principal at the high school. In all this time, she has had fewer than a dozen dates, and those attempts at romance were set up by neighbors, fix-ups that went nowhere but back to her own front door, long before she was expected home. Sally now finds that she's often tired and cranky, and although she's still terrific looking, she's not getting any younger. Lately, she's been so tense that the muscles in her neck feel like strands of wire that someone has been twisting.

When her neck starts to go, when she wakes up from a deep sleep in a panic, and she gets so lonely the ancient janitor at the high school starts to look good, Sally reminds herself of how hard she has worked to make a good life for her girls. Antonia is so popular that for three years running she's been chosen to play the lead in the school play. Kylie, though she seems to have no close friends other than Gideon Barnes, is the Nassau County spelling champion and the president of the chess club. Sally's girls have always had birthday parties and ballet lessons. She has made absolutely certain that they never miss their dentist appointments and that they're at school on time every weekday morning. They are expected to do their homework before they watch TV and are not allowed to stay up past midnight or idly hang out on the Turnpike or at the mall. Sally's children are rooted here; they're treated like anyone else, just normal kids, like any others on the block. This is why Sally left Massachusetts and the aunts in the first place. It's why she refuses to think about what might be missing from her life.

Never look back, that's what she's told herself. Don't think about swans or being alone in the dark. Don't think of storms, or lightning and thunder, or the true love you won't ever have. Life is brushing your teeth and making breakfast for your children and not thinking about things, and as it turns out, Sally is first-rate at all of this. She gets things done, and done on time. Still, she often dreams of the aunts' garden. In the farthest corner there was lemon verbena, lemon thyme, and lemon balm. When Sally sat there cross-legged, and closed her eyes, the citrus scent was so rich she sometimes got dizzy. Everything in the garden had a purpose, even the lush peonies, which protect against bad weather and motion sickness and have been known to ward off evil. Sally isn't sure she can still name all the varieties of the herbs that grew there, although she thinks she could recognize coltsfoot and comfrey by sight, lavender and rosemary by their distinctive scents.

Her own garden is simple and halfhearted, which is just the way she likes it. There is a hedge of listless lilacs, some dogwoods, and a small vegetable patch where only yellow tomatoes and a few spindly cucumbers ever grow. The cucumber seedlings seem dusty from the heat on this last afternoon in June. It is so great to have the summers off. It's worth everything she has to put up with over at the high school, where you have to always keep a smile on your face. Ed Borelli, the vice principal and Sally's immediate superior, has suggested that everyone who works in the office have a grin surgically applied in order to be ready when parents come in and complain. Niceness counts, Ed Borelli reminds the secretaries on awful days, when unruly students are being suspended and meetings overlap and the school board threatens to extend the school year due to snow days. But false cheer is draining, and if you pretend long enough there's always the possibility that you'll become an automaton. By the end of the school term, Sally usually finds herself saying "Mr. Borelli will be right with you" in her sleep. That's when she starts to count the days until summer; that's when she just can't wait for the last bell to ring.

Since the semester ended twenty-four hours earlier, Sally should be feeling great, but she's not. All she can make out is the throbbing of her own pulse and the beat of the radio blaring in Antonia's bedroom upstairs. Something is not right. It's nothing apparent, nothing that will come up and smack you in the face; it's less like a hole in a sweater than a frayed hem that has unraveled into a puddle of thread. The air in the house feels charged, so that the hair on the back of Sally's neck stands up, and her white shirt gives off little sparks.

All afternoon, Sally finds she's waiting for disaster. She tells herself to snap out of it; she doesn't even believe it's possible to foretell future misfortune, since there has never been any scientific documentation that such visionary phenomena exist. But when she does the marketing, she grabs a dozen lemons and before she can stop herself she begins to cry, there in the produce department, as though she were suddenly homesick for that old house on Magnolia Street, after all these years. When she leaves the grocery store, Sally drives by the YMCA field, where Kylie and her friend Gideon are playing soccer. Gideon is the vice president of the chess club, and Kylie suspects he may have thrown the deciding match in her favor so she could be president. Kylie is the only person on earth who seems able to tolerate Gideon. His mother, Jeannie Barnes, went into therapy two weeks after he was born; that's how difficult he was and continues to be. He simply refuses to be like anyone else. He just won't allow it. Now, for instance, he's shaved off all his hair and is wearing combat boots and a black leather jacket, though it must be ninety in the shade.

Sally is never comfortable around Gideon; she finds him rude and obnoxious and has always considered him a bad influence. But seeing him and Kylie playing soccer, she feels a wave of relief. Kylie is laughing as Gideon stumbles over his own boots as he chases after the ball. She's not hurt or kidnapped, she's here on this field of grass, running as fast as she can. It's a hot, lazy afternoon, a day like any other, and Sally would do well to relax. She's silly to have been so certain that something was about to go wrong. That's what she tells herself, but it's not what she believes. When Antonia comes home, thrilled to have gotten a summer job at the ice cream parlor up on the Turnpike, Sally is so suspicious she insists on calling the owner and finding out what Antonia's hours and responsibilities will be. She asks for the owner's personal history as well, including address, marital status, and number of dependents.

"Thanks for embarrassing me," Antonia says coolly when Sally hangs up the phone. "My boss will think I'm real mature, having my mother check on me."

These days Antonia wears only black, which makes her red hair seem even more brilliant. Last week, to test out her allegiance to black clothes, Sally bought her a white cotton sweater trimmed with lace, which she knew any number of Antonia's girlfriends would have died for. Antonia tossed the sweater into the washer with a package of Rit dye, then threw the coal-colored thing into the dryer. The result was an article of clothing so small that whenever she wears it Sally frets that Antonia will wind up running off with someone, just the way Gillian did. It worries Sally to think that one of her girls might follow in her sister's footsteps, a trail that has led to only self-destruction and wasted time, including three brief marriages, not one of which yielded a cent of alimony.

Certainly, Antonia is greedy the way beautiful girls sometimes are, and she thinks quite well of herself. But now, on this hot June day, she is suddenly filled with doubt. What if she isn't as special as she thinks she is? What if her beauty fades as soon as she passes eighteen, the way it does with some girls, who have no idea that they've peaked until it's all over and they glance in the mirror to discover they no longer recognize themselves. She's always assumed she'll be an actress someday; she'll go to Manhattan or Los Angeles the day after graduation and be given a leading role, just as she has been all the way through high school. Now she's not so sure. She doesn't know if she has any talent, or if she even cares. Frankly, she never liked acting much; it was having everyone stare at her that was so appealing. It was knowing they couldn't take their eyes off her.

When Kylie comes home, all sweaty and grass-stained and gawky, Antonia doesn't even bother to insult her.

"Didn't you want to say something to me?" Kylie asks tentatively when they meet in the hallway. Her brown hair is sticking straight up and her cheeks are flushed and blotchy with heat. She's a perfect target and she knows it.

"You can use the shower first," Antonia says in a voice so sad and dreamy it doesn't even sound like her.

"What's that supposed to mean?" Kylie says, but Antonia has already drifted down the hall, to paint her nails red and consider her future, something she has never once done before.

By dinnertime Sally has nearly forgotten the sense of dread she carried around earlier in the day. Never believe what you can't see, that's always been Sally's motto. You have nothing to fear but fear itself, she quoted again and again when her girls were little and convinced monsters resided on the second shelf of the laundry closet in the hall. But just when she's relaxed enough to consider having a beer, the shades in the kitchen snap shut all at once, as if there is a buildup of energy in the walls. Sally has made a bean and tofu salad, carrot sticks, and cold marinated broccoli, with angel food cake for dessert. The cake, however, is now doubtful; when the shades snap closed the cake begins to sink, first on one side, then on the other, until it is as flat as a serving plate.

"It's nothing," Sally says to her daughters about the way the shades seem to have been activated by a strange force, but her voice sounds unsteady, even to herself.

The evening is so humid and dense that laundry left on the line will only get wetter if left out overnight. The sky is deep blue, a curtain of heat.

"It's something, all right," Antonia says, because an odd sort of wind has just started up. It comes in through the screen door and the open windows, rattling the silverware and the dinner plates. Kylie has to run and get herself a sweater. Even though the temperature is still climbing, the wind is giving her the shivers; it's making goose bumps rise along her skin.

Outside, in the neighbors' backyards, swing sets are uprooted and cats claw at back doors, desperate to be let in. Halfway down the block, a poplar tree cracks in two and plummets to the ground, hitting a fire hydrant and crashing through the window of a parked Honda Civic. That's when Sally and her daughters hear the knocking. The girls look up at the ceiling, then turn to their mother.

"Squirrels," Sally assures them. "Nesting in the attic."

But the knocking continues, and the wind does, too, and the heat just rises higher and higher. Finally, near midnight, the neighborhood quiets down. At last people can get some sleep. Sally is one of the few who stay up late, in order to fix an apple tart—complete with her secret ingredients, black pepper and nutmeg—which she'll freeze and have ready to take to the block party on the Fourth of July. But even Sally falls asleep before long, in spite of the weather; she stretches out under a cool white sheet and keeps the bedroom windows open so that the breeze comes in and wraps around the room. The first of the season's crickets have grown quiet and the sparrows are nesting in the bushes, safe within a bower of branches that are too delicate to support a cat's weight. And just when people are beginning to dream, of cut grass and blueberry pie and lions who lie down beside lambs, a ring appears around the moon.

A halo around the moon is always a sign of disruption, either a change in the weather, a fever to come, or a streak of bad fortune that won't go away. But when it's a double ring, all tangled and snarled, like an agitated rainbow or a love affair gone wrong, anything can happen. At times such as this, it's wise not to answer the telephone. People who know enough to be careful always shut their windows; they lock their doors, and they never dare to kiss their sweethearts over a garden gate or reach out to pat a stray dog. Trouble is just like love, after all; it comes in unannounced and takes over before you've had a chance to reconsider, or even to think.

High above the neighborhood, the ring has already begun to twist around itself, an illuminated snake of possibility, double-looped and pulled tight by gravity. If people hadn't been sound asleep, they might have gazed out their windows and admired the beautiful circle of light, but they slept on, oblivious, not noticing the moon, or the silence, or the Oldsmobile that had already pulled into Sally Owens's driveway to park behind the Honda Sally bought a few years ago to replace the aunts' ancient station wagon. On a night such as this, it's possible for a woman to get out of her car so quietly none of the neighbors will hear her. When it's this warm in June, when the sky is this inky and thick, a knock on the screen door doesn't even echo. It falls into your dreams, like a stone into a stream, so that you wake suddenly, heart beating too fast, pulse going crazy, drowning inside your own panic.

Sally sits up in bed, knowing that she should stay exactly where she is. She's been dreaming about the swans again; she's been watching them take flight. For eleven years, she has done all the right things, she's been conscientious and trustworthy, rational and kind, but that doesn't mean she can't recognize the sulfurous odor of trouble. That's what's outside her front door now, trouble, pure and undiluted. It's calling to her, like a moth bumping against a screen, and she just can't ignore it. She pulls on jeans and a white T-shirt and gathers her dark hair into a ponytail. She's going to kick herself for this, and she knows it. She'll wonder why she can't just ignore that jangly feeling that comes over her and why she's always compelled to try to set things right.

Those people who warn that you can't run away because your past will track you down may be right on target. Sally looks out the front window. There on the porch is the girl who could get into more trouble than anyone, all grown up. It's been too many years, it's been an eternity, but Gillian is as beautiful as ever, only dusty and jittery and so weak in the knees that when Sally throws open the door, Gillian has to lean against the brick wall for support.

"Oh, my god, it's you," Gillian says, as if Sally were the unexpected visitor. In eighteen years they have seen each other only three times, when Sally went west. Gillian never once crossed back over the Mississippi, just as she'd vowed when she first left the aunts' house. "It's really, really you!"

Gillian has cut her blond hair shorter than ever; she smells like sugar and heat. She's got sand in the ridges of her red boots and a little green snake tattooed on her wrist. She hugs Sally fast and tight, before Sally can have time to consider the lateness of the hour and the fact that perhaps Gillian might have called, if not to say she was arriving, then just sometime in the past month, only to let Sally know she was still alive. Two days ago Sally mailed off a letter to Gillian's most recent address, in Tucson. She gave Gillian hell in that letter, about her trail of broken plans and missed opportunities; she spoke too strongly and said too much and now she's relieved that it's a letter Gillian will never get.

But her sense of relief surely doesn't last long. As soon as Gillian begins to talk, Sally knows that something is seriously wrong. Gillian's voice is squeaky, which isn't like her at all. Gillian has always been able to think of a good excuse or an alibi in seconds flat because she's had to soothe the egos of all her boyfriends; usually she's cool and composed, but now she's all but jumping out of her skin.

"I've got a problem," Gillian says.

She looks over her shoulder, then runs her tongue over her lips. She's as nervous as a bug, even though having a problem is nothing particularly new. Gillian can create problems just by walking down the street. She is still the kind of woman who cuts through her finger while slicing a cantaloupe, and then is rushed to the hospital, where the ER doctor who has stitched up her finger falls head over heels for her before she's even been sewn back together.

Gillian stops to take a good look at Sally.

"I can't believe how much I've missed you."

Gillian sounds as if she herself was surprised to discover this. She's sticking her fingernails into the palms of her hands, as if to wake herself from a bad dream. If she weren't desperate, she wouldn't be here, running to her big sister for help, when she's spent her whole life trying to be as self-sufficient as a stone. Everyone else had families, and went east or west or just down the block for Easter or Thanksgiving, but not Gillian. She could always be counted on to take a holiday shift, and afterward she always found herself drawn to the best bar in town, where special hors d'oeuvres are set out for festive occasions, hard-boiled eggs tinted pale pink and aqua, or little turkey-and-cranberry burritos. One Thanksgiving Day Gillian went and got the tattoo on her wrist. It was a hot afternoon in Las Vegas, Nevada, and the sky was the color of a pie plate, and the fellow over at the tattoo parlor promised her it wouldn't hurt, but it did.

"Everything is such a mess," Gillian admits.

"Well, guess what?" Sally tells her sister. "I know you won't believe this, and I know you won't care, but I've actually got my own problems."

The electricity bill, for instance, which has begun to reflect Antonia's increased use of the radio, which is never for an instant turned off. The fact that Sally hasn't had a date in almost two years, not even with some cousin or friend of her next-door neighbor Linda Bennett, and can no longer think of love as a reality, or even as a possibility, however remote. For all the time they've been apart, living separate lives, Gillian has been doing as she pleased, fucking whomever she cares to and waking at noon. She hasn't had to sit up all night with little girls who have chicken pox, or negotiate curfews, or set her alarm for the proper hour because someone needs breakfast or a good talking to. Naturally Gillian looks great. She thinks the world revolves around her.

"Believe me. Your problems are nothing like mine. This time it's really bad, Sally."

Gillian's voice is getting smaller and smaller, but it's still the same voice that got Sally through that horrible year when she couldn't bring herself to speak. It's the voice that urged her on every Tuesday night, no matter what, with a fierce devotion, the kind you acquire only when you've shared the past.

"Okay." Sally sighs. "Let me have it."

Gillian takes a deep breath. "I've got Jimmy in the car." She comes closer, so she can whisper in Sally's ear. "The problem is . . ." This is a hard one, it really is. She has to just get it out and say it, whispered or not. "He's dead."

Sally immediately pulls away from her sister. This is nothing anyone wants to hear on a hot June night, when the fireflies are strung across the lawns. The night is dreamy and deep, but now Sally feels as if she's drained a pot of coffee; her heart is beating like mad. Anyone else might assume Gillian is lying or exaggerating or just goofing around. But Sally knows her sister. She knows better. There's a dead man in the car. Guaranteed.

"Don't do this to me," Sally says.

"Do you think I planned it?"

"So you were driving along, headed for my house, figuring we should finally see each other, and he just happened to die?"

Sally has never met Jimmy, and she can't say she's ever really spoken to him. Once he answered the phone when she called Gillian in Tucson, but he certainly wasn't talkative. As soon as he'd heard Sally's voice, he shouted for Gillian to come pick up.

"Get over here, girl." That's what he'd said. "It's your goddamn sister on the phone."

All Sally can remember Gillian telling her about him is that he served some time in the penitentiary for a crime he didn't commit, and that he was so handsome and so smooth he could get into any woman simply by looking at her the right way. Or the wrong way, depending on how you wanted to evaluate the consequences, and whether or not you happened to be married to this woman when Jimmy came along and stole her before you had an inkling of what was going on.

"It happened in a rest area in New Jersey." Gillian is trying to quit smoking, so she takes out a stick of gum and pushes it into her mouth. She has a pouty mouth that's rosy and sweet, but tonight her lips are parched. "He was such a shit," she says thoughtfully. "God. You wouldn't believe the things he did. Once we were house-sitting for some people in Phoenix, and they had a cat that was bothering him—I think it peed on the floor. He put it in the refrigerator."

Sally sits down. She's a little woozy hearing all this information about her sister's life, and the concrete stoop is cool and makes her feel better. Gillian always has the ability to draw her in, even when she tries to fight against the pull. Gillian sits down beside her, knee to knee. Her skin is even cooler than the concrete.

"Even I couldn't believe he'd actually go and do something like that," Gillian says. "I had to get out of bed in the middle of the night and let it out of the fridge or the thing would have frozen to death. It had ice crystals in its fur."

"Why did you have to come here?" Sally says mournfully. "Why now? You're going to ruin everything. I've really worked hard for all this."

Gillian eyes the house, unimpressed. She truly hates being on the East Coast. All this humidity and greenery. She'd do almost anything to avoid the past. Most probably, she'll find herself dreaming about the aunts tonight. That old house on Magnolia Street, with its woodwork and its cats, will come back to her, and she'll start to get fidgety, maybe even panicky to get the hell away, which is how she ended up in the Southwest in the first place. She got on a bus as soon as she left the Toyota mechanic she'd left her first husband for. She had to have heat and sun to counteract her moldy childhood, with its dark afternoons filled with long green shadows and its even darker midnights. She had to be very, very far away.

If she'd had the cash, Gillian would have run out of that rest area in New Jersey and she would have kept running until she got to the airport in Newark, then flown someplace hot. New Orleans, maybe, or Los Angeles. Unfortunately, right before they left Tucson, Jimmy informed her they were penniless. He'd spent every cent she'd earned in the past five years, easy enough to do when you're investing in drugs and alcohol and any jewelry you took a fancy to, including the silver ring he always wore—which had cost nearly a week of Gillian's salary.

The only thing they had after he was done spending was the car, and that was in his name. Where else could she have gone on a night as black as this? Who else would take her in, no questions asked—or, at least, none she can't think up an answer for—until she gets back on her feet?

Gillian sighs and surrenders her fight against nicotine, at least temporarily. She takes one of Jimmy's Lucky Strikes out of her shirt pocket, then lights up and inhales as deeply as she can. She'll quit tomorrow.

"We were about to start a new life, that's why we were heading for Manhattan. I was going to call you once we were settled. You were the first person I planned to have visit our apartment."

"Sure," Sally says, but she doesn't believe a word. When Gillian got rid of her past, she got rid of Sally as well. The last time they were supposed to get together was right before Jimmy and the move to Tucson. Sally had already bought the tickets for herself and the girls to fly to Austin, where Gillian was working as a concierge-in-training at the Hilton. The plan had been to spend Thanksgiving together—which would have been a first—but Gillian called Sally two days before she and the girls were set to take off, and she told Sally to just forget it. In two days, she wouldn't even be in Austin anymore. Gillian never did care to explain what went wrong, whether it was the Hilton, or Austin, or simply some compelling need to move on. When dealing with Gillian, Sally has gotten used to disappointment. She would have worried if there hadn't been a hitch.

"Well, I was planning to call you," Gillian says. "Believe it or not. But we had to get out of Tucson really fast because Jimmy was selling jimsonweed to the kids at the university, telling them it was peyote or LSD, and there was sort of a problem with people dying, which I had no idea about until he said, 'Get packed, pronto.' I would have called before I arrived on your doorstep. I just got freaked out when he collapsed at that rest area. I didn't know where to go."

"You could have taken him to a hospital. Or what about the police? You could have called them." Sally can see in the dark that the azaleas she recently planted are already wilting, their leaves turning brown. In her opinion, everything goes wrong if you give it enough time. Close your eyes, count to three, and chances are you'll have some sort of disaster creeping up on you.

"Yeah, right. Like I could go to the police." Gillian exhales in little, staccato puffs. "They'd give me ten to twenty. Maybe even life, considering it happened in New Jersey." Gillian stares at the stars, her eyes open wide. "If I could just get enough money together, I'd take off for California. I'd be gone before they ever came after me."

It's not just the azaleas Sally could lose. It's eleven years of work and sacrifice. The rings around the moon are now so bright Sally's convinced everyone in the neighborhood will be awake before long. She grabs her sister's arm and digs her fingernails into Gillian's skin. She's got two kids who are dependent on her asleep in the house. She's got an apple tart she has to take to the Fourth of July block party next weekend.

"Why would they come after you?"

Gillian winces and tries to pull away, but Sally won't let go. Finally, Gillian shrugs and lowers her eyes, and as far as Sally's concerned that's not a very comforting way to answer a question.

"Are you trying to tell me that you're responsible for Jimmy's death?"

"It was an accident," Gillian insists. "More or less," she adds when Sally digs her nails in deeper. "All right," she admits when Sally begins to draw blood. "I killed him." Gillian is getting pretty shaky, as if her pressure had started to drop a degree a second. "Now you know. Okay? As usual, everything's my fault."

Maybe it's only the humidity, but the rings around the moon are turning faintly green. Some women believe that a green light in the east can reverse the aging process, and sure enough Sally feels as though she were fourteen. She's having thoughts no grown woman should have, especially not one who's spent her whole life being good. She notices that there are bruises all up and down Gillian's arms; in the dark they look like purple butterflies, like something pretty.

"I'm never getting involved with another man," Gillian says. When Sally gives her a look, Gillian goes on insisting she's through with love. "I've learned my lesson," she says. "Now that it's too damn late. I just wish I could have tonight, and call the police tomorrow." Her voice is sounding strained again, and even littler than before. "I could cover Jimmy with a blanket and leave him in the car. I'm not ready to turn myself in. I don't think I can do it."

Gillian really sounds as if she's cracking up now. She has a tremor in her hand that's making it impossible for her to light another cigarette.

"You have to stop smoking," Sally says. Gillian is still her little sister, even now; she's her responsibility.

"Oh, fuck it." Gillian manages to light the match, then her

cigarette. "I'll probably get a life sentence. Cigarettes will just shorten the time I have to serve. I should smoke two at a time."

Although the girls weren't much more than babies when their parents died, Sally made snap decisions that seemed forceful enough to carry them both along. After the sitter they'd been left with became hysterical, and Sally had to get on the phone with the police officer to hear the news of their parents' death, she told Gillian to choose her two favorite stuffed animals and throw all the others away, because from then on they'd have to travel light, and take only what they could care for themselves. She was the one who told the silly baby-sitter to look for the aunts' phone number in their mother's datebook, and she insisted she be allowed to call and announce that she and Gillian would be made wards of the state unless a relative, however distant, came forward to claim them. She had the same look on her face then as she does now, an unlikely combination of dreaminess and iron.

"The police don't have to know," Sally says. Her voice sounds oddly sure.

"Really?" Gillian examines her sister's face, but at times like this Sally never gives anything away. It's impossible to read her. "Seriously?" Gillian moves closer to Sally, for comfort. She looks over at the Oldsmobile. "Do you want to see him?"

Sally cranes her neck; there's a shape in the passenger seat, all right.

"He really was cute." Gillian stubs out her cigarette and starts to cry. "Oh, boy," she says.

Sally can't believe it, but she actually wants to see him. She wants to see what such a man looks like. She wants to know if a woman as rational as herself could ever be attracted to him, if only for a second.

Gillian follows Sally over to the car and they lean forward to get a good look at Jimmy through the windshield. Tall, dark, handsome, and dead.

"You're right," Sally says. "He was cute."

He is, by far, the best-looking guy Sally has ever seen, dead or alive. She can tell, by the arch of his eyebrows and the smirk that's still on his lips, that he sure as hell knew it. Sally puts her face up to the glass. Jimmy's arm is thrown over the seat and Sally can see the ring on the fourth finger of his left hand—it's a big chunk of silver with three panels: a saguaro cactus is etched into one side panel, a coiled rattlesnake on the other, and in the center there's a cowboy on horseback. Even Sally understands that you wouldn't want to get hit if a man had that ring on; the silver would split your lip right open, it would cut quite deep.

Jimmy cared about the way he looked, that much is clear. Even after hours slumped over in the car, his blue jeans are so crisp it appears that somebody tried hard to iron them just right. His boots are snakeskin and they obviously cost a fortune. They've been very well cared for; if somebody spilled a beer on those boots by accident, or kicked up too much dust, there'd be trouble, you can tell that by looking at the polished leather. You can tell just by looking at Jimmy's face. Dead or alive, he is who he is: somebody you don't want to mess with. Sally steps away from the car. She'd be afraid to be alone with him. She'd be afraid one wrong word would set him off, and then she wouldn't know what to do.

"He looks kind of mean."

"Oh, god, yeah," Gillian says. "But only when he was drinking. The rest of the time he was great. He was good enough to eat, and I'm not kidding. So I got the idea of a way to keep him from being mean—I started giving him a little bit of nightshade in his food every night. It made him go to sleep before he could start drinking. He was perfectly fine all this time, but it must have been building up in his bloodstream, and then he just conked out. We were sitting there in the rest area and he was looking through the glove compartment for his lighter, which I bought for him at the flea market in Sedona last month, and he got bent over and couldn't seem to straighten back up. Then he stopped breathing."

In someone's backyard a dog is barking; it's a hoarse and frantic sound that has already begun to filter into people's dreams.

"You should have phoned the aunts and asked about the correct dosage," Sally says.

"The aunts hate me." Gillian runs her hand through her hair, to give it some fullness, but with this humidity it stays pretty limp. "I've disappointed them in every way."

"So have I," Sally says.

Sally believed the aunts judged her as far too ordinary to be of any real interest. Gillian felt sure they considered her common. Because of this, the girls always felt temporary. They had the sense that they'd better be careful about what they said and what they revealed. Certainly they never shared their fear of storms with the aunts, as if after nightmares and stomach viruses, fevers and food allergies, that phobia might be the last straw for the aunts, who had never particularly wanted children in the first place. One more complaint might send the aunts running to collect the sisters' suitcases, which were stored in the attic, covered with cobwebs and dust, but made of Italian leather and still decent enough to be put to good use. Instead of turning to the aunts, Sally and Gillian turned to each other. They whispered that nothing bad would happen as long as they could count to a hundred in thirty seconds. Nothing could happen if they stayed under the covers, if they did not breathe whenever the thunder crashed above them.

"I don't want to go to jail." Gillian takes out another Lucky Strike and lights it. Because of her family history, she has a real abandonment anxiety, which is why she's always the first to leave. She knows this, she's spent enough time in therapy and paid enough bucks to discuss it in depth, but that doesn't mean anything's changed. There is not one man who's gotten the jump and broken up with her first. That's her claim to fame. Frankly, Jimmy comes the closest. He's gone, and here she still is, thinking about him and paying the price for doing so.

"If they send me to jail, I'll go nuts. I haven't even lived yet. Not really. I want to get a job and have a normal life. I want to go to barbecues. I want to have a baby."

"Well, you should have thought of that before." This is exactly the advice Sally has been giving Gillian all along, which is why their phone conversations have gone from brief to nonexistent in the past few years. This is what she wrote in her most recent letter, the one Gillian never received. "You should have just left him."

Gillian nods. "I should have never said hello to him. That was my first mistake."

Sally carefully searches her sister's face in the green moonlight. Gillian may be beautiful, but she's thirty-six, and she's been in love far too often.

"Did he hit you?" Sally asks.

"Does it really make a difference?" Up close, Gillian certainly doesn't look young. She's spent too much time in the Arizona sun and her eyes are tearing, even though she's no longer crying.

"Yes," Sally says. "It does. It makes a difference to me."

"Here's the thing." Gillian turns her back on the Oldsmobile, because if she doesn't she'll remember that Jimmy was singing along to a Dwight Yoakam tape only a few hours ago. It was that song she could listen to over and over again, the one about a clown, and, in her opinion, Jimmy sang it about a million times better than Dwight ever could, which is saying quite a lot, since she's crazy for Dwight. "I was really in love with this one. Deep down in my heart. It's so sad, really. It's pathetic. I wanted him all the time, like I was crazy or something. Like I was one of those women."

In the kitchen, at twilight, those women would get down on their knees and beg. They'd swear they'd never want anything again in their lives, if they could just have what they wanted now. That was when Gillian and Sally used to lock their pinkies together and vow that they'd never be so wretched and unfortunate. Nothing could do that to them, that's what they used to whisper as they sat on the back stairs, in the dark and the dust, as if desire were a matter of personal choice.

Sally considers her front lawn and the hot and glorious night. She still has goose bumps rising along the back of her neck, but they're not bothering her anymore. In time, you can get used to anything, including fear. This is her sister, after all, the girl who sometimes refused to go to sleep unless Sally sang a lullaby or whispered the ingredients for one of the aunts' potions or charms. This is the woman who phoned her every Tuesday night, exactly at ten, for an entire year.

Sally thinks about the way Gillian held on to her hand when they first followed the aunts through the back door of the old house on Magnolia Street. Gillian's fingers were sticky from gumballs and cold with fear. She refused to let go; even when Sally threatened to pinch her, she just held on tighter.

"Let's take him around the back," Sally says.

They drag him over to where the lilacs grow, and they make certain not to disturb any of the roots, the way the aunts taught them. By now the birds nesting in the bushes are all asleep. The beetles are curled up in the leaves of the quince and the forsythia. As the sisters work, the sound of their shovels has an easy rhythm, like a baby clapping hands or tears falling. There is only one truly bad moment. No matter how hard Sally tries, she cannot close Jimmy's eyes. She's heard this happens when a dead man wishes to see who's next to follow. Because of this, Sally insists that Gillian look away while she begins to shovel the dirt over him. At least this way only one of them will have him staring up at her every night in her dreams.

When they've finished, and returned the shovels to the garage, and there's nothing but freshly turned earth beneath the lilacs, Gillian has to sit down on the back patio and put her head between her legs so she won't pass out. He knew exactly how to hit a woman, so that the marks hardly showed. He knew how to kiss her, too, so that her heart began to race and she'd start to think forgiveness with every breath. It's amazing the places that love will carry you. It's astounding to discover just how far you're willing to go.

On some nights it's best to stop thinking about the past, and all that's been won and lost. On nights like this, just getting into bed, crawling between the clean white sheets, is a great relief. It's only a June night like any other, except for the heat, and the green light in the sky, and the moon. And yet, what happens to the lilacs while everyone sleeps is extraordinary. In May there were a few droopy buds, but now the lilacs bloom again, out of season and overnight, in a single exquisite rush, bearing flowers so fragrant the air itself turns purple and sweet. Before long bees will grow dizzy. Birds won't remember to continue north. For weeks people will find themselves drawn to the sidewalk in front of Sally Owens's house, pulled out of their own kitchens and dining rooms by the scent of lilacs, reminded of desire and real love and a thousand other things they'd long ago forgotten, and sometimes now wish they'd forgotten still.

ON the morning of Kylie Owens's thirteenth birthday, the sky is endlessly sweet and blue, but long before the sun rises, before alarm clocks go off, Kylie is already awake. She has been for hours. She is so tall that she could easily pass for eighteen if she borrowed her sister's clothes and her mom's mocha lipstick and her aunt Gillian's red cowboy boots. Kylie knows she shouldn't rush things, she has her whole life ahead of her; all the same, she's been traveling to this exact moment at warp speed for the duration of her existence, she's been completely focused on it, as if this one morning in July were the center of the universe. Certainly she's going to be a much better teenager than she ever was a child; she's half believed this all her life, and now her aunt has read her tarot cards for her and they predict great good fortune. After all, the star was her destiny card, and that symbol ensures success in every enterprise.

Kylie's aunt Gillian has been sharing her bedroom for the past two weeks, which is how Kylie knows that Gillian sleeps like a little girl, hidden under a heavy quilt even though the temperature has been in the nineties ever since she arrived, as if she's brought some of the Southwest she loves so well along with her in the trunk of her car. They've fixed the place the way two roommates would, everything right down the middle, except that Gillian needs extra closet space and she's asked Kylie to do a tiny bit of redecoration. The black baby blanket that has always been kept at the foot of Kylie's bed is now folded and stored in a box down in the basement, along with the chessboard that Gillian said occupied way too much space. The black soap the aunts send as a present every year has been taken out of the soapdish and has been replaced with a bar of clear, rose-scented soap from France.

Gillian has very particular likes and dislikes and an opinion about everything. She sleeps a lot, she borrows things without asking, and she makes great brownies with M&M's stirred into the batter. She's beautiful and she laughs about a thousand times more than Kylie's mother does, and Kylie wants to be exactly like her. She follows Gillian around and studies her and is thinking of chopping off all her hair, if she has the guts, that is. Were Kylie to be granted a single wish, it would be to wake and discover that her mouse-brown hair has miraculously become the same glorious blond that Gillian is lucky enough to have, like hay left out in the sun or pieces of gold.

What makes Gillian even more wonderful is that she and Antonia don't get along. Given time enough, they may grow to despise each other. Last week, Gillian borrowed Antonia's short black skirt to wear to the Fourth of July block party, spilled a Diet Coke on it accidentally, then told Antonia she was intolerant when she dared to complain. Now Antonia has asked their mother if she can put a lock on her closet door. She has informed Kylie that their aunt is a nothing, a loser, a pathetic creature.

Gillian has taken a job at the Hamburger Shack on the Turnpike, where all the teenage boys have fallen madly in love with her, ordering cheeseburgers they don't want and gallons of ginger ale and Coke just to be near her.

"Work is what people have to do in order to have the bucks to party," Gillian announced last night, an attitude that has already hindered her plan of heading out to California, since she is drawn to shopping malls—shoe stores in particular tend to call out to her—and can't seem to save a cent.

That evening they were having hot dogs made out of tofu and some sort of bean that is supposed to be good for you, even though it tastes, in Kylie's opinion, like the tires of a truck. Sally refuses to have meat, fish, or fowl at their table in spite of her daughters' complaints. She has to close her eyes when she walks past the packaged chicken legs in the market, and still she's always reminded of the dove the aunts used for their most serious love charm.

"Tell that to a brain surgeon," Sally had responded to her

sister's remark about the limited worth of work. "Tell that to a nuclear physicist or a poet."

"Okay." Gillian was still smoking, although she made new plans to quit every morning, and was well aware that the smoke drove everyone but Kylie crazy. She puffed quickly, as though that would lessen anyone's distaste. "Go on and find me a poet or a physicist. Are there any in this neighborhood?"

Kylie was pleased by this putdown of their formless suburb, a place with no beginning and no end, but with plenty of gossips. Everyone is always giving her friend Gideon a hard time, even more so now that he's shaved his head. He said he didn't give a damn and insisted that most of their neighbors had minds as small as weasels', but lately he got flustered when anyone spoke to him directly, and when they walked alongside the Turnpike and a car horn honked he sometimes jumped, as though somehow he'd been insulted.

People were looking to talk, for any reason. Anything different or slightly unusual would do. Already, most people on their street had discussed the fact that Gillian did not wear the top half of her bathing suit when she sunbathed in the backyard. They all knew exactly what the tattoo on her wrist looked like, and that she'd had at least a six-pack at the block party—maybe even more—and then had gone and turned Ed Borelli down flat when he asked her out, even though he was the vice-principal and her sister's boss as well. The Owenses' neighbor Linda Bennett refused to have the optometrist she was dating come to her house to collect her before darkness fell, that's how nervous she was about having someone who looked like Gillian living right next door. Everyone agreed that Sally's sister was confusing. There were times when you'd meet her at the grocery and she'd insist you come on over and let her play around with her tarot cards for you, and other times when you'd say hello to her on the street only to have her look right through you, as if she were a million miles away, say in a place like Tucson, where life was a lot more interesting.

As far as Kylie was concerned, Gillian had the ability to make any place interesting; even a dump like their block could look sparkly in the right kind of light. The lilacs had gone absolutely wild since Gillian's arrival, as though paying homage to her beauty and her grace, and had spilled out from the backyard into the front, a purple bower hanging over the fence and the driveway. Lilacs were not supposed to bloom in July, that was a simple botanical fact, at least it had been until now. Girls in the neighborhood had begun to whisper that if you kissed the boy you loved beneath the Owenses' lilacs he'd be yours forever, whether he wanted to be or not. The State University, in Stony Brook, had sent two botanists to study the bud formations of these amazing plants going mad out of season, growing taller and more lush with every passing hour. Sally had refused to let the botanists into the yard; she had sprayed them with the garden hose to make them go away, but occasionally the scientists would park across from the driveway, mooning over the specimens they couldn't get to, debating whether it was ethical to run across the lawn with some gardening shears and take whatever they wanted.

Somehow, the lilacs have affected everyone. Late last night, Kylie woke and heard crying. She got out of bed and went to her window. There, beside the lilacs, was her aunt Gillian, in tears. Kylie watched for a while, until Gillian wiped her eyes dry and took a cigarette out of her pocket. As she crept back to bed, Kylie felt certain that someday she, too, would be crying in a garden at midnight, unlike her mother, who was always in bed by eleven and who didn't seem to have anything in her life that was even worth crying about. Kylie wondered if her mother had ever cried for their father, or if perhaps the moment of his death was when she'd lost the ability to weep.

Out in the yard, night after night, Gillian was still crying over Jimmy. She just couldn't seem to stop herself, even now. She, who had vowed never to let passion control her, had been hooked but good. She'd been trying to muster the courage and the nerve to walk out the door for so long, almost this whole year. She had written Jimmy's name on a piece of paper and burned it on the first Friday of every month when there was a quarter moon, to try to rid herself of her desire for him. But that didn't help her to stop wanting him. After more than twenty years of flirtations and fucking around and refusing to ever commit, she had to go and fall in love with someone like him, someone so bad that on the day they moved their furniture into their rented house in Tucson, the mice had all fled, because even the field mice had more sense than she did.

Now that he's dead, Jimmy seems much sweeter. Gillian keeps remembering how scorching his kisses were, and the memory alone can turn her inside out. He could burn her up alive; he could do it in a minute flat, and that's not easy to forget. She's been hoping that the damn lilacs will stop blooming, because the scent filters through the house and all along the block, and sometimes she swears she can even smell it at the Hamburger Shack, a good half-mile down the Turnpike. People in the neighborhood are all excited about the lilacs—there's already been a photograph on the front page of *News-*

day—but the cloying smell is driving Gillian nuts. It's getting into her clothes and her hair, and maybe that's why she's been smoking so much, to replace that lilac scent with one that's dirtier and more filled with fire.

She can't stop thinking about how Jimmy used to keep his eyes open when he kissed her—it shocked her to realize he was watching her. A man who doesn't close his eyes, even for a kiss, is a man who wants to keep control at all times. Jimmy's eyes had cold little flecks in the center, and each time she kissed him Gillian wondered if what she was doing wasn't a little like making a pact with the devil. That's what it felt like sometimes, especially when she'd see a woman who could be herself out in public without fearing that her husband or boyfriend would snap at her. "I told you not to park there," some woman would say to her husband outside a movie theater or a flea market, and those words would move Gillian to tears. How wonderful to say whatever you wanted without having to go over it in your mind, again and again, to make certain it wouldn't set him off.

She'll give herself credit for fighting the best battle she could against what she simply couldn't defeat on her own. She tried everything to stop Jimmy from drinking, the old cures as well as the new. Owl eggs, scrambled and disguised with Tabasco sauce and hot pepper as huevos rancheros. Garlic left under his pillow. A paste of sunflower seeds in his cereal. Hiding the bottles, suggesting AA, daring to pick a fight with him, when she knew she couldn't win. She had even tried the aunts' particular favorite of waiting until he was good and plastered, then slipping a tiny live minnow into his bottle of bourbon. The fish's gills stopped dead the instant the poor thing hit the liquor, and Gillian had been racked with guilt about it, but Jimmy hadn't even noticed anything amiss. He drank that minnow in one big gulp, without even blinking, then was violently ill for the rest of the evening, although afterward his taste for alcohol seemed to have doubled. That was when she got the idea for the nightshade, which seemed such a modest plan at the time, just a little something to take the edge off and get him to sleep before he got good and drunk.

When she sits beside the lilacs at night, Gillian is trying to decide whether or not she feels as if she's committed murder. Well, she doesn't. There was no intent and no premeditation. If Gillian could take it all back, she would, although she'd change a few things while she was at it. She actually feels more friendly toward Jimmy than she has in ages; there's a closeness and a tenderness that sure weren't there before. She doesn't want to leave him all alone in the cold earth. She wants to be near and tell him about her day and hear the jokes he used to tell when he was in a good mood. He hated lawyers, since none had ever saved him from serving jail time, and he collected attorney jokes. He had a million of them, and nothing could stop him from telling one when he had a mind to. Just before they'd pulled into the rest area in New Jersey, Jimmy had asked her what was brown and black and looked good on a lawyer. "A rottweiler," he'd told her. He seemed so happy at that moment, as if he'd had his whole life ahead of him. "Think about it," he'd said. "You get it?"

Sometimes, when Gillian sits on the grass and closes her eyes, she could swear Jimmy is beside her. She can almost sense him reaching for her, the way he used to when he was drunk and mad and wanted to hit her or fuck her—she never quite knew which it would be until the very last moment. But as soon as he'd start to twist that silver ring on his finger, she knew she'd better watch out. When he feels too substantial out in the yard, and Gillian begins thinking about the way things used to be—really—Jimmy's presence doesn't feel friendly anymore. When that happens, Gillian runs inside and locks the back door and looks at the lilacs from behind the safety of the glass. He used to scare her pretty good; he used to make her do things she wouldn't even say aloud.

Truthfully, she's glad that she's been sharing a room with her niece; she's scared to sleep alone, so she's happy to make the trade-off of not having much privacy. This morning, for example, when Gillian opens her eyes, Kylie is already sitting on the edge of the bed, staring at her. It's only seven o'clock, and Gillian doesn't have to report to work until lunchtime. She groans and pulls the quilt over her head.

"I'm thirteen," Kylie says with surprise, as though she herself were mystified that this has happened to her. It's the one thing she's wanted her whole life long, and now she's actually got it.

Gillian immediately sits up in bed and hugs her niece. She remembers exactly what a surprise it was to grow up, how disturbing and thrilling it was, how all-of-a-sudden.

"I feel different," Kylie whispers.

"Of course you do," Gillian says. "You are."

Her niece has been confiding in her more and more, maybe because they share a room and can whisper to each other, late at night, after the lights are out. Gillian is touched by the way Kylie studies her, as though she were a textbook on how to be a woman. She can't remember anybody ever looking up to her before, and the experience is intoxicating and puzzling at the same time.

"Happy birthday," Gillian announces. "It will be the best one yet."

The scent of those damn lilacs has mixed in with the breakfast Sally is already cooking in the kitchen. But there's coffee, too, so Gillian crawls out of bed and gathers the clothes she left scattered on the floor last night.

"Wait till later," Gillian tells her niece. "When you get your present from me, you'll be completely transformed. One hundred and fifty percent. People will see you on the street and they'll flip."

In honor of Kylie's birthday, Sally has fixed pancakes and fresh orange juice and fruit salad topped with coconut and raisins. Earlier in the morning, before the birds were awake, she went out to the rear of the yard and cut some of the lilacs, which she's arranged in a crystal vase. The flowers seem to glow, as if each petal emitted a plum-colored ray of light. They're hypnotizing, if you look too long. Sally sat at the table staring at them, and before she knew it she had tears in her eyes and her first batch of pancakes had burned on the griddle.

Last night, Sally dreamed the ground beneath the lilacs turned red as blood, and the grass made a crying sound when the wind rose. She dreamed that the swans that haunt her on restless nights were pulling out their white feathers, one by one; they were building a nest large enough for a man. Sally awoke to find that her sheets were damp with sweat; her forehead felt as though it had been locked in a vise. But that was nothing compared to the night before, when she dreamed there was a dead man here at her table, and he wasn't pleased with what she'd served him for dinner, which was vegetarian lasagna. With one fierce breath he blew every dish off the table; in an instant there was broken china everywhere, a sharp and savage carpet, strewn across the floor.

She's been dreaming about Jimmy so much, seeing his cold, clear eyes, that sometimes she can't think of anything else. She's carrying this guy around with her, when she never even knew him in the first place, and it just doesn't seem fair. The awful thing is, her relationship with this dead man is deeper than anything she's had with any other man in the past ten years, and that's frightening.

This morning Sally isn't certain if she's shaky from her dreams of Jimmy, or if it's the coffee she's already had that's affecting her, or if it's simply because her baby has now turned thirteen. It may be the potency of all three factors combined. Well, thirteen is still young, it doesn't mean Kylie is all grown. At least that's what Sally's telling herself. But when Kylie and Gillian come in for breakfast, their arms looped around each other, Sally bursts into tears. There's one factor she forgot to figure into her anxiety equation, and that's jealousy.

"Well, good morning to you, too," Gillian says.

"Happy birthday," Sally says to Kylie, but she sounds downright gloomy.

"Emphasis on the 'happy,'" Gillian reminds Sally as she pours herself a huge cup of coffee.

Gillian spies her reflection in the toaster; this is not a good hour for her. She smooths out the skin near her eyes. From now on she will not get out of bed until nine or ten at the earliest, although sometime after noon would be preferable.

Sally hands Kylie a small box, wrapped with pink ribbon. Sally has been especially careful, monitoring her grocery spending and avoiding restaurants in order to afford this gold heart on a chain. She can't help but notice that before Kylie allows herself a reaction, she looks over at Gillian.

"Nice." Gillian nods. "Real gold?" she asks.

Sally can feel something hot and red begin to move across her chest and her throat. What if Gillian had said the locket was a piece of junk; what would Kylie have done then?

"Thanks, Mom," Kylie says. "It's really nice."

"Which is amazing, since your mom usually has no taste when it comes to jewelry. But this is really good." Gillian holds the chain up to her neck and lets the heart dangle above her breasts. Kylie has begun to pile pancakes onto a plate. "You're going to eat those?" Gillian asks. "All those carbohydrates?"

"She's thirteen. A pancake won't kill her." Sally would like to strangle her sister. "She's much too young to be thinking about carbohydrates."

"Fine," Gillian says. "She can think about it when she's thirty. After it's too late."

Kylie goes for the fruit salad. Unless Sally is mistaken, she's wearing Gillian's blue pencil streaked beneath her eyes. Kylie carefully scoops two measly spoonfuls of fruit into a bowl and takes teeny, tiny bites, even though she's nearly six feet tall and weighs only a hundred and eighteen pounds.

Gillian takes a bowl of fruit for herself. "Come by the Hamburger Shack at six. That will give us some time before dinner."

"Great," Kylie says.

Sally's back is way up. "Time for what?"

"Nothing," Kylie says, sullen as a full-fledged teenager.

"Girl talk." Gillian shrugs. "Hey," she says, reaching into the pocket of her jeans. "I almost forgot."

Gillian brings forth a silver bracelet that she picked up in a pawnshop east of Tucson for only twelve bucks, in spite of the impressive chunk of turquoise in its center. Someone must have been down-and-out to give this up so easily. She must have had no luck left at all.

"Oh, my gosh," Kylie says when Gillian hands her the bracelet. "It's totally fabulous. I'll never take it off."

"I need to see you outside," Sally informs Gillian.

Sally's face is flushed to the hairline, and she's twisted into jealous knots, but Gillian doesn't notice anything is wrong. She slowly refills her coffee cup, adds half-and-half, then ambles into the yard after Sally.

"I want you to butt out," Sally says. "Do you understand what I'm saying? Is it getting through to you?"

It rained last night and the grass is squishy and filled with worms. Neither of the sisters is wearing shoes, but it's too late to turn back and go into the house.

"Don't yell at me," Gillian says. "I can't take it. I'll flip out, Sally. I'm way too fragile for this."

"I'm not yelling. All right? I'm just simply stating that Kylie is my daughter."

"Do you think I'm not aware of that?" Gillian sounds icy now, except for the tremble in her voice, which gives her away.

In Sally's opinion, Gillian really is fragile, that's the awful part. Or at least she thinks she is, and that's pretty much the same damn thing.

"Maybe you think I'm a bad influence," Gillian says now. "Maybe that's what this is all about."

The tremble is getting worse. Gillian sounds the way she used to when they had to walk home from school late in November. It would already be dark and Sally would wait for her, so she wouldn't get lost, the way she did once in kindergarten. That time she wandered off and the aunts didn't find her until past midnight, sitting on a bench outside the shuttered library, crying so hard she couldn't catch her breath.

"Look," Sally says. "I don't want to fight with you."

"Yes, you do." Gillian is gulping her coffee. Sally is only now noticing how thin her sister is. "Everything I do is wrong. You think I don't know that? I've screwed up my entire existence, and everyone who's close to me gets screwed right along with me."

"Oh, come on. Don't."

Sally means to say something about culpability, as well as all the men Gillian has screwed throughout the years, but she shuts up when Gillian sinks to the grass and begins to cry. Gillian's eyelids always turn blue when she cries, which makes her seem breakable and lost and even more beautiful than usual. Sally crouches down beside her.

"I don't think you're screwed up," Sally tells her sister. A white lie doesn't count if you cross your fingers behind your back, or if you tell it so that someone you love will stop crying.

"Ha." Gillian's voice breaks in two, like a hard piece of sugar.

"I'm really happy that you're here." This is not an outright lie. No one knows you like a person with whom you've shared a childhood. No one will ever understand you in quite the same way.

"Oh, yeah, right." Gillian blows her nose on the sleeve of her white blouse. Antonia's blouse, actually, which she borrowed yesterday, and which, because it fits her so well, Gillian has already begun to consider her own.

"Seriously," Sally insists. "I want you to be here. I want you to stay. Only, from now on, think before you act."

"Understood," Gillian says.

The sisters embrace and get up off the grass. They mean to go inside the house, but their gaze is caught by the hedge of lilacs.

"That's one thing I don't want to think about," Gillian whispers.

"We just have to put it out of our minds," Sally says.

"Right," Gillian agrees, as if she could stop thinking about him.

The lilacs have grown as high as the telephone wires, with blooms so abundant some of the branches have begun to bow toward the ground.

"He was never even here," Sally says. She would probably sound more sure of herself if it weren't for all those bad dreams she keeps having and the line of earth beneath her fingernails that refuses to come clean. This, plus the fact that she can't stop thinking about the way he stared up at her from that hole in the ground.

"Jimmy who?" Gillian says brightly, even though the bruises he left on her arms are still there, like little shadows.

Sally goes inside, to wake Antonia and wash the breakfast dishes, but Gillian stays where she is for a while. She tilts her head back and closes her pale eyes against the sun, and thinks about how crazy love can be. That is how she is, standing barefoot in the grass, with the salt mark of tears left on her cheeks, and a funny sort of smile on her face, when the biology teacher from the high school unlatches the back gate so he can come around and give Sally the notice about the meeting in the cafeteria on Saturday night. He never gets beyond the gate, however—he's stuck there on the path as soon as he sees Gillian, and from then on whenever he smells lilacs he'll think about this moment. How the bees were circling above him, how purple the ink on the leaflets he's been distributing suddenly seemed, how he realized, all at once, just how beautiful a woman can be.

ALL of the teenage boys down at the Hamburger Shack say, "No onions," when Gillian takes their orders. Ketchup is fine, as are mustard and relish. Pickles on the side are all right as well. But when you're in love, when you're so fixated you can't even blink, you don't want onions, and it's not to ensure that your kiss will stay sweet. Onions wake you up, they rattle you and snap right through you and tell you to get real. Go find someone who will love you back. Go out and dance all night, then walk through the dark, hand in hand, and forget about whoever it is who's driving you mad.

Those boys at the counter are too dreamy and young to do anything but drool as they watch Gillian. And, to her credit, Gillian is especially kind to them, even when Ephraim, the cook, suggests she kick them out. She understands that theirs might just be the last hearts she will break. When you're thirty-six and tired, when you've been living in places where the temperature rises to a hundred and ten and the air is so dry you have to use gallons of moisturizer, when you've been smacked around, late at night, by a man who loves bourbon, you start to realize that everything is limited, including your own appeal. You begin to look at young boys with tenderness, since they know so little and think they know so much. You watch teenage girls and feel shivers up and down your arms—those poor creatures don't know the first thing about time or agony or the price they're going to have to pay for just about everything.

And so Gillian has decided that she will come to her niece's rescue. She will be Kylie's mentor as she leaves childhood behind. Gillian has never felt this attached to a kid before; to be honest, she's never even known any, and she's certainly never been interested in anyone else's future or fate. But Kylie brings out some strange instinct to protect and to guide. There are times when Gillian has found herself thinking that if she had had a daughter, she would have wanted her to be like Kylie. Only a little more bold and daring. A bit more like Gillian herself.

Although she is usually late, on the evening of her niece's birthday Gillian has everything ready before Kylie arrives at the Hamburger Shack; she's even spoken to Ephraim about leaving early so they can get to Del Vecchio's for the birthday dinner on time. But first, there is the matter of Gillian's other present, the one that will count for a great deal more than the turquoise bracelet. This present will take a good two hours and will, like most things Gillian is involved with, also make a big mess.

Kylie, who's wearing cutoffs and an old Knicks T-shirt, obediently follows Gillian into the ladies' room, although she hasn't the faintest idea of what's about to transpire. She's wearing the bracelet Gillian gave her, as well as the locket her mother saved for for so long; she has a weird sensation in her legs. She wishes she had time to run around the block once or twice; maybe then she wouldn't feel as if she were about to burn up or shatter.

Gillian turns on the light and locks the door and reaches under the sink for a paper bag. "The secret ingredients," she tells Kylie, as she takes out a pair of scissors, a bottle of shampoo, and a package of bleach. "What do you say?" she asks when Kylie comes to stand beside her. "Want to find out how beautiful you really are?"

Kylie knows her mother will kill her. She'll ground her for the rest of her life and take away her privileges—no movies on weekends, no radio, no TV. Worse, her mom will get that awful look of disappointment on her face—*See what has happened*, that's what her expression will say. *After I've worked so hard to support you and Antonia and bring you up right.*

"Sure," Kylie says, easily, as if her heart weren't going a hundred miles an hour. "Let's do it," she tells her aunt, as if her whole life weren't about to completely flip-flop.

It takes a long time to do almost anything worthwhile to someone's hair, even longer for a change as radical as this, and so Sally and Antonia and Gideon Barnes wait for nearly an hour in a booth at Del Vecchio's, drinking diet Cokes and fuming.

"I missed soccer practice for this," Gideon says mournfully.

"Oh, who cares," Antonia says.

Antonia has been working at the ice cream parlor all day

and she has a pain in her right shoulder from all the scooping she's done. She doesn't even feel like herself this evening, although she has no idea of who else she might be. She hasn't been asked out on a date for weeks. All of a sudden the boys who were so crazy for her seem to be interested either in younger girls—who may not be as pretty as Antonia but who can be impressed by the slightest thing, a stupid award from the computer club or a trophy from the swim team, and go all googly-eyed if a boy pays them the teeniest little compliment—or in an older woman, like her aunt Gillian, who's had so many more sexual experiences than a girl Antonia's age that a high school boy could get hard just by trying to guess what she could teach him in bed.

This summer has not been working out as Antonia hoped. She can already tell that tonight is another totally lost cause. Her mother hurried her so they could be on time for this dinner, and Antonia was in such a rush that she grabbed her clothes from her dresser drawer without looking. And now, what she thought was a black T-shirt has turned out to be a horrible olive-green thing she ordinarily wouldn't be caught dead in. Usually the waiters here wink at Antonia and bring her extra baskets of rolls and garlic bread. This evening not one of them has even noticed she's alive, except for a creepy busboy who asked if she wanted a ginger ale or a Coke.

"This is so typical of Aunt Gillian," she tells her mother when they've been waiting for what seems like an eternity. "It's so inconsiderate."

Sally, who is not completely sure that Gillian wouldn't encourage Kylie to hop a freight train or hitchhike to Virginia

Beach for no particular reason other than a good time, has been drinking wine, something she rarely does.

"Well, to hell with them both," she says now.

"Mother!" Antonia says, shocked.

"Let's order," Sally suggests to Gideon. "Let's get two pepperoni pizzas."

"You don't eat meat," Antonia reminds her.

"Then I'll have another glass of Chianti," Sally says. "And some stuffed mushrooms. Maybe some pasta."

Antonia turns to signal the waiter but immediately turns back. Her cheeks are flushed and she's broken into a sweat. Her biology teacher, Mr. Frye, is at one of the small tables in the back, having a beer and discussing the virtues of eggplant rollatini with the waiter. Antonia is crazy about Mr. Frye. He is so brilliant that Antonia considered flunking Biology I just so she could take it again, until she found out he'd be teaching Biology II in the fall. It doesn't matter that he's way too old for her; he's so incredibly handsome that if all the guys in the senior class were rolled up together and tied with a big bow they still wouldn't come close. Mr. Frye goes running every day at dusk and always circles the reservoir on the far side of the high school three times. Antonia tries to make certain to be there just as the sun is going down, but he never seems to notice her. He never even waves.

Naturally she has to meet up with him on the one evening when she hasn't bothered with makeup and is wearing this horrible olive-green thing, which, she now realizes, doesn't belong to her. She's ludicrous. Even that stupid Gideon Barnes is staring at her shirt.

"What are you staring at?" Antonia asks so savagely that Gideon pulls his head back, as if he expected to be smacked. "What is your problem?" she cries when Gideon continues to stare. God, she can't stand him. He looks like a pigeon when he blinks, and he often makes a weird sound in his throat, as though he's about to spit.

"I think that's my shirt," Gideon says apologetically, and in fact, it is. He got it on a trip to St. Croix last Christmas, and left it at the Owens house last week, which is how it got thrown in with the wash. Antonia would be completely and utterly mortified to know that I'M A VIRGIN is printed across her back in black letters.

Sally calls for a waiter and orders two pizzas—plain, no pepperoni—three orders of stuffed mushrooms, an order of crostini, some garlic bread, and two insalatas.

"Great," Gideon says, since he's starving as usual. "By the way," he tells Antonia, "you don't have to give me the shirt back until tomorrow."

"Gee, thanks." Antonia can't take much more of this. "Like I wanted it in the first place."

She dares to look over her shoulder. Mr. Frye is watching the ceiling fan as though it were the most fascinating thing on earth. Antonia assumes this has to do with some sort of scientific study of speed or light, but in fact it's directly related to the experiences of Ben Frye's youth, when he went out to San Francisco to visit a friend and stayed for nearly ten years, during which time he worked for a rather well-known maker of LSD. Such was his introduction to science. It is also the reason why there are times when he has to slow the world down. That's when he stops and stares, at things like ceiling fans and raindrops on window glass. That's when he wonders what on earth he's been doing with his life.

Now, as he watches the fan spin around, he is thinking about the woman he saw earlier that day, in Sally Owens's backyard. He backed off, the way he always does, but it won't happen a second time. If he ever sees her again he's going to go right up to her and ask her to marry him, that's what he'll do. He's sick of letting fate roll right past him. For years, he's been a lot like this restaurant fan, spinning around and getting noplace. What, when it comes right down to it, is the difference between him and a mayfly, which lives a whole damned adult existence in twenty-four hours? The way Ben sees it, he's just about passing by hour nineteen right now, given the statistics for a man's longevity. If five more hours is what he's got left, he might as well live, he might as well say to hell with it and, for once, just go out and do as he pleases.

Ben Frye is considering all this, as well as deciding whether or not to order a cappuccino, since it will mean he'll be up half the night, when Gillian walks through the door. She's wearing Antonia's best white shirt and a pair of old blue jeans and she has the most beautiful smile on her face. Her smile could knock a dove right out of a tree. It could turn a grown man's head so completely he might spill his beer and never even notice that a pool was spreading across the tablecloth and onto the floor.

"Get ready," Gillian says, as she approaches the booth where three very unhappy customers with low blood sugar and no patience left whatsoever are waiting.

"We've been ready for forty-five minutes," Sally tells her sister. "If you have got an excuse, it better be a good one."

"Don't you see?" Gillian says.

"We see you don't think of anyone but yourself," Antonia says.

"Oh, really?" Gillian says. "Well, you sure would know about such things. You would know better than anyone."

"Holy shit," Gideon Barnes says.

At this moment he has forgotten his empty, growling stomach. He no longer cares that his legs are cramping from being squooshed into this booth for so long. Someone who looks a lot like Kylie is walking toward them, only this person is a knockout. This person has short blond hair and is thin, not in the way that storks are but in the style of women who can make you fall in love with them even when you've known them for what seems like forever though you aren't much more than a kid yourself.

"Holy fucking shit," Gideon says as this person gets closer. It is indeed Kylie. It must be, because when she grins Gideon can see the tooth she chipped last summer when she dove for the ball during soccer practice.

As soon as she notices the way they're all staring at her, open-mouthed, like goldfish whose bowl she's just been dropped into, Kylie feels something tingly which resembles embarrassment, or perhaps it's regret. She slides into the booth next to Gideon.

"I'm famished," she says. "Are we having pizza?"

Antonia has to take a drink of water, and still she feels as though she might faint. Something horrible has happened. Something has changed so intensely that the world doesn't even seem to be spinning on the same axis anymore. Antonia can feel herself fade in the yellow lighting of Del Vecchio's; she is already becoming Kylie Owens's sister, the one with the too-red hair who works down at the ice cream parlor and has fallen arches and a bad shoulder that prevents her from playing tennis or pulling her own weight.

"Well, isn't anybody going to say anything?" Gillian asks. "Isn't anyone going to say, 'Kylie! You look incredible! You're gorgeous! Happy birthday'?"

"How could you do this?" Sally stands up to face her sister. She may have been drinking Chianti for nearly an hour, but she's sober now. "Did you ever think of asking my permission? Did you ever think she might be too young to start dyeing her hair and wearing makeup and doing whatever the hell else will lead her on the same dreadful path you've been on your whole life? Did you ever think that I don't want her to be like you, and if you had any brains you wouldn't want that for her either, especially considering what you just went through, and you know exactly what I mean." By now Sally is hysterical, and she's not about to keep her voice down. "How could you?" she asks. "How dare you!" she cries.

"Don't get so upset." This is definitely not the reaction Gillian expected. Applause, maybe. A pat on the back. But not this sort of indictment. "We can put a brown tint over it, if it's such a big deal."

"It is a big deal." Sally is having trouble breathing. She looks at the girl in the booth who is Kylie, or who used to be Kylie, and feels that she's been hooked through her heart. She breathes in through her nose and out through her mouth, just as they taught her in Lamaze class so long ago. "Robbing someone of her youth and innocence, I'd call that major. I'd say it's a big deal."

"Mother," Antonia pleads.

Antonia has never experienced humiliation quite like this before. Mr. Frye is watching them as though their family is putting on a play. And he's not the only one. There's probably not another conversation going on in the entire restaurant. The better to hear the Owenses. The better to watch the sideshow.

"Can we just eat?" Antonia begs.

The waiter has brought over their order, which he tentatively places on the table. Kylie is doing her best to ignore the adults. She imagined her mother would be mad, but this reaction is in a whole other dimension.

"Aren't you starving?" she whispers to Gideon. Kylie expects Gideon to be the one sane person at the table, but as soon as she sees the expression on his face, she knows it's not food he's thinking of. "What's wrong with you?" she asks.

"It's you," he says, and it sounds like an accusation. "You're all different."

"I am not," Kylie says. "It's just my hair."

"No," Gideon says. The shock is wearing off, and he feels that a theft has been committed. Where is his teammate and friend? "You're just not the same. How could you be so stupid?"

"Go to hell," Kylie says, hurt beyond belief.

"Fine," Gideon shoots back. "Do you mind letting me out so I can get there?"

Kylie moves so Gideon can slide out of the booth. "You are an idiot," she tells him as he leaves, and she sounds so cool she amazes herself. Even Antonia is looking at her with something resembling respect.

"Is that how you treat your best friend?" Sally asks Kylie. "Do you see what you've done?" she says to Gillian.

"He *is* an idiot," Gillian says. "Who leaves a party before it's even happened?"

"It has happened," Sally says. "Don't you see? It's over." She searches through her purse for her wallet, then throws some cash on the table to pay for the uneaten food. Kylie has already grabbed a piece of pizza, which she quickly drops when she sees how grim her mother looks. "Let's go," Sally tells her girls.

It takes Ben Frye this long to realize that he has another chance. Sally and her girls have gotten up and Gillian is alone at the table. Ben walks over casually, just like a man whose blood hasn't heated up to a dangerous degree.

"Hey, Sally," he says. "How are you doing?"

Ben is one of the few teachers who treat Sally like an equal, even though she's only a secretary. Not everyone is so kind—Paula Goodings, the math teacher, orders Sally about, convinced she is some drone behind the desk, available to do errands for anyone who wanders by. Ben and Sally have known each other for years and considered dating when Ben first was hired at the high school, before deciding what they both really could use was a friend. Since then, they have often had lunch together and are allies at school meetings; they like to go out and drink beer and gossip about the faculty and the staff.

"I'm doing really poorly," Sally tells him now before she notices that he's moved on without waiting for an answer. "Since you're asking," she adds.

"Hi," Antonia says to Ben Frye as he walks past her. Brilliant, but it's the best she can do at the moment.

Ben smiles at her blankly, but he keeps right on going, until he's at the table where Gillian is staring at the uneaten food.

"Is there something wrong with your order?" Ben asks her. "Is there anything I can do?"

Gillian looks up at him. There are tears falling from her clear gray eyes. Ben takes a step toward her. He is so gone, he couldn't come back if he wanted to.

"There's nothing wrong," Sally assures him as she collects her girls and begins to troop toward the door.

If Sally's heart weren't so closed up at the moment, she'd feel sorry for Ben. She'd pity him. Ben has already sat down across from Gillian. He's taken the matches out of her hand—which has that damn tremor again—and is lighting her cigarette. As Sally leads her girls out of the restaurant, she believes she hears him say, "Please don't cry," to her sister. She may even hear him say, "Marry me. We can do it tonight." Or maybe she's just imagining that's what he's said, since she knows that's where he's headed. Every man who's ever looked at Gillian the way Ben is looking right now has made a proposal of one sort or another.

Well, the way Sally sees it, Ben Frye is a grown man, he can take care of himself, or, at the very least, he can try. Her girls are another matter entirely. Sally's not about to let Gillian arrive out of nowhere, with three divorces and a dead body in her recent history, to start playing around with her daughters' welfare. Girls like Kylie and Antonia are just too vulnerable; they get broken in two by cruel words alone, they're easily made to believe they're not good enough. Just seeing the back of Kylie's neck as they walk through the parking lot makes Sally want to weep. But she doesn't. And, what's more, she won't.

"My hair's not that bad," Kylie says once they're in the

Honda. "I don't see what's so horrible about what we did." She's sitting alone in the backseat and she feels so weird. There's no space for her legs at all, and in order to fit she has to fold herself up. She almost feels as if she could leap out of the car and walk away. She could start a new life and never look back again.

"Maybe if you think about it, you will," Sally tells her. "You have more sense than your aunt, so you have a better chance of understanding your mistake. Think it over."

That's what Kylie does, and what it all adds up to is spite. Nobody wants her to be happy, except for Gillian. Nobody gives a damn.

They drive home in silence, but after they've pulled into the driveway and are walking toward the front door, Antonia can no longer hold her tongue. "You look so tacky," she whispers to Kylie. "And you know what the worst part is?" She draws this out, as though she were about to utter a curse. "You look like her."

Kylie's eyes sting, but she's not afraid to talk back to her sister. Why should she be? Antonia looks oddly pale tonight, and her hair has turned dry, a bundle of blood-colored straw caught up in barrettes. She's not so pretty. She's not as superior as she's always pretended.

"Well, good," Kylie says. Her voice is honey, so easy and sweet. "If I'm like Aunt Gillian I'm glad."

Sally hears something dangerous in her daughter's voice, but of course thirteen is a dangerous age. It's the time when a girl can snap, when good can turn to bad for no apparent reason, and you can lose your own child if you're not careful.

"We'll go to the drugstore in the morning," Sally says.

"Once we get hold of a package of brown dye you'll look perfectly fine."

"I think that's my decision." Kylie is surprised at herself, but that doesn't mean she's about to give in.

"Well, I disagree," Sally says. There's a lump in her throat. She would like to do something other than stand here—smack Kylie, perhaps, or hug her, but she knows neither of these things is possible.

"Well, that's too bad," Kylie says right back. "Because it's my hair."

Watching all this, Antonia has a big grin on her face.

"Is this any of your business?" Sally says to her. She waits for Antonia to go inside before turning to Kylie. "We'll discuss this tomorrow. Get in the house."

The sky is dark and deep. The stars have begun to come out. Kylie shakes her head no. "I won't."

"Fine," Sally says. There's a catch in her voice, but her posture is straight and unrelenting. For weeks she's been afraid that she might lose her daughter, that Kylie would favor Gillian's careless ways, that she'd grow up too soon. Sally had planned to be understanding, to consider such behavior a passing phase, but now that it's really happened Sally is stunned to find how angry she is. *After all I've done for you* is lodged somewhere in her brain, and, far worse, it's in her heart as well. "If this is the way you want to spend your birthday—fine."

After Sally goes inside, the door closes with a little hissing sound, then slams as it shuts. Kylie has been alive beneath this sky for thirteen years, and only tonight does she really look at all those stars above her. She slips off her shoes, leaves them on the front stoop, then goes around to the backyard. The lilacs have never before been in flower on her birthday, and she takes it as a sign of luck. The bushes are so lush and overgrown, she has to stoop to get by them. For her whole life she has been measuring herself against her sister, and she's not going to do that anymore. That is the gift Gillian has given her tonight, and for that she will always be grateful.

Anything can happen. Kylie sees that now. All across the lawn there are fireflies and heat waves. Kylie stretches out one hand and fireflies collect in her palm. As she shakes them off, and they rise into the air, she wonders if she has something other people don't. Intuition or hope—she wouldn't know what to call it. Perhaps what she has is the simple ability to know that something has changed and is changing still, under this dark and starry sky.

Kylie has always been able to read people, even those who close themselves up tight. But now that she's turned thirteen, her meager talent has intensified. All evening she has been seeing colors around people, as though they were illuminated from within, just like fireflies. The green edge of her sister's jealousy, the black aura of fear when her mother saw that she looked like a woman, not a little girl. These bands of color seem so real to Kylie that she has tried to reach out her hand and touch them, but the colors bleed into the air and disappear. And now, as she stands in her own backyard, she sees that the lilacs, those beautiful things, have an aura all their own, and it's surprisingly dark. It's purple, but it seems like a bloodstained relic, and it drifts upward like smoke.

All of a sudden, Kylie doesn't feel quite so grown-up. She has the desire to be in her own bed, she even finds herself wishing that time could go backward, at least for a bit. But that never happens. Things can't be undone. It's ridiculous, but Kylie could swear there was a stranger out here in the yard. She backs up to the door and turns the handle, and just before she goes inside, she looks across the lawn and sees him. Kylie blinks, but sure enough he's still there, under the arch of the lilacs, and he looks like the sort of man no one in her right mind would want to run into on a night as dark as this. He has a lot of nerve to be on private property, to treat this yard as his own. But, clearly, he doesn't give a damn about such things as decorum and good behavior. He's sitting there waiting, and whether Kylie or anyone else approves or disapproves doesn't much matter. He's there all right, admiring the night through his gorgeous cold eyes, ready to make somebody pay.

CLAIRVOYANCE

If a woman is in trouble, she should always wear blue for protection. Blue shoes or a blue dress. A sweater the color of a robin's egg or a scarf the shade of heaven. A thin satin ribbon, carefully threaded through the white lace hem of a slip. Any of these will do. But if a candle burns blue, that is something else entirely, that's no luck at all, for it means there's a spirit in your house. And if the flame should flicker, then grow stronger each time the candle is lit, the spirit is settling in. Its essence is wrapping around the furniture and the floorboards, it's claiming the cabinets and the closets and will soon be rattling windows and doors.

Sometimes it takes a good while before anyone in a house realizes what has happened. People want to ignore what they can't understand. They're looking for logic at any cost. A woman can easily think she's silly enough to misplace her earrings every single night. She can convince herself that a stray wooden spoon is the reason the dishwasher is constantly jamming, and that the toilet keeps flooding because of faulty pipes. When people snipe at each other, when they slam doors in each other's faces and call each other names, when they can't sleep at night because of guilt and bad dreams, and the very act of falling in love makes them sick to their stomach instead of giddy and joyful, then it's best to consider every possible cause for so much bad fortune.

If Sally and Gillian had been on speaking terms, instead of avoiding each other in the hall and at the supper table, where one would not even ask the other to pass the butter or the rolls or the peas, they would have discovered as July wore on, with white heat and silence, that they were equally unlucky. The sisters could turn on a lamp, leave the room for a second, and return to complete darkness. They could start their cars, drive half a block, and discover they'd run out of gas, even if there'd been nearly a full tank just hours before. When either sister stepped into the shower, the warm water turned to ice, as though someone had played with the faucet. Milk would curdle as it was poured from the container. Toast burned. Letters the postman had carefully delivered were torn in half and their edges turned black, like an old withered rose.

Before long, each sister was losing whatever was most important to her. One morning Sally awoke to find that the photograph of her daughters, which she always kept on her bureau, had disappeared from its silver frame. The diamond earrings the aunts had given to her on her wedding day were no longer in her jewelry box; she searched her entire bedroom and still couldn't find them anywhere. The bills she was supposed to pay before the end of the month, once in a neat pile on the kitchen counter, seemed to be gone, although she was convinced she'd written out the checks and sealed all the envelopes.

Gillian, who could certainly be accused of forgetfulness and disorder, was missing things that seemed almost impossible to lose, even for her. Her prized red cowboy boots, which she always kept beside the bed, simply weren't there when she woke up one morning, as though they'd decided to just walk away. Her tarot cards, which she kept tied up in a satin handkerchief—and which had certainly helped her out of a fix or two, especially after her second marriage, when she didn't have a cent and had to set herself up at a card table in a mall, telling fortunes for $2.95—had evaporated like smoke, all except for the Hanged Man, which can represent either wisdom or selfishness, depending on its position.

Little things were gone, such as Gillian's tweezers and her watch, but major items were missing as well. Yesterday, she had gone out the front door still half asleep, and when she went to get into the Oldsmobile, it wasn't anywhere in sight. She was late for work and figured that some teenage boy had stolen her car and she'd phone the police when she got to the Hamburger Shack. But when she arrived there, her feet killing her since she wasn't wearing shoes meant for walking, there was the Oldsmobile, parked right out front, as though it were waiting for her, propelled by a mind of its own.

When Gillian questioned Ephraim, who'd been working behind the grill since early that morning, demanding to know whether he'd seen someone drop off her car, she sounded on edge, maybe even hysterical.

"It's a practical joke," Ephraim guessed. "Or somebody stole it, then got cold feet."

Well, cold feet was certainly something Gillian knew about lately. Every time the phone rang, at work or at Sally's house,

Gillian thought it was Ben Frye. She got the shivers just thinking about him; she got them all the way down to her toes. Ben had sent her flowers, red roses, the morning after they'd met at Del Vecchio's, but when he phoned she told him she couldn't accept them, or anything else.

"Don't call me," she told him. "Don't even think about me," she cried.

What on earth was wrong with Ben Frye—didn't he see her for the loser that she was? Lately, everything she touched fell apart—animal, vegetable, mineral, it didn't matter in the least. It all fell apart equally beneath her touch. She opened Kylie's closet and the door came right off its hinges. She put up a can of tomato-rice soup to cook on the back burner and the kitchen curtains caught on fire. She walked out to the patio, to have a cigarette in peace, only to step on a dead crow, which seemed to have fallen directly from the sky into her path.

She was bad luck, ill-fated and unfortunate as the plague. When she dared to glance into the mirror she looked the same—high cheekbones, wide gray eyes, generous mouth—all of it familiar and, many would say, beautiful. Still, once or twice she had caught sight of her image a little too quickly, and then she didn't like what she found staring back at her. From certain angles, in certain sorts of light, she saw what she imagined Jimmy must have seen, late at night, when he was plastered and she was backing away from him, her hands up, to protect her face. That woman was a silly, vain creature who didn't stop to think before she opened her mouth. That woman believed she could change Jimmy, or, if worse came to worst, rearrange him somehow. The absolute fool. No wonder she couldn't work the stove or find her boots. No wonder she'd managed to kill Jimmy, when all she'd really wanted was a little tenderness.

Gillian had been crazy to sit in the booth at Del Vecchio's with Ben Frye in the first place, but she'd been so upset she'd stayed until midnight. By the end of that evening, they had eaten every bit of the food Sally had ordered and had fallen for each other so hard they didn't notice they had each consumed an entire pizza. Even then, it wasn't enough. They ate the way people who'd been hypnotized might have, not bothering to glance at the bits of salad and mushroom they speared with their forks, not wanting to leave the table if that meant leaving each other.

Gillian still can't quite believe that Ben Frye is for real. He's unlike any other man she has ever been with. He listens to her, for one thing. He's so kindhearted that people are drawn to him. People just assume he's trustworthy; whenever he visits cities he's never been to before he's always asked for directions, even by natives. He has a degree in biology from Berkeley, but he also puts on magic shows in the children's ward of the local hospital every Saturday afternoon. The kids aren't the only ones who gather around when Ben arrives, with his silk scarves and carton of eggs and his decks of cards. It's impossible to get the attention of any of the nurses on the floor; some of them swear Ben Frye is the best-looking single man in New York State.

Because of all this, Gillian Owens is definitely not the first to have Ben on her mind. There are women in town who have been after him for so long they've memorized his daily schedule and all the facts of his life, and are so obsessed that when asked for their phone number they often recite his instead. There are teachers in the high school who bring him casseroles every Friday evening, and newly divorced neighbors who call him late at night because their fuses have all blown and they insist they're afraid they'll electrocute themselves without his scientific know-how.

These women would give anything to have Ben Frye sending them roses. They'd say Gillian needs her head examined for sending them back. You're lucky, that's what they'd tell her. But it's a perverse sort of luck: The second Ben Frye fell in love with her, Gillian knew she could never allow someone as wonderful as he is to get involved with a woman like her. Considering the messes she's made, falling in love is now permanently out of the question. The only way anyone could force her to become a wife again would be to chain her to a chapel wall and aim a shotgun at her head. When she came home from Del Vecchio's on the night she met Ben, she took a vow never to marry again. She locked herself in the bathroom and lit a black candle and tried to remember some of the aunts' incantations. When she could not, she repeated "Single forever" three times, and that seems to have done the trick because she keeps refusing him, in spite of how she feels inside.

"Go away," she tells Ben whenever he calls. She doesn't think about the way he looks, or about the feel of the calluses on his fingers, the ones caused by practicing knots for his magic act nearly every day. "Find someone who will make you happy."

But that's not what Ben wants. He wants her. He phones and phones, until they all assume he's the one calling each and every time. Now whenever the phone rings in the Owens house, whoever grabs the receiver doesn't say a word, not even a hello. Each one of them just breathes and waits. It's gotten so that Ben can discern their breathing styles: Sally's matter-of-fact intake of air. Kylie's snort, like a horse who has no patience for the idiot on the other side of the fence. Antonia's sad, fluttery inhalation. And, of course, the sound he's always wishing for—the exasperated and beautiful sigh that escapes from Gillian's mouth before she tells him to leave her alone, get a life, get lost. Do whatever you want, just don't call me anymore.

Still, there's a catch in her voice, and Ben can tell that when she hangs up on him, she's sad and bewildered. He truly can't stand the thought of her unhappiness. Just the idea of tears in her eyes makes him so frenzied that he doubles the miles he usually runs. He traipses around the reservoir so often that the ducks have begun to recognize him and no longer take flight when he passes by. He is as familiar as twilight and cubed white bread. Sometimes he sings "Heartbreak Hotel" while he runs, and then he knows he's in deep trouble. A fortuneteller at a magicians' convention in Atlantic City once told him that when he fell in love it would be forever, and he laughed at the notion, but now he sees that reading was completely on target.

Ben is so mixed up that he's begun to do magic tricks involuntarily. He reached for his credit card at the gas station and pulled out the queen of hearts. He made his electricity bill disappear and set the rosebush in his backyard on fire. He took a quarter from behind an elderly woman's ear as he was helping her cross the Turnpike and nearly sent her into cardiac arrest. Worst of all, he's no longer allowed into the Owl Café at the north end of the Turnpike, where he usually has breakfast, since lately he sets all the soft-boiled eggs spinning and rips the tablecloths off each table he passes on the way to his regular booth.

Ben can't think of anything but Gillian. He's started to carry a rope around with him, in order to tie and untie Tom Fool and Jacoby knots, a bad habit that comes back to him whenever he's nervous or when he can't get what he wants. But even the rope isn't helping. He wants her so much that he's fucking her inside his head when he should be doing things like putting on his brakes at a stoplight or discussing the influx of Japanese beetles with his next-door neighbor, Mrs. Fishman. He's so overheated that the cuffs of his shirts are singed. He's hard constantly, ready for something that looks as if it's never going to happen.

Ben doesn't know what to do to win Gillian over, he has no idea, so he goes to see Sally, ready to beg for her help. But Sally won't even open the door for him. She speaks through the screen, with a distant tone, as if he'd appeared on her front stoop with a vacuum to sell, instead of arriving with his heart in his hand.

"Take my advice," Sally suggests. "Forget Gillian. Don't even think about her. Marry some nice woman."

But Ben Frye made up his mind the minute he saw Gillian standing beneath the lilacs. Or maybe it wasn't his mind that was so intensely affected, but now every piece of him wants her. And so when Sally tells him to go home, Ben refuses to leave. He sits down on the porch as though he had something to protest or all the time in the world. He's there all day, and when the six o'clock whistle at the fire station over on the Turnpike blows, he still hasn't moved. Gillian will not even speak to him when she comes home from work. Already, today, she has lost her watch and her favorite lipstick. At work, she dropped so many hamburgers on the floor she could have sworn someone was tipping the plates right out of her hands. Now, Ben Frye is here and in love with her and she can't even kiss him or wrap her arms around him, because she's poison and she knows it, which is just her luck.

She rushes past him and locks herself in the bathroom, where she runs the water so that no one can hear her cry. She is not worth his devotion. She wishes he would evaporate into thin air. Maybe then she wouldn't have this feeling deep inside, a feeling she can deny all she wants, but that won't stop it from being desire. Still, in spite of her constant refusals, she can't help but peek out the bathroom window, just to get a look at Ben. There he is, in the fading light, certain of what he wants, certain of her. If Gillian were speaking to her sister, or, more correctly, if Sally were speaking to her, Gillian would draw her over to the window to get a look. *Isn't he beautiful?* That's what she would have said if she and Sally had been talking. *I wish I deserved him*, she would have whispered into her sister's ear.

It chills Antonia through and through to see Mr. Frye on the front porch, so obviously in love it seems he's placed his pride and his self-respect on the concrete for anyone to trample. Antonia finds this display of devotion extremely disgusting, she really does. When she walks past him, on her way to work, she doesn't even bother to say hello. Her veins are filled with ice water instead of blood. Lately Antonia doesn't bother with carefully choosing her clothes. She doesn't brush her hair a thousand times at night, or pluck her eyebrows, or bathe with sesame oil so her skin will stay smooth. In a world without love, what is the point of any of that? She broke her mirror and put away her high-heeled sandals. From now on she will concentrate on working as many hours as she can at the ice cream parlor. At least things are tangible there: You put in your time and pick up your paycheck. No expectations and no letdowns, and right now that's what Antonia wants.

"Are you having a nervous breakdown?" Scott Morrison asks when he sees her at the ice cream parlor later that night.

Scott is home from Harvard for summer vacation and is delivering chocolate syrup and marshmallow topping, as well as sprinkles and maraschino cherries and wet walnuts. He'd been the smartest boy ever to graduate from their high school, and the only one to ever be accepted at Harvard. But so what? All the time he was growing up in this neighborhood, he was so smart that no one talked to him, least of all Antonia, who considered him to be a pitiful drip.

Antonia has been methodically cleaning the ice cream scoopers, which she's lined up all in a row. She hasn't even bothered to glance at Scott while he delivered buckets of syrup. She certainly seems different from the way she used to be—she was beautiful and snooty, but tonight she looks like something that's been left out in a storm. When he asks her the completely innocent question about the nervous breakdown, Antonia bursts into tears. She dissolves into them. She is nothing but water. She lets herself slip to the floor, her back against the freezer. Scott leaves his metal dolly and comes to kneel beside her.

"A simple yes or no would have been just fine," he says.

Antonia blows her nose on her white apron. "Yes."

"I can see that," Scott tells her. "You're definitely psychiatric material."

"I thought I was in love with someone," Antonia explains. Tears continue to leak from her eyes.

"Love," Scott says with contempt. He shakes his head, disgusted. "Love is worth the sum of itself, and nothing more."

Antonia stops crying and looks at him. "Exactly," she agrees.

At Harvard, Scott had been shocked to find out that there were hundreds, if not thousands, of people as smart as he was. He'd been getting away with murder for years, using a tenth of his brain power, and now he actually had to work. He'd been so busy competing all year he hadn't had time for daily life—he'd repudiated things like breakfast and haircuts, the consequences of which are that he's lost twenty pounds and has shoulder-length hair, which his boss makes him tie back with a piece of leather so he doesn't offend the customers.

Antonia stares at him, hard, and discovers that Scott looks completely different and exactly the same. Out in the parking lot, Scott's summer partner, who's been driving this delivery route for twenty years and has never before had an assistant who received a 790 on his verbal SATs, leans on the horn.

"Work," Scott says ruefully. "Hell with a paycheck."

That does it. Antonia follows him when he goes to collect his metal dolly. Her face feels hot, even though the air conditioner is switched on.

"See you next week," Scott says. "You're low on hot fudge."

"You could come in before that," Antonia tells him. There are some things she hasn't forgotten, in spite of her depression and this mess with her aunt Gillian and Mr. Frye.

"I could," Scott agrees, realizing, before he heads for the truck, that Antonia Owens is much deeper than he would have ever imagined.

That night Antonia runs all the way home after work. She is suddenly filled with energy; she's absolutely charged. When she turns the corner onto her street she can smell the lilacs, and the odor makes her laugh at the silly reactions caused by some ridiculous out-of-season blooms. Most people in the neighborhood have gotten used to the incredible size of the flowers. They no longer notice that there are whole hours of the day when the entire street echoes with the sound of buzzing bees and the light turns especially purple and sweet. Yet some people return again and again. There are women who stand on the sidewalk and weep at the sight of the lilacs for no reason at all, and still others who have plenty of reasons to cry out loud, although none they'd admit to if questioned.

A hot wind is threading through the trees, shaking the branches, and heat lightning has begun to appear in the east. It's a curious night, so hot and so heavy it seems better suited to the tropics, but despite the weather Antonia sees that two women, one whose hair is white and the other who is not much more than a girl, have come to see the lilacs. As Antonia hurries past, she can hear weeping, and she quickens her pace, goes inside, then locks the door behind her.

"Pathetic," Antonia decrees as she and Kylie peer out the front window to watch the women on the sidewalk cry.

Kylie has been more withdrawn than usual since her birthday supper. She misses Gideon; she has to force herself not to break down and phone him. She feels terrible, but, if anything, she's become even more beautiful. Her cropped blond hair is no longer as shocking. She has stopped slouching to hide how tall she is, and now that she's claimed her full posture, her chin usually tilts up, so that she seems to be considering the blue sky or the cracks in the living room ceiling. She squints her gray-green eyes to see through the glass. She has a particular interest in these two women, since they've come to stand on the sidewalk each night for weeks. The older woman has a white aura around her, as though snow were falling above her alone. The girl, who is her granddaughter and who has just graduated from college, has little pink sparks of confusion rising off her skin. They are here to weep for the same man—the older woman's son, the girl's father—someone who went from boyhood to manhood without ever changing his attitude, convinced till the last that the universe revolved around him alone. The women on the sidewalk spoiled him, both of them, then blamed themselves when he was careless enough to kill himself in a motorboat in Long Island Sound. Now, they're drawn to the lilacs because the flowers remind them of a June night, years ago, when the girl was still tender and awkward and the woman still had thick black hair.

On that night there was a pitcher of sangría on the table, and the lilacs in the grandmother's yard were all in bloom, and the man they both loved, so dearly that they ruined him, took his daughter in his arms and danced with her on the grass. At that moment, beneath the lilacs and the clear sky, he was everything he could have been, if they hadn't given in to him night and day, if they had once suggested that he get a job or act with kindness or think about someone other than himself. They're crying for all he might have been, and all they might have been in his presence and by his side. Watching them, sensing that they've lost what they had for only a brief time, Kylie cries right along with them.

"Oh, please," Antonia says.

Since her encounter with Scott, she can't help but feel a little smug. Unrequited love is so boring. Weeping under a blue-black sky is for suckers or maniacs.

"Will you get real?" she advises her sister. "They're two total strangers who are probably complete nut cases. Ignore them. Pull the window shade down. Grow up."

But that is exactly what has happened to Kylie. She's grown up to discover that she knows and feels too much. No matter where she goes—to the market on an errand, or the town pool for an afternoon swim—she is confronted with people's innermost emotions, which seep from their skins to billow out and float above them, like clouds. Just yesterday, Kylie passed an old woman walking her ancient poodle, which was crippled by arthritis and could barely move. This woman's grief was so overpowering—she would take the dog to the animal hospital by the end of the week to put it out of its misery—that Kylie found she could not take another step. She sat down on the curb and she stayed there until dusk, and when she finally walked home she felt dizzy and weak.

She wishes that she could go out and play soccer with Gideon and not feel other people's pain. She wishes that she were twelve years old again, and that men didn't shout out their car windows whenever she walks along the Turnpike about how much they'd like to fuck her. She wishes she had a sister who acted like a human being, and an aunt who didn't cry herself to sleep so often that her pillow has to be wrung out each morning.

Most of all, Kylie wishes that the man in their backyard would go away. He's out there right now, as Antonia heads for the kitchen, humming, to fetch herself a snack. Kylie can see him from the window that allows a view of both the front and the side yards. Bad weather never affects him; if anything, he relishes black skies and wind. The rain doesn't bother him in the least. It seems to go right through him, with each drop turning a luminous blue. His polished boots have just the slightest film of dirt. His white shirt looks starched and pressed. All the same, he's been making a mess of things. Every time he breathes, horrible things come out of his mouth: Little green frogs. Drops of blood. Chocolates wrapped in pretty foil, but with poisonous centers that give off a foul odor each time he breaks one in half. He's wrecking things just by snapping his fingers. He's making things fall apart. Inside the walls, the pipes are rusting. The tile floor in the basement is turning to dust. The coils of the refrigerator have been twisted, and nothing will stay fresh; the eggs are spoiling inside their shells, the cheeses have all turned green.

This man in the garden has no aura of his own, but he often reaches to dip his hands into the purple-red shadow above him, then smears the aura of the lilacs all over himself. No one but Kylie can see him, but he's still able to call all these women out of their houses. He's the one who whispers to them late at night while they're sleeping in their beds. *Baby*, he says, even to the ones who never thought they'd hear a man talk to them this way again. He gets inside a woman's mind, and he stays there, until she finds herself crying on the sidewalk, crazy for the scent of lilacs, and even then he's not going anywhere. At least not anytime soon. He's definitely not through.

Kylie has been watching him ever since her birthday. She understands that no one else can see him, although the birds sense him and avoid the lilacs, and the squirrels stop dead in their tracks whenever they get too close. Bees, on the other hand, have no fear of him. They seem attracted to him; they hover near, and anyone who came too close to him would surely risk a sting, maybe even two. The man in the garden is easier to see on rainy days, or late at night, when he appears out of thin air like a star you've been staring at but only now see, right in the center of the sky. He doesn't eat or sleep or drink, but that doesn't mean there aren't things he wants. His wanting is so strong Kylie can feel it, like bands of electricity shaking up the air around him. Just recently, he has taken to staring back at her. She gets terrified whenever he does this. She gets cold right through her skin. He's doing it more and more, staring and staring. It doesn't matter where she is, behind the kitchen window or on the path to the back door. He can watch her twenty-four hours a day if he likes, since he never has to blink—not even for a second, not anymore.

Kylie has begun to set dishes of salt on the windowsills. She sprinkles rosemary outside all the doors. Still, he manages to get into the house when everyone's asleep. Kylie stays up after everyone else is in bed, but she can't stay awake forever, although it's not for lack of trying. Often she falls asleep while she's still dressed in her clothes, a book open beside her, the overhead light kept on, since her aunt Gillian, who's still sharing her room, refuses to sleep in the dark and has lately insisted that the windows be closed tight as well, even on sweltering nights, to keep out the scent of those lilacs.

Some nights everyone in the house has a bad dream at the

very same instant. Other nights they all sleep so deeply their alarm clocks can't get them out of bed. Either way, Kylie always knows he's been close by when she wakes to find that Gillian is crying in her sleep. She knows when she goes down the hall to the bathroom and sees that the toilet is clogged and when it's flushed the body of a dead bird or a bat rises up in the water. There are slugs in the garden, and waterbugs in the cellar, and mice have begun to nest in a pair of Gillian's high heels, the black patent leather ones she bought in L.A. Look into a mirror and the image starts to shift. Pass by a window and the glass will rattle. It's the man in the garden who's responsible when the morning begins with a curse muttered under someone's breath, or a toe stubbed, or a favorite dress torn so methodically you'd think someone had sliced through the fabric with a pair of scissors or a hunting knife.

On this morning, the bad fortune rising from the garden is particularly nasty. Not only has Sally discovered the diamond earrings she was given on her wedding day tucked into Gillian's jacket pocket, but Gillian found her paycheck from the Hamburger Shack torn into a thousand pieces, spread across the lace doily on the coffee table.

The silence Sally and Gillian mutually agreed upon at Kylie's birthday dinner, when they snapped their mouths shut in fury and despair, is now over. During these days of silence, both sisters have had migraine headaches. They've had sour expressions and puffy eyes, and both have lost weight, since they now bypass breakfast so they won't have to face one another first thing. But two sisters cannot live in the same house and ignore each other for long. Sooner or later they will break down and have the fight they should have had at the start. Helplessness and anger make for predictable behavior: Children are certain to shove each other and pull hair, teenagers will call each other names and cry, and grown women who are sisters will say words so cruel that each syllable will take on the form of a snake, although such a snake often circles in on itself to eat its own tail once the words are said aloud.

"You dishonest piece of garbage," Sally says to her sister, who has stumbled into the kitchen in search of coffee.

"Oh, yeah?" Gillian says. She's more than ready for this fight. She's got the torn paycheck in the palm of her hand, and now she lets it fall to the floor, like confetti. "Deep down, under all that goody-goody stuff, is a grade-A bitch."

"That's it," Sally says. "I want you out. I've wanted you out from the moment you arrived. I never asked you to stay. I never invited you. You take whatever you want, just the way you always have."

"I'm desperate to go. I'm counting the seconds. But it would be faster if you didn't tear up my checks."

"Listen," Sally says. "If you need to steal my earrings to pay for your departure, well, then good. Fine." She opens her fist and the diamonds fall onto the kitchen table. "Just don't think you're fooling me."

"Why the hell would I want them?" Gillian says. "How stupid can you be? The aunts gave you those earrings because no one else would ever wear such horrible things."

"Fuck you," Sally says. She tosses the words off, easy as butter in her mouth, but in fact she doesn't think she's ever cursed out loud in her own house before.

"Fuck you twice," Gillian says. "You need it more."

That's when Kylie comes down from her bedroom. Her face is pale and her hair is sticking straight up. If Gillian stood before a mirror that was stretched to present someone younger and taller and more beautiful, she'd be looking at Kylie. When you're thirty-six and you're confronted with this, so very early in the morning, your mouth can suddenly feel parched, your skin can feel prickly and worn out, no matter how much moisturizer you've been using.

"You have to stop fighting." Kylie's voice is matter-of-fact, and much deeper than that of most girls her age. She used to think about scoring goals and being too tall; now she's thinking about life and death and men you'd better not dare to turn your back on.

"Says who?" Gillian counters haughtily, having decided, perhaps a little too late, that it might actually be best if Kylie were to remain a child, at least for another few years.

"This is none of your business," Sally tells her daughter.

"Don't you understand? You make him happy when you fight. It's just what he wants."

Sally and Gillian immediately shut up. They exchange a worried look. The kitchen window has been left open all night, and the curtain flaps back and forth, drenched from last night's downpour.

"Who are you talking about?" Sally asks in a calm and steady tone, as though she were not speaking with someone who might have just flipped her lid.

"The man under the lilacs," Kylie says.

Gillian nudges Sally with her bare foot. She doesn't like the sound of this. Plus, Kylie's got a funny look about her, as if she's seen something, and she's not telling, and they're just going to have to play this guessing game with her until they get it right.

"This man who wants us to fight—is he someone bad?" Sally asks.

Kylie snorts, then takes out the coffeepot and a filter. "He's vile," she says—a vocabulary word from last semester that she's putting to good use for the very first time.

Gillian turns to Sally. "Sounds like someone we know."

Sally doesn't bother to remind her sister that only Gillian knows this man. She's the one who dragged him into their lives simply because she had nowhere else to go. Sally can't begin to guess how far her sister's bad judgment will go. Since she's been sharing a room with Kylie, who knows what she's confided?

"You told her about Jimmy, didn't you?" Sally's skin feels much too hot; before long her face will be flushed and red, her throat will be dry with fury. "You just couldn't keep your mouth shut."

"Thanks a lot for trusting me." Gillian is really insulted. "For your information, I didn't tell her anything. Not a word," Gillian insists, although at this moment she's not sure. She can't be angered by Sally's suspicions, because she doesn't even trust herself. Maybe she's been talking in her sleep, maybe she's been telling all while in the very next bed Kylie listens to every word.

"Are you talking about a real man?" Sally asks Kylie. "Someone who's sneaking around our house?"

"I don't know if he's real or not. He's just there."

Sally watches her daughter spoon decaf into the white paper filter. At this moment, Kylie seems like a stranger, a grown woman with secrets to keep. In the dark morning light, her gray eyes look completely green, as though they belonged to a cat that can see in the dark. All that Sally wanted for her, a good and ordinary life, has gone up in smoke. Kylie is anything but ordinary. There is no way around that. She is not like the other girls on the block.

"Tell me if you see him now," Sally says.

Kylie looks at her mother. She's afraid, but she recognizes her mother's tone of voice as one to be obeyed and she goes to the window in spite of her fear. Sally and Gillian come to stand beside her. They can see their reflections in the glass, and the wet lawn. Outside are the lilacs, taller and more lush than would seem possible.

"Under the lilacs." Little knobs of fear are rising on Kylie's arms and her legs and everywhere in between. "Where the grass is the greenest. He's right there."

It is the spot exactly.

Gillian stands close behind Kylie and squints, but all she can make out are the shadows of the lilacs. "Can anyone else see him?"

"The birds." Kylie blinks back tears. What she wouldn't have given to look out and find he's gone. "The bees."

Gillian is ashen. She is the one who should be punished. She deserves it, not Kylie. Jimmy should be haunting her; each time she closes her eyes, it should be his face she sees. "Oh, fuck," she says, to no one in particular.

"Was he your boyfriend?" Kylie asks her aunt.

"Once," Gillian says. "If you can believe it."

"Is that why he hates us so much?" Kylie asks.

"Honey, he just hates," Gillian says. "It doesn't matter if

it's us or them. I just wish I'd learned that when he was still alive."

"And now he won't go away." Kylie understands that much. Even girls of thirteen can figure out that a man's ghost reflects who he was and everything he's ever done. There's a lot of spite under those lilacs. There's a whole lot of get-even.

Gillian nods. "He won't go."

"You're talking about this as if it were real," Sally says. "And it just isn't. It can't be! No one is out there."

Kylie turns to look outside. She wants her mother to be right. It would be such a relief to look and see only the grass and the trees, but that's not all that is out in the yard.

"He's sitting up and lighting a cigarette. He just threw the burning match on the grass."

Kylie's voice sounds breakable, and there are tears in her eyes. Sally has gone very cold and very quiet. It's Jimmy her daughter is in contact with, all right. Every once in a while, Sally herself has felt something out in the yard, but she's dismissed the dark shape seen from the corner of her eye, she's refused to recognize the chill in her bones when she goes to water the cucumbers in the garden. It's nothing, that's what she's told herself. A shadow, a cool breeze, nothing but a dead man who can't hurt anyone.

Now as she considers her own backyard, Sally accidentally bites her lip, but she pays no attention to the blood she's drawn. In the grass there is a spiral of smoke, and the scent of something acrid and burning, as if, indeed, someone had carelessly tossed a match onto the wet lawn. He could burn the house down, if he wanted to. He could take over the backyard, leaving them too frightened to do anything but peer through the window. The lawn is rife with crabgrass and weeds, and not mowed nearly often enough. Still, the fireflies come here in July. The robins always find worms after a storm. This is the garden where her girls grew up, and Sally will be damned if she lets Jimmy force her out, considering he wasn't worth two cents even back when he was alive. He's not going to sit in her yard and threaten her daughters.

"You don't have to worry about this," Sally says to Kylie. "We'll take care of it." She goes to the back door and opens it, then nods to Gillian.

"Me?" Gillian has been trying to get a cigarette out of the pack with her hands shaking like a bird's wings. She has no intention of going into that yard.

"Now," Sally says, with that strange authority she gets at these times, the worst times, moments of panic and confusion when Gillian's first instinct is always to run in the other direction, as fast and heedlessly as possible.

They go outside together, so close each can feel the beat of the other's heart. It rained all night, and now the sticky air is moving in thick mauve-colored waves. The birds aren't singing this morning, it's too dark for that. But the humidity has brought the toads away from the creek behind the high school, and they have a sort of song, a deep humming that rises up through the sleepy neighborhood. The toads are crazy about Snickers, which teenagers sometimes throw to them at lunch hour. It's candy they're looking for as they wind along the neighborhood, hopping across the squishy lawns and through pools of rainwater that have collected in the gutters. Less than half an hour ago, the newspaper delivery boy joyfully biked right over one of the largest toads, only to discover his bike was headed straight for a tree, which crumpled his front wheel and broke two bones in his left ankle and ensured that there'd be no more newspaper deliveries for today.

One of the toads from the creek is halfway across the lawn, on a path toward the hedge of lilacs. Now that they're outside, both of the sisters feel cold; they feel the way they used to on winter days, when they would wrap themselves up in an old quilt in the aunts' parlor and watch the windows as ice formed inside the panes of glass. Just looking at the lilacs makes Sally's voice naturally drop.

"They're bigger than they were yesterday. He's making them grow. He's doing it with hate or spite, but it sure is working."

"God damn you, Jimmy," Gillian whispers.

"Never speak ill of the dead," Sally tells her. "Besides, we're the ones who put him here. That piece of shit."

Gillian's throat goes dry as dust. "Do you think we should dig him back up?"

"Oh, that's good," Sally says. "That's brilliant. Then what do we do with him?" Most probably, they've overlooked a million details. A million ways for him to make them pay. "What if someone comes looking for him?"

"Nobody will. He's the kind of guy you avoid. Nobody gives enough of a shit about Jimmy to look for him. Believe me. We're safe when it comes to that."

"You looked for him," Sally reminds her. "You found him."

Out in a neighboring backyard, a woman is hanging white sheets and blue jeans on a laundry line. It won't rain anymore, that's what they're saying on the radio. It will be beautiful and sunny all week long, till the end of July.

"I got what I thought I deserved," Gillian says.

It is such a deep and true statement Sally cannot believe the words have come out of Gillian's careless mouth. They both measured themselves harshly, and they still do, as if they have never been anything but those two plain little girls, waiting at the airport for someone to claim them.

"Don't worry about Jimmy," Sally tells her sister.

Gillian wants to believe this is possible, she'd pay good money to, if she had any, but she shakes her head, unconvinced.

"He's as good as gone," Sally assures her. "Wait and see."

The toad in the middle of the lawn has come closer. In all honesty, it's quite pretty, with smooth, watery skin and green eyes. It's watchful and patient, and that's more than can be said for most human beings. Today, Sally will follow the toad's example, and will use patience as her weapon and her shield. She will go about her business; she'll vacuum and change the sheets on the beds, but all the while she's doing these things she'll really be waiting for Gillian and Kylie and Antonia to go out for the day.

As soon as she's finally alone, Sally heads for the backyard. The toad is still there; it's been waiting right along with Sally. It settles more deeply into the grass when Sally goes to the garage for the hedge clippers, and it's there when she brings them over, along with the stepladder she uses whenever she wants to change light bulbs or search the top shelves of the pantry.

The clippers are rusty and old, left behind by the house's previous owners, but they'll certainly do the job. The day is already turning hot and sultry, with steam rising from the rain puddles as they evaporate. Sally expects interference. She's never had any experience with restless spirits before, but she assumes they want to hang on to the real world. She half expects Jimmy to reach up through the grass and grab her ankle; she wouldn't be surprised if she clipped off the tip of her thumb or was toppled right off the ladder. But her work goes ahead with surprising ease. A man like Jimmy, after all, never does well in this sort of weather. He prefers air-conditioning and several six-packs. He prefers to wait until night falls. If a woman wants to work in the hot sun, he'd never be the one to stop her; he'd be flat out on his back, relaxed in the shade, before she'd even have time to set up her stepladder.

Sally, however, is used to hard work, especially in the dead of winter, when she sets her alarm for five a.m. so she can wake up early enough to shovel snow and do at least one load of laundry before she and the girls head out. She considered herself lucky to get the job at the high school so she could have time with her children. Now she sees she was smart. Summers have always belonged to her, and they always will. That's why she can take her time cutting down the hedges. She can take all day, if need be, but by twilight those lilacs will be gone.

In the far section of the yard only a few stumps will be left behind, so dark and knotty they'll be good for nothing other than a toad's home. The air will be so still it will be possible to hear a single mosquito; the last call of the mockingbird will echo, then fade. When night falls, there will be armloads of branches and flowers on the street, all neatly tied with rope, ready for the trash pickup in the morning. The women who are called to the lilacs will arrive to see that the hedges have been chopped to the ground, their glorious flowers nothing but garbage strewn along the gutter and the street. That is the moment when they'll throw their arms around one another and praise simple things and, at long last, consider themselves to be free.

Two hundred years ago, people believed that a hot and steamy July meant a cold and miserable winter. The shadow of a groundhog was carefully studied as an indicator for bad weather. The skin of an eel was commonly used to prevent rheumatism. Cats were never allowed inside a house, since it was well known that they could suck the breath right out of an infant, killing the poor baby in his cradle. People believed that there were reasons for everything, and that they could divine these reasons easily. If they could not, then something wicked must be at work. Not only was it possible to converse with the devil, but some in their midst actually made bargains with him. Anyone who did was always found out in the end, exposed by his or her own bad fortune or the dreadful luck of those close by.

When a husband and wife were unable to have a child, the husband placed a pearl beneath his wife's pillow, and if she still failed to conceive, there'd be talk about her, and concern about the true nature of her character. If all the strawberries in every patch were eaten by earwigs, suddenly and overnight, then the old woman down the road, who was cross-eyed and drank until she was as unmovable as a stone, was brought into the town hall for questioning. Even after a woman proved herself innocent of any wrongdoing—if she managed to walk through water and not dissolve into smoke and ashes or if it was discovered that the strawberries in the entire Commonwealth had been affected—that still didn't mean she'd be welcome in town or that anyone believed she wasn't guilty of something.

These were the prevailing attitudes when Maria Owens first came to Massachusetts with only a small satchel of belongings, her baby daughter, and a packet of diamonds sewn into the hem of her dress. Maria was young and pretty, but she dressed all in black and didn't have a husband. In spite of this, she possessed enough money to hire the twelve carpenters who built the house on Magnolia Street, and she was so sure of herself and what she wanted that she went on to advise these men in such matters as what wood to use for the mantel in the dining room and how many windows were needed to present the best view of the back garden. People became suspicious, and why shouldn't they be? Maria Owens's baby girl never cried, not even when she was bitten by a spider or stung by a bee. Maria's garden was never infested with earwigs or mice. When a hurricane struck, every house on Magnolia Street was damaged, except for the one built by the twelve carpenters; not one of the shutters was blown away, and even the laundry forgotten out on the line stayed in place, not a single stocking was lost.

If Maria Owens chose to speak to you, she looked you straight in the eye, even if you were her elder or better. She was known to do as she pleased, without stopping to deliberate what the consequences might be. Men who shouldn't have fell in love with her and were convinced that she came to them in the middle of the night, igniting their carnal appetites. Women found themselves drawn to her and wanted to confess their own secrets in the shadows of her porch, where the wisteria had begun to grow and was already winding itself around the black-painted railings.

Maria Owens paid attention to no one but herself and her daughter and a man over in Newburyport who none of her neighbors even knew existed, although he was well known and quite well respected in his own town. Three times every month, Maria bundled up her sleeping baby, then she put on her long wool coat and walked across the fields, past the orchards and the ponds filled with geese. Drawn by desire, she traveled quickly, no matter what the weather might be. On some nights, people thought they saw her, her coat billowing out behind her, running so fast it seemed she was no longer touching the ground. There might be ice and snow, there might be white flowers on every apple tree; it was impossible to tell when Maria might walk through the fields. Some people never even knew she was passing right by their houses; they would simply hear something out beyond where they lived, out where the raspberries grew, where the horses were sleeping, and a wash of desire would filter over their own skins, the women in their nightgowns, the men exhausted from the hard work and boredom of their lives. Whenever they did see Maria in daylight, on the road or in a shop, they looked at her carefully, and they didn't trust what was before them—the pretty face, the cool gray eyes, the black coat, the scent of some flower no one in their town could name.

And then one day, a farmer winged a crow in his cornfield, a creature that had been stealing from him shamelessly for months. When Maria Owens appeared the very next morning with her arm in a sling and her right hand wound up in a white bandage, people felt certain they knew the reason why. They were polite enough when she came into their stores, to buy coffee or molasses or tea, but as soon as her back was turned they made the sign of the fox, raising pinky and forefinger in the air, since this motion was known to unravel a spell. They watched the night sky for anything strange; they hung horseshoes over their doors, hammered in with three strong nails, and some people kept bunches of mistletoe in their kitchens and parlors, to protect their loved ones from evil.

Every Owens woman since Maria has inherited those clear gray eyes and the knowledge that there is no real defense against evil. Maria was no crow interested in harassing farmers and their fields. It was love that had wounded her. The man who was the father of her child, whom Maria had followed to Massachusetts in the first place, had decided he'd had enough. His ardor had cooled, at least for Maria, and he'd sent her a large sum of money to keep her quiet and out of the way. Maria refused to believe he would treat her this way; still he had failed to meet her three times, and she just couldn't wait any longer. She went to his house in Newburyport, something he'd absolutely forbidden, and she'd bruised her own arm and broken a bone in her right hand by pounding on his door. The man she loved would not answer her cries; instead he shouted at her to go away, with a voice so distant anyone would have guessed they were little more than strangers. But Maria would not go away, she knocked and she knocked, and she didn't even notice that her knuckles were bloody; welts had already begun to appear on her skin.

Finally, the man Maria loved sent his wife to the door, and when Maria saw this plain woman in her flannel nightgown, she turned and ran all the way home, across the fields in the moonlight, fast as a deer, faster even, entering into people's dreams. The next morning most people in town awoke out of breath, with their legs shaking from exertion, so tired it seemed as though they hadn't slept a wink. Maria didn't even realize what she'd done to herself until she tried to move her right hand and couldn't, and she thought it only fitting that she'd been marked this way. From then on, she kept her hands to herself.

Of course, bad fortune should be avoided whenever possible, and Maria was always prudent when it came to matters of luck. She planted fruit trees in the dark of the moon, and some of the hardier perennials she tended continue to sprout among the rows in the aunts' garden; the onions are still so fiery and strong it's easy to understand why they were thought to be the best cure for dog bites and toothaches. Maria always made certain to wear something blue, even when she was an old lady and couldn't get out of bed. The shawl across her shoulders was blue as paradise, and when she sat on the porch in her rocking chair it was difficult to tell where she ended and where the sky began.

Until the day she died, Maria wore a sapphire the man she'd loved had given her, just to remind herself of what was important and what was not. For a very long time after she was gone, some people insisted they saw an icy blue figure in the fields, late at night, when the air was cold and still. They swore that she walked past the orchards, traveling north, and that if you were very quiet, if you didn't move at all, but stayed down on one knee beside the old apple trees, her dress would brush against you, and from that day forward you'd be lucky in all matters, as would your children after you, and their children as well.

In the small portrait the aunts have sent Kylie for her birthday, which arrives in a packing crate two weeks late, Maria is wearing her favorite blue dress and her dark hair is pulled back with a blue satin ribbon. This oil painting hung on the staircase in the Owens house for one hundred and ninety-two years, in the darkest corner of the landing, beside the damask drapes. Gillian and Sally passed by it a thousand times on their way up to bed, without giving it a second look. Antonia and Kylie played games of Parcheesi on the landing during their August vacations and never even noticed that there was anything on the wall, other than spiderwebs and dust.

They notice now. Maria Owens is hanging above Kylie's bed. She is so alive on the canvas, it's obvious that the painter was in love with her by the time he had finished this portrait. When the hour is late and the night very quiet, it's almost possible to see her breathing in and out. If a ghost were to consider climbing in the window, or seeping through the plaster, he might think twice about facing Maria. You can tell just by looking at her that she never backed down or valued anyone's opinion above her own. She always believed that experience was not simply the best teacher, it was the only one, which is why she insisted the painter include the bump on her right hand, where it had never quite healed.

The day the painting arrived, Gillian came home from work smelling of french fries and sugar. Since Sally had chopped down the lilacs, every day was better than the one before. The sky was bluer, the butter set out on the table was sweeter, and it was possible to sleep through the night without nightmares or fears of the dark. Gillian sang while she wiped off the counters at the Hamburger Shack; she whistled on her way to the post office or the bank. But when she went upstairs and opened the door to Kylie's room to find herself face to face with Maria, she let out a screech that frightened all the sparrows in the neighbors' yards and set the dogs howling.

"What a dreadful surprise," she said to Kylie.

Gillian went as close to Maria Owens as she dared. She had the urge to drape a towel over the portrait, or to replace it with something cheerful and ordinary, a brightly toned painting of puppies playing tug of war, or children at a tea party setting out cakes for their teddy bears. Who needed the past right there on the wall? Who needed anything that had once been in the aunts' house, up on the gloomy landing, beside the threadbare drapes.

"This is way too creepy to have in the bedroom," Gillian informed her niece. "We're taking it down."

"Maria is not creepy," Kylie said. Kylie's hair was growing out, leaving her with a brown streak half an inch wide in the center of her head. She should have looked odd and unfinished; instead she was growing even more beautiful. In fact, she resembled Maria; side by side, they might even appear to be twins. "I like her," Kylie told her aunt, and since it was her bedroom, that was that.

Gillian claimed she would be too nervous to sleep with Maria hanging above them, she'd have nightmares and perhaps even the shakes, but that's not the way it's turned out. She's stopped thinking about Jimmy completely and no longer worries that someone will come looking for him; if he owed money or had cut a bad deal, the men who'd been wronged would have been there by now, they would have come and taken what they wanted and already been gone. Now that the portrait of Maria is on the wall, Gillian has been sleeping even more deeply. Each morning she wakes with a smile on her face. She's not as frightened of the backyard as she used to be, although every now and then she drags Kylie to the window, just to make certain Jimmy hasn't come back. Kylie always insists she has nothing to worry about. The garden is clear and green. The lilacs have been cut so close to their roots it may be years before they sprout again. Once in a while something casts a shadow across the lawn, but it's probably the toad who has taken up residence in the roots of the lilacs. They'd know if it was Jimmy, wouldn't they? They'd feel more threatened and much more vulnerable.

"No one is out there," Kylie has promised. "He's gone." And maybe he really is, because Gillian isn't crying anymore, not even in her sleep, and those bruises he left on her arms have disappeared, and she's started to date Ben Frye.

The decision to take a chance with Ben came upon her suddenly, as she was driving home from work in Jimmy's Oldsmobile, which still had beer cans rattling around somewhere under the seat. Ben continued to call several times a day, but that couldn't go on forever, even though he had amazing patience. As a boy, he had taken eight months to teach himself to escape from a pair of iron handcuffs. Before he mastered the art of putting a match out under his tongue, he burned the roof of his mouth, again and again, so that for weeks afterward he could consume nothing but buttermilk and pudding. Illusions that lasted only seconds on a stage took months or even years to understand and execute. But love was not about practice and preparation, it was pure chance; if you took your time with it you ran the risk of having it evaporate before it had even begun. Sooner or later, Ben was bound to give up. He'd be on his way to see her, he'd have a book under his arm in order to pass the time while he waited for her on the porch, and he'd suddenly think, Nope, just like that, out of the blue. All Gillian had to do was close her eyes and she could see the expression of doubt that would spread across his face. *Not today*, he'd decide and he'd turn around to head for home and he probably wouldn't ever come back.

Speculating about the time when Ben finally stopped chasing after her made Gillian sick to her stomach. The world without him, without his phone calls and his faith, didn't interest her in the least. And who was she protecting him from, really? That careless girl who broke people's hearts and asked for nothing more than a good time was gone. Jimmy had seen to that. That girl was so long ago and so far away that Gillian couldn't even remember why she'd thought she'd ever been in love before, or what she'd thought she was getting from all those men, who never knew who she was in the first place.

On that evening when the sky was pale and blue and the beer cans were rolling around each time she stepped on the brake, Gillian made an illegal U turn and drove to Ben Frye's house before her nerve failed her. She told herself she was an adult and could handle an adult encounter. It wasn't necessary for her to run away, or protect someone at her own expense, or do anything more than take one baby step at a time in any direction she chose. All the same, she thought she might faint when Ben came to answer his door. She'd planned to tell him that she wasn't looking for a commitment or anything serious—she wasn't sure if she was going to kiss him, let alone get into bed with him—but she never got to say any of it, because once she stepped into the front hallway, Ben wasn't about to wait.

He'd done enough time with patience, he'd served his sentence, now he didn't intend to look past what he wanted. He started kissing Gillian before she could mention that she was still thinking it over. His kisses made her feel things she didn't want to feel, at least not yet. He got her up against the wall and slipped his hands under her blouse, and that was that. She didn't say "Stop it," she didn't say "Wait," she kissed him back until she was too far gone to think anything over. Ben was driving her crazy, and he was testing her, too—every time he got her really hot, he'd stop just to see what she would do, and how much she wanted it. If he didn't take her into the bedroom soon, she'd find herself begging him to fuck her. She'd wind up saying, *Please, baby*, which is what she used to say to Jimmy, although she never really meant it. Not back then. It's never possible for a woman to concentrate on making love when she's that scared. Too scared to breathe, too frightened to consider saying, *Not like that. It hurts too much when you do it like that.*

She talked dirty to Jimmy because she knew it helped to make him hard. If he'd been drinking all night and couldn't get it up, he'd turn on her so fast she'd be reeling. One minute everything would be fine, and the next second the air all around him would be set on fire from the fury of whatever was inside him. When this happened, either he'd start to slap her or she'd have to start telling him how much she wanted him inside her.

At least he'd have something to do with his anger when Gillian told him that she wanted him to fuck her all night, she wanted him so much she'd do anything, he could make her do anything. And didn't he have a perfect right to be angry and do whatever he pleased? Wasn't she so bad she needed to be punished, and only he could do it, he could do it right?

Talk and violence always turned Jimmy on, and so Gillian always started talking right away. She was smart enough to get him hard fast, to talk nasty and suck his dick, before he started to get really mad. He'd fuck her then, but he could be mean about it, and selfish, too, and he liked it when she cried. When she cried, he knew he had won, and for some reason that was important to him. He didn't seem to know he'd won from the start, when she first saw him, when she first looked into his eyes.

As soon as they were done with sex, Jimmy would be nice to her again, and it was worth almost anything to have him when he was that way. When he was feeling all right and didn't have anything to prove, he was the man she'd fallen for so hard, he was the one who could make nearly any woman believe whatever he wanted. It's easy to forget what you do in the dark, if you need to. Gillian knew that other women thought she was lucky, and she agreed with them. She'd gotten confused, that's what had happened. She'd started to accept that love had to be like this, and in a way she was right, because with Jimmy that's the way it did have to be.

Gillian was so used to having someone get her down on her hands and knees first thing; she was so ready to be struck and then told she'd better suck hard, that she couldn't believe Ben was spending this much time kissing her. All this kissing was making her crazy; it was reminding her of what she could feel, and how it could be when you wanted someone as much as he wanted you. Ben was about as different from Jimmy as anyone could be. He wasn't interested in making anyone cry, then sweet-talking her afterward, the way Jimmy used to, and he didn't need any help the way Jimmy always did. By the time Ben pulled her panties off, Gillian was completely weak in the knees. She didn't give a damn about going into the bedroom, she wanted it there, she wanted it now. She no longer had to debate the possibility of being with Ben Frye; this relationship had already happened, she'd walked straight into it, and she wasn't about to start walking away.

They made love for as long as they could, right there in the hallway, and then they went to Ben's bed and slept for hours, as though they'd been drugged. As they were falling asleep, Gillian could have sworn she heard Ben say *Fate*—as if they were meant to be together from the start and every single thing they'd ever done in their lives had been leading to this moment. If you thought that way, you could fall asleep without regret. You could put your whole life in place, with all the sadness and the sorrow, and still feel that at last you had everything you'd ever wanted. In spite of the lousy odds and all the wrong turns, you might actually discover that you were the one who'd won.

When Gillian woke, it was evening and the room was dark, except for something that appeared to be a white cloud poised at the foot of the bed. Gillian wondered if she was dreaming, if perhaps she'd risen out of her body to float above herself and the bed she'd been sharing with Ben Frye. But when she pinched herself, it hurt. This was still her, all right. She ran her hand along Ben's back, just to make certain he was real too. In fact, he was real enough to startle her; his muscles and his skin and the heat from his sleeping body made her want him all over again, and she felt foolish, like a schoolgirl who doesn't stop to consider any consequences.

Gillian sat up, the white sheet pulled around her, and found that the cloud at the foot of the bed was nothing more than Ben's pet rabbit, Buddy, who hopped into her lap. Only a few weeks ago, Gillian had been out in the Sonoran desert, her hands over her ears, as Jimmy and two of his friends shot prairie dogs. They killed thirteen of them, and Gillian had thought it was terrible luck. She'd gotten shaky and pale, too upset to hide it. Luckily, Jimmy was in a great mood, since he'd bagged more prairie dogs than his pals had, shooting eight, if you included the two babies. He came over and put his arms around Gillian. When he looked at her in this way, she understood why she'd been so drawn to him, and why she was still. He could make it seem as though you were the only person in the universe; a bomb could fall, lightning could strike, he simply would not take his eyes off you.

"The only good rodent is a dead rodent," Jimmy had told her. He smelled of cigarettes and heat and was just about as alive as a human being could be. "Trust me on this. When you see one, shoot to kill."

Jimmy would have gotten a good laugh catching her in bed with a rodent. Gillian pushed the rabbit away, then got up and found her way to the kitchen for a glass of water. She was disoriented and confused. She didn't know what she was doing in Ben's house, although it was surprisingly comfortable, with nice old pine furniture and shelves filled with books. Most of the men Gillian had been involved with had avoided the kitchen, some hadn't even seemed to be aware that their own houses had such rooms, complete with stoves and sinks, but here the kitchen was well used—a weathered pine table was piled high with science textbooks and menus from Chinese restaurants, and, when she looked, Gillian discovered that there was actually food in the refrigerator: several casserole pans of lasagna and broccoli-with-cheese soufflé, a carton of milk, cold cuts, bottled water, bunches of carrots. Right before they had to leave Tucson in such a hurry, there was nothing in their refrigerator but six-packs of Budweiser and Diet Coke. One package of frozen burritos was wedged way in the back near the ice trays, but anything left in their freezer always defrosted, then refroze, and was better left alone.

Gillian got herself a bottle of fancy water, and when she turned she saw that the rabbit had followed her.

"Go away," she told him, but he wouldn't.

Buddy had taken to Gillian in a major way. He thumped his leg, the way rabbits in love always do. He paid no attention to her frown, or the fact that she waved her hands at him, as if he were a cat to be shooed away. He trailed behind her into the living room. When Gillian stopped, Buddy sat down on the rug and looked up at her.

"You quit this right now," Gillian said.

She wagged her finger and glared at him, but Buddy stayed where he was. He had big brown eyes that were rimmed with pink. He looked serious and dignified, even when he washed his paws with his tongue.

"You're just a rodent," Gillian told him. "That's all you are."

Gillian felt like crying, and why shouldn't she? She could never live up to Ben's version of her; she had a whole secret, horrible past to hide. She used to fuck men in parked cars just to prove she didn't give a damn; she used to count her conquests and laugh. She sat on the couch that Ben had ordered from a catalogue when his old one became threadbare. It was a really nice couch, made out of some plum-colored corduroy fabric. Just the kind of couch Gillian would have spotted in a magazine and wanted for herself, if she had a house, or money, or even a permanent address to which she could have catalogues and magazines mailed. She wasn't even certain that she could be in a normal relationship. What if she got tired of someone's being nice to her? What if she couldn't make him happy? What if Jimmy had been right and she'd asked to be hit—maybe not out loud, but in some nameless way she wasn't aware of. What if he'd fixed it so she actually needed it now?

The rabbit hopped over and sat at her feet.

"I'm fucked up," Gillian told him.

She curled up on the couch and wept, but even that didn't scare the rabbit away. Buddy had spent a great deal of time at the children's ward at the hospital over on the Turnpike. Every Saturday, during Ben's magic act, he was pulled out of a hat that was old and smelled of alfalfa and sweat. Buddy was used to bright lights and people crying, and he was always well behaved. He had never once bitten a child, not even when he'd been poked or teased. Now, he rose onto his back legs and balanced carefully, just as he'd been taught.

"Don't try to cheer me up," Gillian said, but all the same he did. By the time Ben came out of the bedroom, Gillian was sitting on the floor with Buddy, feeding him some seedless grapes.

"This is one smart character," Gillian said. The sheet she'd taken from the bed was wrapped around her carelessly and her hair was sticking out like a halo. She felt calmer now, and lighter than she had for quite a while. "Why, he can put on the floor lamp by jumping on the switch. He can hold this bottle of water between his paws and drink some without spilling a drop. No one who hadn't seen it would believe it. Next thing I know, you'll tell me he's litter-trained like a cat."

"He is."

Ben was standing by the window, and in the pale new light he looked as if he'd slept the deep sleep of angels; no one would guess how he had panicked when he awoke to find Gillian gone from his bed. He'd been ready to run down the street, to call the police and demand a search party. In those moments when he'd climbed from his bed he'd guessed he had somehow managed to lose her, as he'd lost everything else in his life, but here she was, wrapped up in the sheet from his bed. If he was honest with himself, he'd have to admit that he had a real fear of people disappearing on him, which is why he turned to magic in the first place. In Ben Frye's act, what vanished always reappeared, whether it was a ring or a quarter or Buddy himself. In spite of all this, Ben had gone and fallen in love with the most unpredictable woman he'd ever met. And he couldn't fight it; he didn't even want to try. He wished he could tie her up in his room, with ropes made of silk; he wished he never had to let her go. He crouched down beside Gillian with the full knowledge that he was the one tied in knots. He wanted to ask her to marry him, to never leave him; instead he reached beneath the couch pillow, then waved his arm around and pulled a carrot out of thin air. For the first time ever, Buddy ignored food; he edged closer to Gillian.

"I see I have a rival," Ben said. "I may have to cook him."

Gillian scooped the rabbit into her arms. All the while Ben had been sleeping, she'd been dissecting her past. Now, she was through with it. She was not going to let that little girl sitting on the dusty back steps of the aunts' kitchen control her. She was not going to let that idiot who'd gotten herself entangled with Jimmy rule her life. "Buddy is probably the most intelligent bunny in the entire country. He's so smart that he'll probably ask me over for dinner tomorrow night."

It was clear to Ben that he owed the rabbit a debt of gratitude. If not for Buddy, perhaps Gillian would have left without saying good-bye; instead she stayed, and wept, and reconsidered. And so, in honor of Buddy, Ben fixed carrot soup the next evening, a salad of leaf lettuce, and a pot of Welsh rabbit, which Gillian was extremely relieved to hear was nothing more than melted cheese served with bread. A plate of salad and a small bowl of soup had been placed on the floor for Buddy. The rabbit was petted and thanked, but after dinner he was taken to his carrying crate for the night. They didn't want him scratching at the bedroom door; they didn't want to be disturbed, not by Buddy or anyone else.

Since then, they have been together every night. Just about the time when Gillian gets off from work, Buddy heads for the front door, and he paces, agitated, until Gillian arrives, smelling of french fries and herbal soap. The teenage boys from the Hamburger Shack follow her halfway down the Turnpike, but they stop when she turns onto Ben's street. In the fall, these boys will sign up for Ben Frye's biology course, even the lazy and stupid ones who have always failed science before. They figure that Mr. Frye knows something, and that they'd better learn whatever it is, and learn fast. But these boys can study all semester, they can be on time for every single lab, they still won't learn what Ben knows until they fall head over heels in love. When they don't care if they make fools of themselves, when taking a risk seems the safest thing to do, and walking a tightrope or throwing themselves into white-water rapids feels like child's play compared with a single kiss, then they'll understand.

But for now, these boys don't know the first thing about love, and they sure don't know women. They would never have imagined that the reason Gillian has been dropping steaming cups of hot coffee while she's waiting on people at the Hamburger Shack is that she can't stop thinking about the things Ben does to her when they're in his bed. She gets lost driving home whenever she thinks about the way he whispers to her; she's as hot and confused as a teenager.

Gillian has always considered herself an outsider, so it's been a big relief to discover that Ben is not as normal as she originally thought. He can easily spend three hours at the Owl Café on a Sunday morning, ordering plates of pancakes and eggs; most of the waitresses there have dated him and they get all dreamy when he comes in for breakfast, bringing him free coffee and ignoring whoever his companion might be. He keeps late hours; he is amazingly quick because of all his practice with cards and scarves, and can catch a sparrow or a chickadee in midflight just by reaching into the air.

The unexpected facets of Ben's personality have truly surprised Gillian, who never would have imagined that a high school biology teacher would be such a fanatic about knots, and that he would want to tie her to the bed or that after her previous experience, she would consider, then agree, and finally find herself begging for it. Whenever Gillian sees a package of shoelaces or a ball of string in the hardware store, she gets totally excited. She has to run home to Sally's so she can scoop some ice cubes out of the freezer and run them along her arms and inside her thighs just to chill her desire.

After she found several pairs of handcuffs in Ben's closet—which he often uses in his magic act—ice cubes weren't enough. Gillian had to go into the yard, turn on the hose, and run a shower of water over her head. She was burning up at the thought of what Ben could do with those handcuffs. She wishes she could have seen his smile when he walked into the room to discover that she'd left them out on his bureau, but he took the hint. That night he made certain the key was far enough away so that neither of them could reach it from the bed. He made love to her for so long that she ached, and still she wouldn't have thought of asking him to stop.

She wants him never to stop, that's the thing, that's what's making her nervous, since it was always the other way around. Even with Jimmy—it was the man who wanted her, and that's the way she liked it. When you want someone you're in his power. Feeling the way she does, Gillian has actually gone over to the high school, where Ben has been setting up his classroom for the fall, to ask him to make love to her. She can't wait for him to come home, she can't wait for night to fall, for bedrooms and closed doors. She comes to put her arms around him and then she tells him she wants it right now. It's not like

Jimmy; she really means it. She means it so much that she can't even remember saying these same words to anyone else. As far as she's concerned, she never did.

Everyone in the school district knows about Ben and Gillian; the news has gone through the neighborhood like a grass fire. Even the janitor has congratulated Ben on his good fortune. They're the couple watched by neighbors and discussed at the hardware store and at the bar of Bruno's Tavern. Dogs follow them when they go out for a walk; cats congregate in Ben's backyard at midnight. Each time Gillian sits on a rock at the reservoir with a stopwatch to time Ben as he runs, the toads climb out of the mud to sing their deep, bloodless song, and by the time Ben has finished with his run he has to step over a mass of damp gray-green bodies in order to help Gillian down from her rock.

If they're out together and Ben accidentally meets one of his students, he gets serious and starts to talk about last year's final exam or the new equipment he'll be setting up in the lab or the countywide science fair in October. The girls who have been in his classes become wide-eyed and mute in his presence; the boys are so busy staring at Gillian they don't pay attention to a word he says. But Gillian listens to him. She loves to hear Ben talk about science. It makes her stomach flip over with desire when he starts to discuss cells. If he mentions the pancreas or the liver, it's all she can do to keep her hands off him. He's so smart, but that's not the only thing that gets to Gillian—he acts like she is, too. He assumes she can understand what the hell he's talking about, and just like a miracle, she does. For the first time she grasps the difference between a vein and an artery. She knows all the major organs, and what's more, she can actually recite the function of each, not to mention its placement in the human body.

One day, Gillian completely surprises herself by driving to the community college and signing up for two classes that start in the fall. She doesn't even know whether she'll be here in September, but if she should happen to stay on, she'll be studying earth science and biology. At night, when she comes home from being with Ben, Gillian goes to Antonia's room and borrows her Biology I textbook. She reads about blood and bones. She traces the digestive system with the tip of her finger. When she gets to the chapter on genetics she stays up all night. The notion that there is a progression and a sequence of possibilities when dealing with who a human can and will be is thrilling. The portrait of Maria Owens above Kylie's bed now seems as certain and as clear as a mathematical equation; on some nights Gillian finds herself staring at it and she has the feeling she's looking into a mirror. *Of course*, she always thinks then. Math plus desire equals who you are. For the first time she has begun to appreciate her own gray eyes.

Now when she sees Kylie, who looks enough like her that strangers assume they're mother and daughter, Gillian senses the connection in her blood. What she feels for Kylie is equal parts science and affection; she would do anything for her niece. She'd step in front of a truck and trade away several years of her life to ensure Kylie's happiness. And yet Gillian is so busy with Ben Frye, she doesn't notice that Kylie is barely speaking to her in spite of all this affection. She'd never guess that Kylie has been feeling used and cast aside ever since Ben entered the picture, which is especially painful for her, since she took her aunt's side against her mother in the birthday debacle. Even though Gillian took her side, too, and is the only one on earth to treat Kylie like a grownup rather than a baby, Kylie has felt betrayed.

Secretly, Kylie has done mean things, nasty tricks worthy of Antonia's malice. She put ashes in Gillian's shoes, so her aunt's toes would be dirty and smudged, and even added some glue for good measure. She poured a can of tunafish down the bathtub drain, and Gillian wound up bathing in oily water that had such a strong scent four stray cats jumped in through the open window.

"Is something wrong?" Gillian asked one day when she turned to see Kylie glaring at her.

"Wrong?" Kylie blinked. She knew how innocent she could seem if she wanted to. She could be an extremely good girl, just the way she used to be. "What would make you ask that?"

The very same night Kylie had five anchovy pizzas delivered to Ben Frye's house. Being resentful was an awful feeling; she wanted to be happy for Gillian, really she did, but she just couldn't seem to manage it until one day she happened to see Gillian and Ben walking together by the high school. Kylie was on her way to the town pool, with a towel draped over her shoulder, but she stopped where she was, on the sidewalk outside Mrs. Jerouche's house, even though Mrs. Jerouche was known to come after you with a hose if you walked across her lawn, and she had an evil cocker spaniel, a prize bitch named Mary Ann, who ate sparrows and drooled and bit little boys on the ankles and knees.

A circle of pale yellow light seemed to hover around Ben and Gillian; the light rose higher, then fanned out, across the street and above the rooftops. The air itself had turned lemony, and when Kylie closed her eyes she felt she was in the aunts' garden. If you sat there in the shade during the heat of August, and rubbed the lemon thyme between your fingers, the air turned so yellow you'd swear a swarm of bees had gathered above you, even on days when it had done nothing but rain. In that garden, on hot, still days, it was easy to think about possibilities that had never crossed your mind before. It was as if hope had appeared out of nowhere, to settle beside you, and it wasn't going anywhere, it wasn't going to desert you now.

On the afternoon when Kylie stood in front of Mrs. Jerouche's house, she wasn't the only one to sense something unusual in the air. A group of boys playing kickball all stopped, stunned by the sweet scent wafting down from the rooftops, and they rubbed at their noses. The youngest turned and ran home and begged his mother for lemon pound cake, heated, and spread with honey. Women came to their windows, leaned their elbows on the sills, and breathed more deeply than they had in years. They didn't even believe in hope anymore, but here it was, in the treetops and the chimneys. When these women looked down at the street and saw Gillian and Ben, arms looped around each other, something inside them started to ache, and their throats got so dry only lemonade could quench their thirst, and even after a whole pitcherful, they still wanted more.

It was hard to be angry with Gillian after that, it was impossible to resent her or even feel slighted. Gillian was so intense when it came to Ben Frye that the butter in Sally's house kept melting, the way it does whenever love is under a roof.

Even the sticks of butter in the refrigerator would melt, and anyone who wanted some would have to pour it on a piece of toast or measure it out with a tablespoon.

On nights when Gillian lies in bed and reads biology, Kylie stretches out on her own bed and leafs through magazines, but really she's watching Gillian. She's feeling lucky to be learning about love from someone like her aunt. She's heard people talking; even the ones who feel the need to point out that Gillian is trash seem envious of her somehow. Gillian may be a waitress at the Hamburger Shack, she may have little lines around her eyes and mouth from all that Arizona sun, but she's the one Ben Frye's in love with. She's the one who has that smile on her face, night and day.

"Guess what the largest organ in the human body is," Gillian asks Kylie one evening when they're both in bed reading.

"Skin," Kylie says.

"Wise guy," Gillian tells her. "Know-it-all."

"Everybody's jealous that you got Mr. Frye," Kylie says.

Gillian goes on reading her Bio I book, but that doesn't mean she isn't listening. She has the ability to talk about one thing and concentrate on another. She learned it from all that time she spent with Jimmy.

"That makes him sound like he was something I picked up in a store. Like he was a grapefruit, or something on sale, and I got him half-price." Gillian wrinkles her nose. "Anyway, it wasn't luck."

Kylie rolls onto her stomach so she can study her aunt's dreamy face. "Then what was it?"

"Destiny." Gillian closes her biology textbook. She has the

best smile in the world, Kylie will certainly grant her that. "Fate."

Kylie thinks about destiny all night long. She thinks about her father, whom she remembers only from a single photograph. She thinks about Gideon Barnes, because she could fall in love with him if she let herself, and she knows he could fall in love with her, too. But Kylie's not so certain that's what she wants. She's not sure if she's ready yet, or if she'll ever be. Lately, she's so sensitive and tuned in she can pick up Gillian's dreams as she sleeps in the next bed, dreams so scandalous and hot that Kylie wakes up aroused, and then she's more embarrassed and confused than ever.

Being thirteen is not what she hoped it would be. It's lonely and not any fun whatsoever. Sometimes she feels she's stumbled onto a whole secret world she doesn't understand. When she stares at herself in the mirror she just can't decide who she is. If she ever does figure it out, she'll know whether she should dye her hair blond or brown, but for now, she's in the middle. She's in the middle about everything. She misses Gideon; she goes to the basement and takes out her chessboard, which always reminds her of him, but she can't bring herself to call him. When she runs into any of the girls she goes to school with and they invite her to go swimming or to the mall, Kylie isn't interested. It's not that she dislikes them; it's just that she doesn't want them to see who she really is, when she herself doesn't know.

What she does know is that awful things can happen if you don't watch out. The man in the garden has taught her this, and it's a lesson she won't soon forget. Grief is all around; it's just invisible to most people. Most people will figure out a way to stop themselves from being aware of agony—they'll have a good stiff drink, or swim a hundred laps, or not eat anything all day, except for a small polished apple and a head of lettuce—but Kylie isn't like that. She's too sensitive, and her ability to feel others' pain is getting stronger. If she passes a baby in his stroller, and he's wailing until he's bright red with frustration and neglect, Kylie herself is grumpy for the rest of the day. If a dog limps by with a stone embedded in its paw, or a woman buying fruit in the supermarket closes her eyes and stops to recall a boy who drowned fifteen years ago, the one she loved so much, Kylie starts to feel as if she's going to pass out.

Sally watches her daughter and worries. She knows what happens when you bottle up your sorrow, she knows what she's done to herself, the walls she's built, the tower she's made, stone by stone. But they're walls of grief, and the tower is drenched in a thousand tears, and that's no protection; it will all fall to the ground with one touch. When she sees Kylie climb the stairs to her bedroom Sally senses another tower being built, a single stone perhaps, yet it's enough to chill her. She tries to talk to Kylie, but each time she approaches her, Kylie runs from the room, slamming the door behind her.

"Can't I have any privacy?" is what Kylie answers to almost any question Sally asks. "Can't you just leave me alone?"

The mothers of other thirteen-year-old girls assure Sally such behavior is normal. Linda Bennett, next door, insists this adolescent gloom is temporary, even though her daughter, Jessie—whom Kylie has always avoided, describing her as a loser and a nerd—recently changed her name to Isabella and has pierced her navel and her nose. But Sally hasn't expected to go through this with Kylie, who's always been so open and good-natured. Thirteen with Antonia was no great shock, since she'd always been selfish and rude. Even Gillian didn't go wild until high school, when the boys realized how beautiful she was, and Sally never gave herself permission to be moody and disrespectful. She didn't think she had the luxury to talk back; as far as she knew, nothing was legal. The aunts didn't have to keep her. They had every right to cast her out, and she wasn't about to give them a reason to do so. At thirteen, Sally cooked dinner and washed the clothes and went to bed on time. She never thought about whether or not she had privacy or happiness or anything else. She never dared to.

Now, with Kylie, Sally holds herself back, but it isn't easy to do. She keeps her mouth closed, and all her opinions and good advice to herself. She flinches when Kylie slams doors; she weeps to see her pain. Sometimes Sally listens outside her daughter's bedroom, but Kylie no longer bothers to confide in Gillian. Even that would be a relief, but Kylie has pulled away from everyone. The most Sally can do is watch as Kylie's isolation becomes a circle: the lonelier you are, the more you pull away, until humans seem an alien race, with customs and a language you can't begin to understand. This Sally knows better than most. She knows it late at night, when Gillian is at Ben Frye's, and the moths tap against the window screens, and she feels so separated from the summer night that those screens might as well be stones.

It appears that Kylie will spend her whole summer alone in her room, serving time just as certainly as if she were in prison. July is ending with temperatures in the nineties, day in and day out. The heat has caused white spots to appear behind Kylie's eyelids whenever she blinks. The spots become clouds, and the clouds rise high, and the only way to get rid of them is to do something. Quite suddenly she knows this. If she doesn't do something, she could get stuck here. Other girls will continue, they'll go on and have boyfriends and make mistakes, and she will be exactly the same, frozen. If she doesn't make a move soon, they're all going to pass her by and she'll still be a child, afraid to leave her room, afraid to grow up.

At the end of the week, when the heat and humidity make it impossible to close windows or doors, Kylie decides to bake a cake. It is a small concession, a tiny step back into the world. Kylie goes out to buy the ingredients, and when she gets home it's ninety-six in the shade, but that doesn't stop her. She's driven about this project of hers, almost as if she believes she'll be saved by this one cake. She turns the oven to four hundred degrees and gets to work, but it's not until the batter is ready and the pans are greased that she realizes she's about to bake Gideon's favorite cake.

All afternoon the cake sits on the kitchen counter, frosted and untouched, on a blue platter. When evening falls, Kylie still doesn't know what to do. Gillian is at Ben's, but no one answers the phone when Kylie calls to ask Gillian if she thinks it's foolish for her to go to Gideon's. Why does she even want to? What does she care? He was the one who was rude; shouldn't he be the one to make the first move? He should be bringing her the damn cake, as a matter of fact—a chocolate chip pound cake with maple frosting, or mocha if that's the best he can do.

Kylie goes to sit by her bedroom window in search of cool,

fresh air, and instead discovers a toad sitting on the sill. A crab apple tree grows just outside her window, a wretched specimen that hardly ever flowers. The toad must have found its way along the trunk and the limbs, then leapt into her window. It's bigger than most of the toads you can find near the creek, and it's amazingly calm. It doesn't seem frightened, not even when Kylie lifts it and holds it in her hand. This toad reminds her of the ones she and Antonia used to find in the aunts' garden each summer. They loved cabbage and leaf lettuce and would hop after the girls, begging for treats. Sometimes Antonia and Kylie would take off running, just to see how fast the toads could go; they'd race until they collapsed with laughter, in the dust or between the rows of beans, but no matter how far they'd gone, when they turned around, the toads would be right on their heels, eyes unblinking and wide.

Kylie leaves the toad on her bed, then heads off to look for some lettuce. She feels guilty and foolish about having listened to Antonia all those times when they forced the toads to chase them. She's not that silly anymore; she's got more sense and a whole lot more compassion. Everyone is out and the house is more peaceful than usual. Sally is at a meeting Ed Borelli has called, to plan for the opening of school in September, a reality none of the office staff cares to recognize as inevitable. Antonia is at work, watching the clock and waiting for Scott Morrison to appear. Down in the kitchen, it's so quiet that the water from the dripping faucet echoes. Pride is a funny thing; it can make what is truly worthless appear to be a treasure. As soon as you let go of it, pride shrinks to the size of a fly, but one that has no head, and no tail, and no wings with which to lift itself off the ground.

Standing there in the kitchen, Kylie can barely remember some of what mattered so much only a few hours ago. All she knows is that if she waits much longer, the cake will begin to go stale, or ants will get to it, or someone will wander in and cut a piece. She'll go to Gideon's right now, before she can change her mind.

There's no lettuce in the refrigerator, so Kylie takes the first interesting edible she spies—half of an uneaten Snickers that Gillian left to melt on the counter. Kylie's about to rush back upstairs, but when she turns she sees that the toad has followed her.

Too hungry to wait, Kylie guesses.

She takes the toad in her hand and breaks off a tiny sliver of the candy bar. But then the oddest thing happens: When she goes to feed the toad, it opens its mouth and spits out a ring.

"Gee." Kylie laughs. "Thanks."

The ring is heavy and cold when she holds it in her hand. The toad must have found it in the mud; damp earth is caked over the band so thickly it's impossible for Kylie to see this gift for what it really is. If she stopped to examine it, if she held it up to the light and took a good look, she'd discover that the silver has a strange purple tint. Drops of blood are hidden beneath the patina of dirt. If she hadn't been in such a hurry to get to Gideon's, if she realized what it was she had, she would have taken that ring out to the backyard and buried it, beneath the lilacs, where it belongs. Instead, Kylie goes ahead and tosses it into the little Fiestaware saucer on which her mother keeps a pathetic example of a cactus. She grabs the cake and pushes the screen door open with her hip, and as soon as she's outside she leans to place the toad in the grass.

"There you go," she tells it, but the toad is still there, motionless on the lawn, when Kylie has already turned the corner onto the next block.

Gideon lives on the other side of the Turnpike, in a development that pretends to be fancier than it is. The houses in his neighborhood have decks and finished basements and French doors leading to well-tended gardens. Usually it takes Kylie twelve minutes to get there from her house, but that's if she's running and not carrying a large chocolate cake. Tonight, she doesn't want to drop the cake, so her pace is measured as she walks past the gas station and the shopping center, where there are a supermarket, a Chinese restaurant, and a deli, side by side, as well as the ice cream parlor where Antonia works. Then she has a choice; she can walk past Bruno's, the tavern at the end of the shopping center, which has a pink neon sign and a nasty feel to it, or she can cross the Turnpike and take a shortcut across the overgrown field, where everyone says a health club will soon be built, complete with an Olympic-size pool.

Since there are two guys coming out of Bruno's, talking to each other in too-loud voices, Kylie opts for the field. She can cut through, and be two blocks away from Gideon's. The weeds are so high and scratchy that Kylie wishes that she were wearing jeans instead of shorts. Still, it's a pretty night, and the foul smell of the puddles at the far end of the field, where mosquitoes have been breeding all summer, is replaced by the scent of chocolate frosting from the cake Kylie's about to deliver. Kylie is wondering if it will be too late for her to stay and play a game of one-on-one—Gideon has a regulation basketball hoop set up in his driveway, a gift of guilt from his father, right after he divorced Gideon's mother—when she notices that the air around her is growing murky and cold. There's a black edge to this field. Something is wrong. Kylie starts to walk faster, and that's when it happens. That's when they call out for her to wait up.

She sees exactly who they are and what they want when she looks over her shoulder. The two men from the tavern have crossed the Turnpike and are following her; they're big and their shadows have a crimson cast and they're calling her Baby. They're saying, "Hey, don't you understand English? Wait up. Just wait."

Kylie can already feel her heart beating too hard, even before she starts to run. She knows what kind of men they are; they're like the one they had to get rid of out in the garden. They get mad the way he does, for no reason at all, except some pain deep inside that they're not even aware of anymore, and they want to hurt somebody. They want to do it right now. The cake hits against Kylie's chest; the weeds are thorny and scratch at her. The men let out a whoop when she starts to run, as if she's made it more fun to track her. If they're smashed, they won't bother to run after her, but they're not that drunk yet. Kylie throws the cake away, and it splatters when it hits the ground, where it will be food for the field mice and the ants. She can still smell the frosting, though; it's all over her hands. She will never again be able to eat chocolate. The scent of it will set her heart racing. The taste will turn her stomach.

They're following her, forcing her to run toward the darkest part of the field, where the puddles are, where no one from the Turnpike can see her. One of the men is fat, and he's fallen behind. He's cursing at her, but why should she listen? Her long legs are worth something to her now. Out of the corner of her eye she sees the lights of the shopping center, and she knows if she keeps on going in the direction she's headed now, the one who's still after her will get her. That's what he's been telling her, and when he gets her, he's going to fuck her brains out. He's going to make certain she never runs away from anyone again. He's going to take care of that little pussy of hers, and she won't ever forget it.

He's been calling out horrible things to her all along, but suddenly he stops talking, he's dead silent, and Kylie knows this is it. He's running really fast, she can feel him; he's going to get her now, or he's not going to get her at all. Kylie's breathing is shallow and panicky, but she takes a single deep breath, and then she turns. She turns quickly, she's almost running to him, and he sticks his arms out, to catch her, but she loops around, toward the Turnpike. Her legs are so long she could sidestep ponds and lakes. With one good leap she could be up there where there are stars, where it's cold and clear and constant, and things like this never, ever happen.

By the time he's close enough to reach out and grab her shirt, Kylie has made it to the Turnpike. A man walking his golden retriever is just down the street. At the corner, a gang of sixteen-year-old boys is heading home from the town pool after swim team practice. They would surely hear Kylie if she screamed, but she doesn't have to. The man who's been following her stays where he is, then retreats, back into the weeds. He'll never get her now, because Kylie is still running. She runs through the traffic, and along the opposite side of the street; she runs past the tavern and the supermarket. She doesn't feel she can stop, or even slow down, until she's inside the ice cream parlor and the bell over the door jingles to signify that the door has opened and is now closed tight behind her.

She has mud all over her legs, and her breathing is so shallow that each time she inhales she wheezes in some strangled way, like rabbits when they pick up the scent of a coyote or a dog. An elderly couple sharing a sundae look up and blink. The four divorced women at the table by the window appraise what a mess Kylie is, then think of the difficulties they've been having with their own children, and decide, all at once, that they'd better set out for home.

Antonia hasn't been paying much attention to the customers. She's smiling and leaning her elbows on the counter, the better to gaze into Scott Morrison's eyes as he explains the difference between nihilism and pessimism. He's here every night, eating rocky road ice cream and falling more deeply in love. They have spent hours making out in the front and back seats of Scott's mother's car, kissing until their lips are fevered and bruised, getting their hands into each other's pants, wanting each other so much that they're not thinking of anything else. In the past week, Scott and Antonia have both had incidents where they crossed the street without looking both ways and were frightened back to the sidewalk by a blaring horn. They're in their own world, a place so dreamy and complete they don't have to pay attention to traffic, or even to the fact that other human beings exist.

Tonight, it takes a while for Antonia to realize it's her sister standing there, dripping mud and weeds onto the linoleum floor that Antonia is responsible for keeping clean.

"Kylie?" she says, just to make certain.

Scott turns to look and then understands that the weird noise he's been hearing behind him, which he thought was the rattling air conditioner, is someone's ragged breathing. The scratches along Kylie's legs have begun to bleed. Chocolate frosting is smeared over her shirt and her hands.

"Jesus," Scott says. He's been thinking on and off about med school, but, when it comes right down to it, he doesn't like the surprises human beings can throw at you. Pure science is more his speed. It's a whole lot safer and more exact.

Antonia comes out from behind the counter. Kylie just stares at her, and in that instant, Antonia knows exactly what's happened.

"Come on." She grabs Kylie's hand and pulls her toward the back room, where the cans of syrup and the mops and brooms are kept. Scott is following.

"Maybe we'd better take her over to the emergency room," he says.

"Why don't you go behind the counter?" Antonia suggests. "Just in case there are any customers."

When Scott hesitates, Antonia has no doubt that he's fallen in love with her. Another boy would turn and run. He'd be grateful to be released from a scene like this.

"Are you sure?" Scott asks.

"Oh, yes." Antonia nods. "Very." She pulls Kylie into the storeroom. "Who was it?" she asks. "Did he hurt you?"

Kylie can smell chocolate, and it's making her so nauseated she can barely stand up straight. "I ran," she says. Her voice is funny. It sounds as if she were about eight years old.

"He didn't touch you?" Antonia's voice sounds funny, too.

Antonia hasn't turned on the light in the storeroom. Moonlight filters through the open window in waves, turning the girls as silver as fish.

Kylie looks at her sister and shakes her head no. Antonia considers the countless horrible things she's said and done, for reasons she herself doesn't understand, and her throat and face become scarlet with shame. She never even thought to be generous or kind. She would like to comfort her sister and give her a hug, but she doesn't. She's thinking, *I'm sorry*, but she can't say the words out loud. They stick in her throat because she should have said them years ago.

All the same, Kylie understands what her sister means, and that's the reason she can finally cry, which is what she's wanted to do since she first began running in the field. When she's done crying, Antonia closes up the shop. Scott gives them a ride home, through the dark, humid night. The toads have come out from the creek, and Scott has to swerve as he drives, and still he can't avoid hitting some of the creatures. Scott knows something major has happened, although he's not clear on what. He notices that Antonia has a band of freckles across her nose and cheeks. If he saw her every single day for the rest of his life, he would still be surprised and thrilled each time he looked at her. When they get to the house, Scott has the urge to get down on his knees and ask her to marry him, even though she has another year of high school to go. Antonia's not the girl he thought she was, a bratty, spoiled kid. Instead, she's somebody who can make his pulse go crazy simply by resting her hand on his leg.

"Turn your lights off," Antonia tells Scott as he pulls into the driveway. She and Kylie exchange a look. Their mother has come home and left the porch light on for them, and they have no way of knowing that she's gone off to bed exhausted. For all they know, she may be waiting up for them, and they don't want to face someone whose worry will outweigh their own fear. They don't want to have to explain. "We're avoiding dealing with our mom," Antonia tells Scott.

She kisses him quickly, then carefully opens the car door, so it won't creak as it usually does. There's a toad trapped beneath one of Scott's tires, and the air feels watery and green as the sisters run across the lawn, then sneak into the house. They find their way upstairs in the dark, then lock themselves in the bathroom, where Kylie can wash the mud and chocolate off her arms and face, and the blood off her legs. Her shirt is ruined, and Antonia hides it in the trash basket, beneath some tissues and an empty shampoo bottle. Kylie's breathing is still off; there's a ripple of panic when she inhales.

"Are you all right?" Antonia whispers.

"No," Kylie whispers back, and that makes them both laugh. The girls put their hands over their mouths to ensure that their voices won't reach their mother's bedroom; they wind up doubled over and out of breath, with tears in their eyes.

They may never talk about tonight, and yet, all the same, it will change everything. Years from now, they'll think of each other on dark nights; they'll telephone one another for no particular reason, and they won't want to hang up, even when there's nothing left to say. They're not the same people they were an hour ago, and they never will be. They know each other too well to turn back now. By the very next morning that edge of jealousy Antonia has been dragging around with her will be gone, leaving only the faintest green outline on her pillow, in the place where she rests her head.

In the days that follow, Kylie and Antonia laugh when they meet accidentally, in the hallway or in the kitchen. Neither hogs the bathroom or calls the other names. Every evening after supper, Kylie and Antonia clear the table and wash the dishes together, side by side, without even being asked. On nights when the girls are both at home, Sally can hear them talking to each other. Whenever they think someone might be listening, they stop speaking all at once, and yet it still seems as though they are communicating with each other. Late at night Sally could swear that they tap out secrets on their bedroom walls in Morse code.

"What do you think is going on?" Sally asks Gillian.

"Something weird," Gillian says.

Just that morning, Gillian noticed that Kylie was wearing one of Antonia's black T-shirts. "If she catches you wearing that, she'll tear it right off your back," Gillian informed Kylie.

"I don't think so." Kylie shrugged. "She's got too many black shirts. And anyway, she gave this one to me."

"What do you mean by weird?" Sally asks Gillian. She was up half the night making lists of what could be affecting the girls. Cults, sex, criminal activity, a pregnancy scare—she's been through every possibility in the past few hours.

"Maybe it's nothing," Gillian says, not wanting Sally to worry. "Maybe they're just growing up."

"What?" Sally says. Just the suggestion makes her feel skittish and upsets her in a way pregnancies and cults simply can't. This is the possibility she's avoided considering. She cannot believe Gillian's talent for always saying the exact wrong thing. "What the hell is that supposed to mean? They're kids."

"They've got to grow up, eventually," Gillian says, stumbling in deeper. "Before you know it, they'll be out of here."

"Well, thanks for your expert parenting advice."

Gillian doesn't catch the sarcasm; now that she's begun, she has another recommendation for her sister. "You need to stop focusing so much on being just a mom, before you shrivel into dust and we have to sweep you up with a broom. You should start to date. What's holding you back? Your kids are going out—why not you?"

"Any more words of wisdom?" Sally is such pure ice even Gillian can't fail to notice she's getting frozen out.

"Not one." Gillian backs off now. "Not a syllable."

Gillian has the urge for a cigarette, then realizes she hasn't had one in nearly two weeks. The funny thing is, she's stopped trying to quit. It's looking at all those illustrations of the human body. It's seeing those drawings of lungs.

"My girls are babies," Sally says. "For your information."

She sounds a little hysterical. For the past sixteen years—except for the one year when Michael died and she went so inside herself she couldn't find her way out—she has been thinking about her children. Occasionally she has thought about snowstorms and the cost of heat and electricity and the fact that she often gets hives when September closes in and she knows she has to go back to work. But mostly she's been preoccupied with Antonia and Kylie, with fevers and cramps, with new shoes to buy every six months and making sure everyone gets well-balanced meals and at least eight hours of sleep every night. Without such thoughts, she's not certain she will continue to exist. Without them, what exactly is she left with?

That night Sally goes to bed and sleeps like a stone, and she doesn't get up in the morning.

"The flu," Gillian guesses.

From beneath her quilt, Sally can hear Gillian making coffee. She can hear Antonia talking to Scott on the phone, and Kylie running the shower. All that day, Sally stays where she is. She's waiting for someone to need her, she's waiting for an accident or an emergency, but it never happens. At night, she gets up to use the toilet and wash her face with cold water, and the following morning she goes on sleeping, and she's still sleeping at noon, when Kylie brings her some lunch on a wooden tray.

"A stomach virus," Gillian suggests when she comes home from work and is informed that Sally will not touch her chicken noodle soup or her tea and has asked for the curtains in her room to be drawn.

Sally can hear them still; she can hear them right now. How they whisper and cook dinner, laughing and cutting up carrots and celery with sharp knives. How they wash all the laundry and hang the sheets out to dry on the line in the yard. How they comb their hair and brush their teeth and go on with their lives.

On her third day in bed, Sally stops opening her eyes. She will not consider toast with grape jelly, or Tylenol and water, or extra pillows. Her black hair is tangled; her skin pale as paper. Antonia and Kylie are frightened; they stand in the doorway and watch their mother sleep. They're afraid any chatter will disturb her, so the house grows quieter and quieter still. The girls blame themselves, for not being well behaved when they should have been, for all those years of arguing and acting like selfish, spoiled brats. Antonia phones the doctor, but he doesn't make house calls and Sally refuses to get dressed and go to his office.

It is nearly two a.m. when Gillian gets home from Ben's house. It's the last night of the month, and the moon is thin and silvery; the air is turning to mist. Gillian always comes back to Sally's place; it's like a safety net. But tonight Ben told her he was tired of the way she always left as soon as they were finished in bed. He wanted her to move in with him.

Gillian thought he was kidding, she really did. She laughed and said, "I'll bet you say that to all the girls, after you've fucked them twenty or thirty times."

"No," Ben said. He wasn't smiling. "I've never said it before."

All day long Ben had had the feeling that he was about to either lose or win, and he couldn't tell which it would be. He put on a show at the hospital this morning, and one of the children, a boy of eight, wept when Ben made Buddy disappear into a large wooden box.

"He'll be back," Ben assured this most distraught member of his audience.

But the boy was convinced that Buddy's reemergence was impossible. Once someone was gone, he told Ben, that was the end of him. And in the case of this boy, the theory was irrefutable. He'd been in the hospital for half his life, and this time he would not be going home. Already, he was leaving his body; Ben could see it just by looking at him. He was disappearing by inches.

And so Ben did what a magician almost never does: he took

the boy aside and revealed how Buddy sat quietly and snugly within a false bottom of the disappearing box. But the boy refused to be consoled. Perhaps this wasn't even the same rabbit; there was no proof, after all. A white rabbit was an everyday thing, you could buy a dozen at a pet store. And so the boy continued to cry, and Ben might have wept right along with this child had he not been lucky enough to possess the tricks of his trade. Quickly, he reached to pull a silver dollar from behind the boy's ear.

"See." Ben grinned. "Presto," he announced.

The boy stopped crying all at once; he was startled out of his tears. When Ben told him the silver dollar was his to keep, this boy looked, for a brief instant, the way he might have if awful things had not happened to him. At noon, Ben left the hospital and went to the Owl Café, where he had three cups of black coffee. He didn't have lunch; he didn't order the hash and eggs that he liked, or the bacon, lettuce, and tomato on whole wheat. The waitresses watched him carefully, hoping he'd soon be up to his old tricks, setting the salt shakers on end, starting fires in the ashtrays with a snap of his fingers, snatching tablecloths from beneath their place settings, but Ben just went on drinking coffee. After he'd paid and left a large tip, he drove around for hours. He kept thinking about the life span of a mayfly, and all the time he had wasted, and frankly he wasn't willing to waste any more.

Ben has spent his whole life afraid that whoever he loves will disappear, and there'll be no finding her: not behind the veils, not in the false bottom of the largest wooden box, the red lacquer one he keeps in the basement but cannot bring himself to use, even though he's been assured he can drive swords through the wood without causing a single wound. Well, that had changed. He wanted an answer, right then, before Gillian got dressed and ran back to the safety of her sister's house.

"It's very simple," he said. "Yes or no?"

"This isn't a yes-or-no kind of thing," Gillian hedged.

"Oh, yes," Ben said with absolute certainty. "It is."

"No," Gillian insisted. Looking at his solemn face, she wished then that she'd known him forever. She wished that he had been the first one to kiss her, and the first to make love to her. She wished she could say yes. "It's more of a thinking-it-over kind of thing."

Gillian knew where this argument would lead. Start living with someone, and before you knew it you were married, and that was a human condition Gillian planned to avoid repeating. In that arena, she was something of a jinx. As soon as she said "I do," she always realized that she didn't at all, and that she never had, and she'd better get out fast.

"Don't you understand?" Gillian told Ben. "If I didn't love you I'd move in today. I wouldn't think twice."

Actually, she's been thinking about it ever since she left him, and she'll keep right on thinking about it, whether she wants to or not. Ben doesn't understand how dangerous love can be, but Gillian certainly does. She's lost at this too many times to sit back and relax. She has to stay on her toes, and she has to stay single. What she really needs is a hot bath and some peace and quiet, but when she sneaks in the back door she finds Antonia and Kylie waiting up for her. They're frantic and ready to call for an ambulance. They're beside themselves with worry. Something has happened to their mother, and they don't know what.

The bedroom is so dark that it takes Gillian a while to realize that the lump beneath the blankets is indeed a human life form. If there's anything Gillian knows, it's self-pity and despair. She can make that particular diagnosis in two seconds flat, since she's been there herself about a thousand times, and she knows what the cure is, too. She ignores the girls' protests and sends them to bed, then she goes to the kitchen and fixes a pitcher of margaritas. She takes the pitcher, along with two glasses dipped in coarse salt, out to the backyard and leaves it all beside the two lawn chairs set up near the little garden where the cucumbers are doing their best to grow.

This time when she goes to stand in Sally's doorway, the jumble of blankets doesn't fool her. There's a person hiding in there.

"Get out of bed," Gillian says.

Sally keeps her eyes shut. She's drifting somewhere quiet and white. She wishes she could shut her ears as well, because she can hear Gillian approaching. Gillian pulls down the sheet and grabs Sally's arm.

"Out," she says.

Sally falls off the bed. She opens her eyes and blinks.

"Go away," she tells her sister. "Don't bother me."

Gillian helps Sally to her feet and guides her out of the room and down the stairs. Leading Sally is like dragging a bundle of sticks; she doesn't resist, but she's dead weight. Gillian pushes the back door open, and once they're outside, the rush of moist air slaps Sally in the face.

"Oh," she says.

She really does feel weak and is relieved to sink into a lawn chair. She leans her head back and is about to close her eyes, but then she notices how many stars are visible tonight. A long time ago, they used to go up to the roof of the aunts' house on summer nights. You could get out through the attic window, if you weren't afraid of heights or easily scared by the little brown bats who came to feast on the clouds of mosquitoes drifting through the air. They both always made certain to wish on the first star, always the same wish, which of course they could never tell.

"Don't worry," Gillian says. "They'll still need you after they're all grown up."

"Yeah, right."

"I still need you."

Sally looks at her sister, who's pouring them both margaritas. "For what?"

"If you hadn't been here for me when all that happened with Jimmy, I'd be in jail right now. I just wanted you to know that I couldn't have done it without you."

"That's because he was heavy," Sally says. "If you'd had a wheelbarrow, you wouldn't have needed me."

"I mean it," Gillian insists. "I owe you forever."

Gillian raises her glass in the direction of Jimmy's grave. "Adios, baby," Gillian says. She shivers and takes a sip of her drink.

"Good-bye and good riddance," Sally tells the damp, humid air.

After being cooped up for so long, it's good to be outside. It's good to be here together on the lawn at this hour, when the crickets have begun their slow, late-summer call.

Gillian has salt on her fingers from her margarita. She has that beautiful smile on her face, and she seems younger tonight. Maybe the New York humidity is good for her skin, or maybe it's the moonlight, but something about her seems brand new. "I never even believed in happiness. I didn't think it existed. Now look at me. I'm ready to believe in just about anything."

Sally wishes she could reach out and touch the moon and see whether it feels as cool as it looks. Lately, she's been wondering if perhaps when the living become the dead they leave an empty space behind, a hollow that no one else can fill. She was lucky once, for a very brief time. Maybe she should just be grateful for that.

"Ben asked me to move in with him," Gillian says. "I pretty much told him no."

"Do it," Sally tells her.

"Just like that?" Gillian says.

Sally nods with certainty.

"I might consider it," Gillian admits. "For a while. As long as there are no commitments."

"You'll move in with him," Sally assures her.

"You're probably just saying all this because you want to get rid of me."

"I wouldn't be getting rid of you. You'd be three blocks away. If I wanted to get rid of you, I'd tell you to go back to Arizona."

A circle of white moths has gathered around the porch light. Their wings are so heavy and damp the moths seem to be flying in slow motion. They're as white as the moon, and when they fly off, suddenly, they leave a powdery white trail in the air.

"East of the Mississippi." Gillian runs her hand through her hair. "Yikes."

Sally stretches out flat in the lawn chair and looks into the sky. "Actually," she says, "I'm glad you're here."

They both always wished for the same thing when they were sitting on the roof of the aunts' house on those hot, lonely nights. Sometime in the future, when they were both all grown up, they wanted to look up at the stars and not be afraid. This is the night they had wished for. This is that future, right now. And they can stay out as long as they want to, they can remain on the lawn until every star has faded, and still be there to watch the perfect blue sky at noon.

LEVITATION

ALWAYS keep mint on your windowsill in August, to ensure that buzzing flies will stay outside, where they belong. Don't think the summer is over, even when roses droop and turn brown and the stars shift position in the sky. Never presume August is a safe or reliable time of the year. It is the season of reversals, when the birds no longer sing in the morning and the evenings are made up of equal parts golden light and black clouds. The rock-solid and the tenuous can easily exchange places until everything you know can be questioned and put into doubt.

On especially hot days, when you'd like to murder whoever crosses you, or at least give him a good slap, drink lemonade instead. Go out and buy a first-rate ceiling fan. Make certain never to step on one of the crickets that may have taken refuge in a dark corner of your living room, or your luck will change for the worse. Avoid men who call you Baby, and women who have no friends, and dogs that scratch at their bellies and refuse to lie down at your feet. Wear dark glasses; bathe with lavender oil and cool, fresh water. Seek shelter from the sun at noon.

It is Gideon Barnes's intention to ignore August completely and sleep for four weeks, refusing to wake up until September, when life is settled and school has already begun. But less than a week into this difficult month, his mother informs him that she's getting married, to some guy Gideon has been only dimly aware of.

They'll be moving several miles down the Turnpike, which means that Gideon will be going to a new school, along with the three new siblings he'll meet at a dinner his mother is giving next weekend. Afraid of what her son's reaction might be, Jeannie Barnes has put this announcement off for some time, but now that she's told him, Gideon only nods. He thinks it over while his mother nervously waits for a response, and finally he says, "Great, Mom. I'm happy for you."

Jeannie Barnes can't believe she's heard correctly, but she doesn't have time to ask Gideon to repeat himself, because he ducks into his room and thirty seconds later he's gone. He's out of there, pronto, just as he's going to be in five years, only then it will be for real. Then he'll be at Berkeley or UCLA, instead of racing down the Turnpike, desperate to be gone. He's driven by instinct; there's no need to think, because inside he knows where he wants to be. He arrives at Kylie's house less than ten minutes later, drenched with sweat, and finds her sitting on an old Indian bedspread under the crab apple tree, drinking a glass of iced tea. They haven't seen each other since Kylie's birthday, yet when Gideon looks at her she is unbelievably familiar. The arch of her neck, her shoulders, her lips, the shape of her hands, Gideon sees all this and his throat goes dry. He must be an idiot to feel this way, but there's nothing he can do. He doesn't even know if he can manage to speak.

It is so hot the birds aren't flying, so humid not a single bee can rise into the air. Kylie is startled to see Gideon; the ice cube she's been crunching on drops out of her mouth and slides down her knee. She pays no attention to it. She doesn't notice the plane flying above, or the caterpillar making its way across the bedspread, or the fact that her skin feels even hotter than it did a minute ago.

"Let's see how fast I can put you in check," Gideon says. He has his chessboard with him, the old wooden one his father gave him on his eighth birthday.

Kylie bites down on her lip, considering. "Ten bucks to the winner," she says.

"Sure." Gideon grins. He has shaved his head again, and his scalp is as smooth as a stone. "I could use the cash."

Gideon flops down on the grass beside Kylie, but he can't quite bring himself to look at her. She may think this is just a game they're about to play, but it's much more. If Kylie doesn't go for the jugular, if she doesn't pull out all her best moves, he'll know they're not friends anymore. He doesn't want it to be that way, but if they can't be their true selves with each other, they might as well walk away now.

This sort of test can make a person nervous, and it's not until Kylie is considering her third move that Gideon has the guts to look at her. Her hair isn't as blond as it was. Maybe she dyed it, or maybe the blond stuff washed out; it's a pretty color now, like honey.

"Looking at something?" Kylie says when she catches him staring.

"Die," Gideon says, and he moves his bishop.

He takes her glass of iced tea and gulps some of it down, the way he used to do when they were friends.

"My sentiments exactly," Kylie says right back.

She has a big smile on her face and her chipped tooth shows. She knows what he's thinking, but then, who wouldn't? He's about as transparent as a piece of glass. He wants it all to be the same and all to have changed. Well, who doesn't? The difference between him and Kylie is that she already knows they can't have it both ways, whereas Gideon still hasn't a clue.

"I missed you." Kylie's voice is offhand.

"Yeah, right." When Gideon looks up he sees that she's staring at him. Quickly, he shifts his gaze to the place where the lilacs used to grow. There are only some twiggy-looking things with black bark. On each twig is a row of tiny thorns so sharp even the ants don't dare to come near.

"What the hell happened to your yard?" Gideon asks.

Kylie looks over at the branches. They're growing so quickly they'll reach the height of a good-sized apple tree before long. But for now they seem harmless, just wispy shoots of brambles. It's so easy to ignore what grows in one's own garden; look away for too long and anything can turn up—a vine, a weed, a hedge of thorns.

"My mom cut the lilacs down. Too much shade." Kylie bites down harder on her lip. "Check."

She's taken Gideon by surprise, moving a pawn he hadn't paid much attention to. She's got him surrounded, allowing him one last turn out of kindness before she moves in for the kill.

"You're going to win," Gideon says.

"That's right," Kylie says. The expression on his face makes her feel like crying, but she's not going to lose on purpose. She just can't do that.

Gideon makes the only move he can—sacrificing his queen—but it's not enough to save him, and when Kylie puts him in checkmate, he salutes her. This is what he wanted, but he's all confused anyway.

"Do you have the ten with you?" Kylie asks, even though she couldn't care less.

"Over at my place," Gideon says.

"We don't want to go there."

On this they both agree. Gideon's mother never leaves them alone, she's constantly asking if they want something to eat or drink; maybe she figures if she leaves them alone for a second they'll find themselves in big trouble.

"You can owe me until tomorrow," Kylie says. "Bring it over then."

"Let's just go for a walk," Gideon suggests. He looks at her then, finally. "Let's get out of here for a while."

Kylie pours the rest of the iced tea on the grass and leaves the old bedspread where it is. She doesn't care if Gideon isn't like anyone else. He has so much energy and so many ideas percolating inside his head that a band of orange light rises off him. There's no point being afraid to see people for who they really are, because every once in a while you see into someone like Gideon. Deception and dishonesty are alien to him; sooner or later he'll have to take a crash course in the ABCs of bullshit to ensure that he won't get eaten alive out in the world he's so anxious to get into.

"My mom's getting married to some guy, and we're moving

to the other side of the Turnpike." Gideon coughs once, as if something had stuck in his throat. "I've got to switch schools. Lucky me. I get to matriculate with an entire building full of shit-eating imbeciles."

"School doesn't matter." Kylie scares herself when she gets so sure of things. Right now, for instance, she is absolutely certain Gideon won't find a better friend than the one he's found in her. She'd bet her savings on it, and still be willing to add her clock radio and the bracelet Gillian gave her for her birthday into the bargain.

They've begun to walk down the street, in the direction of the YMCA field.

"Where I go to school doesn't matter?" Gideon is pleased and he doesn't know quite why. Maybe it's just that Kylie doesn't seem to think they'll see each other any less—that's what he hopes she believes. "You're sure about that?"

"Positive," Kylie tells him. "One hundred percent."

When they get to the field they'll find shade and green grass and they'll have time to think things over. For a moment, as they turn the corner, Kylie has the feeling that she should stay in her own yard. She looks back at the house. By morning they'll be gone, on their way to the aunts'. They've tried to talk Gillian into coming along, but she simply refuses.

"You couldn't pay me to go. Well, I'd agree to do it for a million bucks, but nothing less." That's what she's told them. "And even then you'd have to break both my kneecaps so I couldn't leap out of the car and run away. You'd have to anesthetize me, maybe perform a lobotomy, and I'd still recognize the street and jump out the window before you pulled up to the house."

Although the aunts have no idea that Gillian is east of the Rockies, Kylie and Antonia both insist they'll be devastated when they discover how near Gillian is and that she chose not to visit.

"Believe me," Gillian tells the girls, "the aunts won't care if I'm there or not. They didn't then and they certainly wouldn't now. They'll say, 'Gillian who?' if you mention my name. I'll bet they don't remember what I look like. We could probably pass on the street and be nothing more than strangers. Do not worry about the aunts and me. Our relationship is just what we want it to be—absolute and utter zero, and we like it that way."

And so tomorrow they'll be leaving for vacation without Gillian. They'll fix a picnic lunch of cream cheese and olive sandwiches, pita pockets stuffed with salad, Thermoses filled with lemonade and iced tea. They'll pack up the car the way they do every August, and get on the highway before seven, to avoid traffic. Only this year Antonia has vowed she will cry all the way to Massachusetts. She's already confided to Kylie that she doesn't know what she'll do when Scott goes back to Cambridge. She'll probably spend most of her time studying, since she needs to get into a school somewhere in the Boston area, Boston College, maybe, or, if she can get her grades up, Brandeis. On the trip to the aunts' she'll insist on stopping at rest areas to buy postcards, and after they've settled into the aunts' house she plans to spend every morning lying on a scratchy wool blanket set out in the garden. She'll rub sunscreen on her shoulders and legs, then she'll get to work, and when Kylie looks over at the message her sister is writing to Scott she'll see *I love you* scrawled a dozen different times.

This year, Gillian will wave good-bye to them from the front porch, if she isn't already moved in to Ben Frye's house by then. She's been moving in slowly, afraid that Ben will go into shock when he realizes she has a zillion and one bad habits; it won't take long before he notices that she never rinses out her cereal bowls or bothers to make the bed. Sooner or later he'll discover that the ice cream is always disappearing from the freezer because Gillian is feeding it to Buddy as a special treat. He'll see that Gillian's sweaters often are crumpled into balls of wool and chenille on the floor of a closet or under the bed. And if Ben grows disgusted, if he should decide to kick her out, say good-bye, rethink his options, well, then let him. There's no marriage license and no commitment, and Gillian wants to keep it like that. Options, that's what she's always wanted. A way out.

"I want you to understand one thing," she's told Kylie. "You're still my favorite kid. In fact, if I'd had a daughter I would have wanted her to be you."

Kylie was so stricken by love and admiration that she almost felt guilty enough to admit that she'd been the one who'd had all those anchovy pizzas delivered to Ben's house, back when she'd felt so betrayed; she'd been the one who'd put ashes in Gillian's shoes. But some secrets are best kept to oneself, particularly when they cover up a silly act of childish pique. So Kylie said nothing, not even about how much she would miss Gillian. She hugged her aunt and then helped load up another box of clothes to haul over to Ben's place.

"More clothes!" Ben held a hand to his forehead as though his closets couldn't stand any more additions, but Kylie could see how delighted he was. He reached into the box and pulled out some black lace panty hose, and with three quick knots he turned them into a dachshund. Kylie was so surprised that she applauded.

Gillian had arrived with another box—this one filled with shoes—which she balanced on her hip so she could applaud as well. "You see why I fell for him," she whispered to Kylie. "How many men can do that?"

When they leave in the morning, Gillian will wave until they turn the corner, and then, Kylie is sure, she'll drive over to Ben's. By then they'll be headed for Massachusetts; they'll start to sing along with the radio, just as they always do. There's never any question about how they will spend their summer vacation, so why is it that Kylie suddenly has the notion that they may not even carry their suitcases out to the car?

Walking to the field with Gideon on this clear hot day, Kylie tries to imagine leaving for the aunts', and she can't. Usually she can picture every part of vacation, from packing up to watching rainstorms from the safety of the aunts' porch, but today when she tries to envision their week in Massachusetts, it all comes up blank. And then, when Kylie looks back at her house, she has the strangest feeling. The house seems lost to her in some way, as though she were looking at a memory, a place she used to live in and will never forget but one she can't go back to, not anymore.

Kylie stumbles over a crack in the sidewalk, and Gideon automatically reaches out, in case she falls.

"Are you okay?" he asks.

Kylie thinks about her mother, cooking in the kitchen, her black hair tied back, so that no one would ever guess how thick and beautiful it is. She thinks about the nights when she was feverish and her mother sat beside her in the dark, with cool hands and cups of water. She thinks of those times when she locked herself in the bathroom because she was too tall, and her mother calmly spoke to her from the other side of the door without once calling her foolish or silly or vain. Most of all, she remembers that day when Antonia was pushed down in the park and the white swans, spooked by the commotion, spread their wings and flew right toward Kylie. She can remember the look on her mother's face as Sally ran across the grass, waving her arms and shouting so fiercely the swans didn't dare to come closer. Instead, they rose into the air, flying so low to the pond that their wings broke the water into ripples, and they never returned, not ever, not once.

If Kylie continues to walk along this leafy street, things will never be the same. She feels this as deeply as she's ever felt anything. She's stepping over a crack in the concrete into her own future, and there won't be any going back. The sky is cloudless and white with heat. Most people are inside, with fans or air conditioners turned to high. Kylie knows that it's hot in the kitchen where her mother is fixing a special dinner for tonight. Vegetarian lasagna and green bean salad with almonds, and cherry cheesecake for dessert, all homemade. Antonia has invited her sweetie pie, Scott, to a farewell meal, since she'll be gone for a whole week, and Ben Frye will be there, and Kylie just may ask Gideon as well. These thoughts make Kylie feel sad—not the dinner, but the image of her mother at the stove. Her mom always purses her lips when she's reading a recipe; she reads it twice, out loud, to ensure that she won't make any mistakes. The sadder Kylie feels, the more convinced she is that she shouldn't turn back. She's been waiting all summer to feel like this, she's been waiting to encounter her future, and she's not going to wait a second longer, no matter whom she has to leave behind.

"Race you," Kylie says, and she takes off running; she's down the block before Gideon comes to his senses and charges after her. Kylie is amazingly fast, she always has been, although now she doesn't seem even to be touching the ground. Following her, Gideon wonders if he'll ever catch up, but of course he will, if only because Kylie will throw herself onto the grass at the far end of the field, where the tall, leafy maples cast deep pools of shade.

To Kylie these trees are comforting and familiar, but to anyone accustomed to the desert, to a man who's used to seeing for miles, past the saguaro and the purple dusk, these maples can seem like a mirage, rising above the green field from out of the heat waves and the rich, dark soil. Natives say that more lightning occurs in Tucson, Arizona, than anywhere else on earth; if you've grown up close to the desert you can easily chart a storm by the location of the lightning; you know how long you have before you'd better call in your dog, and see to your horse, and get yourself under a safe, grounded roof.

Lightning, like love, is never ruled by logic. Accidents happen, and they always will. Gary Hallet is personally acquainted with two men who've been hit by lightning and have lived to tell the tale, and that's who he's been thinking about as he navigates the Long Island Expressway at rush hour, then tries to find his way through a maze of suburban streets, passing the Y field when he makes a wrong turn off the Turnpike. Gary went to school with one of these survivors, a boy who was only seventeen at the time he was hit, and it messed up his life from that day on. He walked out of his house, and the next thing he knew, he was sprawled out in the driveway, staring up at the indigo sky. The fireball had passed right through him, and his hands were as charred as a grilled steak. He heard a clattering, like keys being jangled or somebody drumming, and it took a while for him to realize that he was shaking so hard the sound he was hearing was being made by his bones as they hit against the asphalt.

This fellow graduated from high school the same year Gary did, but only because the teachers let him pass through his courses out of kindness. He'd been a terrific shortstop and was hoping for a try at the minors, but now he was too nervous for that. He would no longer play baseball out on the field. Too much open space. Too much of a chance he'd be the tallest thing around if lightning should decide to strike twice. That was the end for him; he wound up working in a movie theater, selling tickets and sweeping up popcorn and refusing to give any patrons their money back if they didn't like the film they'd paid to see.

The other guy who was hit was even more affected; lightning changed his life and every single thing about it. It lifted him up, right off his feet, and spun him around, and by the time it set him back on the ground, he was ready for just about anything. This man was Gary's grandfather, Sonny, and he spoke about being struck by what he called "the white snake" every single day until the day he died, two years ago, at the age of ninety-three. Long before Gary had ever come to live with him, Sonny had been out in the yard where the cottonwoods grew, and he'd been so drunk he didn't notice the oncoming storm. Being drunk was his natural state at that point. He couldn't recall what it felt like to be sober, and that alone was enough of a reason for him to figure he'd better go on avoiding it, at least until they put him in his grave. Maybe then he'd consider abstinence; but only if a good foot of dirt had been shoveled on top of him, to keep him in the ground and out of the package store over on Speedway.

"There I was," he told Gary, "minding my own business, when the sky came down and slapped me."

It slapped him and tossed him into the clouds, and for a second he felt he might never come back to earth. He got hit with enough voltage for his clothes to be burned to ashes as he wore them, and if he hadn't had the presence of mind to jump into the scummy green pond where he kept two pet ducks, he'd have burned up alive. His eyebrows never grew back, and he never again had to shave, but after that day he never had a drink again. Not a single shot of whiskey. Not one short, cold beer. Sonny Hallet stuck to coffee, never less than two pots of thick, black stuff a day, and because of this he was ready, willing, and able to take Gary in when his parents couldn't care for him any longer.

Gary's parents were well intentioned, but young and addicted to trouble and alcohol; they both ended up dead long before they should have. Gary's mother had been gone for a year when the news came through about his father, and that very day Sonny walked into the courthouse downtown and announced to the county clerk that his son and daughter-in-law had killed themselves—which was more or less the truth, if you consider a drinking-related death a suicide—and that he wished to become Gary's legal guardian.

As Gary drives through this suburban neighborhood, he's

thinking that his grandfather wouldn't have liked this area of New York much. Lightning could come up and surprise you here. There are too many buildings, they're endless, they block out what you ought to see, which, in Sonny's opinion, and in Gary's as well, should always be the sky.

Gary is working on a preliminary inquiry begun by the attorney general's office, where he's been an investigator for seven years. Before that he had a background of wrong choices. He was tall and lanky and could have considered basketball as a possibility, but although he was dogged enough, he didn't have the raw aggression needed for professional sports. In the end, he went back to college, thought about law school, then decided against spending all those years studying in closed rooms. The result is that he's doing what he's best at anyway, which is figuring things out. What sets him apart from most of his colleagues is that he likes murder. He likes it so well that his friends rib him and call him the Mexican Turkey Vulture, a carrion creature that hunts by scent. Gary doesn't mind the kidding and he doesn't mind that most people have an easy answer that allows them to believe they've gotten a fix on the reason why he's so interested in homicide. They point straight to his family history—his mother died of liver failure, and his father probably would have done so as well, if he hadn't been murdered first, over in New Mexico. The fellow who did it never was found, and, frankly, nobody seemed to look very hard for him. But the circumstances of Gary's past aren't what drives him, no matter what his friends think. It's figuring out the why of things; the final factor that makes a person act can be so damn elusive, but you can always find some motivation, if you look hard enough. The wrong word said at the wrong time, a gun in the wrong hand, the wrong woman who kisses you just right. Money, love, or fury—those are the causes for most everything. You can usually uncover the truth, or a version of it at any rate, if you ask enough questions; if you close your eyes and imagine the way it might have been, how you might have reacted if you'd had enough, if you just couldn't find it in you to care anymore.

The why in the case he's working on is clearly money. Three kids from the university are dead because someone wanted bucks badly enough to sell them rattlesnake seeds and jimsonweed without once giving a good goddamn about the consequences. Kids will buy anything, especially East Coast kids who haven't been warned their whole life long about what grows in the desert. One seed of rattlesnake weed makes you euphoric, it's like LSD growing free. The problem is, two can cause your death. Unless, of course, the first has already done that job nicely, which was the case with one of the kids, a history major from Philadelphia who had just turned nineteen. Gary was called in early by his friend Jack Carillo in homicide, and he saw the history major on the floor of his dorm room. The boy had had awful convulsions before he died; the whole left side of his face was black and blue, and Gary suggested that no one would consider it tampering with the evidence if they put some makeup on the kid before his parents arrived.

Gary has read the file on James Hawkins, who's been selling drugs in Tucson for twenty years. Gary is thirty-two, and he vaguely remembers Hawkins, an older guy the girls used to whisper about. After dropping out of high school, Hawkins got into trouble in various states, Oklahoma for a while, then Tennessee, before returning to his hometown and getting sent to the lockup on charges of criminal assault, which, along with drugs, seems to be his forte. When he couldn't bullshit his way out of a bad situation, Hawkins was known to go for his opponent's eyes, using the heavy silver ring he wore to gouge and dig. He acted as though no one could stop him, but it's pretty much the end of Mr. Hawkins's criminal career now. The history major's roommate positively identified him—from his snakeskin boots to the silver ring decorated with a cactus and a rattlesnake and the cowboy he may have imagined himself to be—and they're not the only ones to have picked out his photo. Seven other students, who were lucky enough not to take the bogus drugs they bought from him, have identified this loser as well—and that should be that, except no one can find Hawkins. They can't find his live-in girlfriend, either, from all accounts a good-looking woman who seems to have been a hostess at every half-decent restaurant in town. They've checked the bars Hawkins frequented and questioned all three of his alleged friends, and no one's seen him since late June, when the university let out.

Gary has been getting into Hawkins's life, trying to figure him. He's been frequenting the Pink Pony, which was Hawkins's favorite place to get drunk, and sitting on the front patio of the last house Hawkins rented, which is why Gary happened to be there when the letter arrived. He was sitting in a metal chair, his long legs stretched out so he could prop his feet up on the patio's white metal railing, when the mailman walked right over and dropped the letter on his lap and demanded the postage due, since the stamp had fallen off somewhere along the way.

The letter was crumpled and torn in one corner, and if the

flap hadn't already been open, Gary would have just taken it over to the office. But an opened letter is hard to resist, even for someone like Gary, who's resisted a lot in his life. His friends know enough not to offer him a beer, just as they know not to ask him about the girl he was married to, briefly, right after high school. They're willing to do this because his friendship is worth it. They know that Gary will never deceive them or disappoint them—that's the way he's built; that's the way his grandfather raised him. But this letter was something else; it tempted him, and he gave in to it, and, if he's going to be honest, he still doesn't regret it.

Summer in Tucson is seriously hot, and it was a hundred and seven degrees as Gary sat out on the patio of the house Hawkins used to rent and read that letter addressed to Gillian Owens. The creosote plant that grew beside the patio was all but popping with the heat, yet Gary just sat there and read the letter Sally had written to her sister, and when he was done he read it again. As the afternoon heat finally began to ease up, Gary took off his hat and dropped his boots down from the metal railing. He's a man who's willing to take chances, but he has the courage to walk away from impossible odds. He knows when to back off and when to keep trying, but he'd never felt like this before. Sitting out on that patio in the purple dusk, he was long past considering the odds.

Until Sonny died, Gary had always shared a house with his grandfather, except for his brief marriage and the first eight years with his parents, which he doesn't remember out of sheer willpower. But he remembers everything about his grandfather. He knew what time Sonny would get out of bed in the morning, and when he'd go to sleep, and what he'd eat for breakfast, which was invariably shredded wheat on weekdays, and on Sundays pancakes, spread with molasses and jam. Gary has been close to people and has a whole town full of friends, but he'd never once felt he'd known anyone the way he felt he knew the woman who wrote this letter. It was as if someone had ripped off the top of his head and hooked a piece of his soul. He was so involved with the words she'd written that anyone passing by could have pushed him off his chair with one finger. A turkey vulture could have landed on the back rung of the chair he was sitting in, screamed right in his ear, and Gary wouldn't have heard a sound.

He went home then and packed his bag. He called to tell his buddy Arno at the AG's office that he had found a great lead and was going after Hawkins's girlfriend, but of course that wasn't the whole truth. Hawkins's girlfriend wasn't the one he was thinking about when he asked his closest neighbor's twelve-year-old boy to hike by each morning and set out some food and water for the dogs, then took his horses over to the Mitchells' ranch, where they'd be turned out with a bunch of Arabians much prettier than themselves, and maybe learn a lesson or two.

Gary was at the airport that evening. He caught the 7:17 to Chicago, and he spent the night with his long legs folded up on a bench at O'Hare, where he had to change planes. He read Sally's letter twice more in midair, and then again while he ate eggs and sausage for lunch in a diner in Elmhurst, Queens. Even when he folds it back into its envelope and places it deep inside the pocket of his jacket, the letter keeps coming back to him. Whole sentences Sally has written form inside his head, and for some reason he's filled with the strangest sense of acceptance, not for anything he's done but for what he might be about to do.

Gary picked up directions and a cold can of Coke at a gas station on the Turnpike. In spite of his wrong turn near the Y field, he manages to find the correct address. Sally Owens is in the kitchen when he's parking his rented car. She's stirring a pot of tomato sauce on the back burner when Gary circles the Honda in the driveway, gets a good look at the Oldsmobile parked in front, and matches its Arizona license plate number to the one in his files. She's pouring hot water and noodles into a colander when he knocks at the door.

"Hold on," Sally calls in her matter-of-fact, no-nonsense way, and the sound of her voice knocks Gary for a loop. He could be in trouble here, that much is certain. He could be walking into something he cannot control.

When Sally swings the door open, Gary looks into her eyes and sees himself upside down. He finds himself in a pool of gray light, drowning, going down for the third time, and there's not a damn thing he can do about it. His grandfather told him once that witches caught you in this way—they knew how much most men love themselves and how deeply they'll let themselves be drawn in, just for a glimpse of their own image. If you ever come face to face with a woman like this, his grandfather told him, turn and run, and don't judge yourself a coward. If she comes after you, if she has a weapon or screams your name like bloody murder, quickly grab her by the throat and shake her. But of course, Gary has no intention of doing anything like that. He intends to go on drowning for a very long time.

Sally's hair has slipped out of its rubber band. She's wearing a pair of Kylie's shorts and a black sleeveless T-shirt of Antonia's and she smells like tomato sauce and onions. She's out of sorts and impatient, as she is every summer when she has to pack for the trip to the aunts'. She's beautiful, all right, at least in Gary Hallet's estimation; she's exactly the way she is written down in her letter, only better and right here in front of him. Gary's got a lump in his throat just looking at her. He's already thinking about the things they could do if the two of them were alone in a room. He could forget the reason he's come here in the first place if he's not careful. He could make a very stupid mistake.

"Can I help you?" This man who's arrived at her door wearing cowboy boots coated with dust is lean and tall, like a scarecrow come to life. She has to tilt her head to get a glimpse of his face. Once she sees how he's looking at her, she takes two steps back. "What do you want?" Sally says.

"I'm from the attorney general's office. Out in Arizona. I just flew in. I had to transfer in Chicago." Gary knows this all sounds awfully stupid, but most things he'd say at this moment probably would.

Gary hasn't had an easy life, and it shows in his face. There are deep lines he's too young to have; there's a good deal of loneliness, in full view, for anyone to see. He's not the kind of man who hides things, and he's not hiding his interest in Sally right now. In fact, Sally can't believe the way he's staring at her. Would somebody really have the nerve to stand in her doorway and look at her like this?

"I think you must be at the wrong address," she tells him. She's sounding flustered, even to herself. It's how dark his eyes are, that's the problem. It's the way he can make someone feel she's being seen from the inside out.

"Your letter arrived yesterday," Gary says, as if he were the one she'd actually written to rather than her sister, who, as far as Gary can tell from the advice Sally gave her, doesn't have a brain in her head, or—if she does—it's not one she pays much attention to.

"I don't know what you're talking about," Sally says. "I never wrote to you. I don't even know who you are."

"Gary Hallet," he introduces himself. He reaches into his pocket for her letter, although he hates to give it up. If they examined this letter in Forensics they'd find his fingerprints all over it; he's folded and unfolded it more times than he can count.

"I mailed that to my sister ages ago." Sally looks at the letter, then at him. She has the funny feeling that she may be in for more than she can handle. "You opened it."

"It was opened already. It must have gotten lost at the post office."

While Sally is deciding whether or not to judge him a liar, Gary can feel his heart flopping around like a fish inside his chest. He's heard about this happening to other men. They're going about their business one minute, and suddenly there's no hope for them. They fall in love so hard they never again get up off their knees.

Gary shakes his head, but that doesn't clear up the matter. All it does is make him see double. Momentarily there are two Sallys before him, and each one makes him wish he weren't here in an official capacity. He forces himself to think about the kid at the university. He thinks about the bruises up and down the kid's face and the way his head must have hit against the metal bed frame and the wooden floor as he thrashed about in convulsions. If there's one thing in this world Gary knows for a fact, it's that men like Jimmy Hawkins never pick fair fights.

"Would you know where your sister might be?"

"My sister?" Sally narrows her eyes; maybe this is just one more heart Gillian broke, arriving to plead for mercy. She wouldn't have taken this fellow for such a fool. She wouldn't have figured him to be her sister's type. "You're looking for Gillian?"

"Like I said, I'm doing some work for the attorney general's office. It's an investigation that concerns one of your sister's friends."

Sally feels something wrong in her fingers and toes that is a whole lot like the edge of panic. "Where did you say you were from?"

"Well, originally, Bisbee," Gary says, "but I've been in Tucson for nearly twenty-five years."

It is panic that Sally is feeling, that much is certain, and it's creeping along her spine, spreading into her veins, moving toward her vital organs.

"I pretty much grew up in Tucson," Gary is saying. "I guess you could say I'm chauvinistic, because I'm convinced it's the greatest place on earth."

"What's your investigation about?" Sally interrupts before Gary can say more about his beloved Arizona.

"Well, there's a suspect we're looking for." Gary hates to do this. The joy he gets out of a murder investigation isn't happening for him this time around. "I'm sorry to inform you of this, but his car is parked out there in your driveway."

The blood drains out of Sally's head all at once, leaving her faint. She leans against the doorway and tries to breathe. She's seeing spots before her eyes, and every spot is red, hot as a cinder. That goddamn Jimmy just doesn't let go. He keeps coming back and coming back, trying to ruin someone's life.

Gary Hallet stoops down toward Sally. "Are you okay?" he asks, although he knows from her letter that Sally's the kind of woman who wouldn't tell you right away if something was wrong. It took her nearly eighteen years before she gave her sister a piece of her mind, after all.

"I'm going to sit down," Sally says, casually, as if she weren't about to collapse.

Gary follows her into the kitchen, and watches as she drinks a glass of cool tap water. He's so tall he has to duck in order to pass through the kitchen doorway, and when he sits down he has to stretch his legs straight out so his knees will fit under the table. His grandfather always said he had the makings of a worrywart, and this pronouncement has turned out to be true.

"I didn't mean to upset you," he tells Sally.

"You didn't upset me." Sally fans herself with her hand, and still she's flushed. Thank goodness the girls are out of the house; she has that to be grateful for at least. If they get dragged into this, she'll never forgive Gillian, and she'll never forgive herself. How did they ever think they could get away with it? What idiots, what morons, what self-destructive fools. "You didn't upset me a bit."

It takes everything she has to keep her nerve and look at

Gary. He looks right back at her, so she quickly lowers her gaze to the floor. You have to be extremely careful when you look into eyes like his. Sally drinks more water; she goes on fanning herself. In a predicament such as this, it's best to appear normal. Sally knows that from her childhood. Don't give anything away. Don't let them know what you feel deep inside.

"Coffee?" Sally says. "I've got some that's hot."

"Sure," Gary says. "Great." He has to talk to the sister, and he knows it, but he doesn't have to rush. Maybe the sister just took off with the car, but it's just as likely she knows where Hawkins is, and Gary can wait to deal with that.

"You're looking for one of Gillian's friends?" Sally says. "Is that what you said?"

She has such a sweet voice; it's the New England vowels she's never quite lost, it's the way she purses her lips after each word, as though tasting the very last syllable.

"James Hawkins." Gary nods.

"Ah," Sally says thoughtfully, because if she says any more she'll scream, she'll curse Jimmy and her sister and everyone who ever lived in or traveled through the state of Arizona.

She serves the coffee, then sits down and starts to think about how the hell she's going to get them out of this. She's already done the laundry for their trip to Massachusetts; she's gassed up the car and had the oil checked. She has to get her girls out of here; she has to figure out a really good story. Something about how they bought the Oldsmobile at auction, or how they found it abandoned in a rest area, or maybe it was just left sitting in the driveway in the middle of the night.

Sally looks up, ready to start lying, and that's when she sees that this man at her table is crying. Gary is too tall to be anything but awkward in most situations, but he's got a graceful way of crying. He just lets it happen.

"What's wrong?" Sally says. "What's the matter?"

Gary shakes his head; it always takes a while before he can talk. His grandfather used to say that holding tears back makes them drain upward, higher and higher, until one day your head just explodes and you're left with a stub of a neck and nothing more. Gary has cried more than most men ever will. He's done it at rodeos and in courts of law; he's stood by the side of the road and wept at the sight of a hawk someone has shot out of the sky, before going to get a shovel from the back of his truck so he can bury the carcass. Crying in a woman's kitchen doesn't embarrass him; he's seen his grandfather's eyes fill with tears nearly every time he looked at a beautiful horse or a woman with dark hair.

Gary wipes at his eyes with one of his big hands. "It's the coffee," he explains.

"Is it that bad?" Sally takes a sip. It's just her same old regular coffee that hasn't killed anyone yet.

"Oh, no," Gary says. "The coffee's great." His eyes are as dark as a crow's feathers. He has the ability to catch someone by the way he looks at her, and make her wish he would go on looking. "It's coffee in general that does this to me. I get reminded of my grandfather, who died two years ago. He sure was addicted to coffee. He had three cups before he opened his eyes in the morning."

Something is truly wrong with Sally. She can feel a tightness inside her throat and her belly and her chest. This could well be what a heart attack feels like; for all she knows she could end up unconscious on the floor in seconds flat, her blood boiling, her brain fried.

"Will you excuse me for a minute?" Sally says. "I'll be right back."

She runs upstairs to Kylie's room and switches on the light. It was nearly dawn when Gillian got home from Ben's, where half of her belongings are now taking up most of his closet space. Since she has today off, her plan was to sleep as long as possible, go shopping for shoes, then swing by the library for a book on cell structure. Instead, the shades are being cast open and sunlight is spilling across the room in thick yellow stripes. Gillian squirms beneath the quilt; if she's quiet enough, maybe this will all go away.

"Wake up," Sally tells Gillian and she gives her a good shake. "Someone's here looking for Jimmy."

Gillian sits up so fast that she hits her head on the bedpost. "Does he have a lot of tattoos?" she asks, thinking of the last person from whom Jimmy borrowed too much money, a guy named Alex Devine, who was said to be the singular human life form able to exist without a heart.

"I wish," Sally says.

The sisters stare at each other.

"Oh, god." Gillian is whispering now. "It's the police, isn't it? Oh, my god." She reaches to the floor to grab for the nearest pile of clothes.

"He's an investigator from the attorney general's office. He found the last letter I sent you and traced you here."

"That's what happens when you write letters." Gillian is out of bed now, pulling on jeans and a soft beige blouse. "You want to communicate? Use the damn phone."

"I gave him some coffee," Sally says. "He's in the kitchen."

"I don't care what room he's in." Gillian looks at her sister. Sometimes Sally really doesn't get it. She certainly doesn't seem to understand what it means to bury a body in your backyard. "What are we going to tell him?"

Sally clutches at her chest and goes white. "I may be having a heart attack," she announces.

"Oh, terrific. That's all we need." Gillian slips on a pair of flip-flops, then stops to consider her sister. Sally can have a fever of a hundred and three before she thinks to complain. She can spend the whole night in the bathroom, brought to her knees by a stomach virus, and be cheery by the first light of morning, down in the kitchen, already fixing a fruit salad or some blueberry waffles. "You're having a panic attack," Gillian decides. "Get over it. We have to go convince that damn investigator we don't know anything."

Gillian runs a comb through her hair, then starts for the door. She turns when she senses that Sally isn't following her.

"Well?" Gillian says.

"Here's the thing," Sally says. "I don't think I can lie to him."

Gillian walks right up to her sister. "Yes, you can."

"I don't know. I may not be able to sit there and just lie. It's the way he looks at you. . . ."

"Listen to me." Gillian's voice is thin and high. "We will go to jail unless you lie, so I think you'll be able to do it. When he talks to you, don't look at him." She takes Sally's hands in her own. “He’ll ask a few questions, then he’ll go back to Arizona and everyone will be happy.”

“Right,” Sally says.

“Remember. Don’t look at him.”

“Okay.” Sally nods. She thinks she can do this, or at the very least she can try.

“Just follow my lead,” Gillian tells her.

The sisters cross their hearts and hope to die, then swear they’re in this together, forever, till the absolute very end. They’ll give Gary Hallet simple facts; they won’t say too much or too little. By the time they have their story worked out and go downstairs, Gary has finished his third cup of coffee and has memorized every item on the kitchen shelves. When he hears the women on the stairs, he wipes his eyes with the back of his hand and pushes his coffee cup away.

“Hey there,” Gillian says.

She’s good at this, that’s for sure. When Gary stands to greet her she sticks her hand out for him to shake just like this was a regular old social event. But when she really looks at him, when she feels his grip on her hand, Gillian gets nervous. This guy won’t be easy to fool. He’s seen a lot of things, and heard a lot of stories, and he’s smart. She can tell that just by looking at him. He may be too smart.

“I hear you want to talk to me about Jimmy,” Gillian says. Her heart feels too big for her chest.

“I’m afraid I do.” Gary sizes Gillian up fast—the tattoo on her wrist, the way she takes one step back when he addresses her, as if she expects to be hit. “Have you seen him recently?”

“I ran away in June. I took his car and hit the road and haven’t heard from him since.”

Gary nods and makes some notes, but the notes are just scribbles, nothing but nonsense words. *Ivory Snow*, he's written at the top of the page. *Wolverine. Apple pie. Two plus two equals four. Darling.* He's jotting down anything in order to appear concentrated on official business. This way, Sally and her sister won't be able to look into his eyes and sense that he doesn't believe Gillian. She wouldn't have had the nerve to take off with her boyfriend's car, and Hawkins wouldn't have let it go so easy. No way. He would have caught up with her before she reached the state line.

"Probably a smart move," Gary says. He's done this before, smoothed out the doubt so it doesn't seep through his voice. He reaches into his jacket pocket, takes out Hawkins's legal record and spreads it across the table for Gillian to see.

Gillian sits down to get a better look. "Wow," she says.

Jimmy's first arrest for drugs was so many years back he couldn't have been more than fifteen years old. Gillian runs her finger down a list of crimes that goes on and on; the misdemeanors becoming more violent with every year, until they veer into felonies. It looks as if they were living together when he was picked up for his last aggravated assault, and he never bothered to mention it. Unless Gillian is mistaken, Jimmy told her he'd gone to Phoenix to help his cousin move some furniture on the day of his court date.

She cannot believe what an idiot she was for all those years. She knew more about Ben Frye after two hours than she knew about Jimmy after four years. Jimmy seemed mysterious back then, with deep secrets he had to keep. Now the facts are apparent; he was a thief and a liar, and she went and sat still for it for longer than would seem humanly possible.

"I had no idea," Gillian says. "I swear to you. All that time, I never asked him any questions about where he went and what he did." Her eyes feel hot, and when she blinks it doesn't do any good. "Not that that's any excuse."

"You don't have to make any excuses for who you love," Gary says. "Don't apologize."

Gillian will have to pay even more attention to this investigator. He's got a particular way of observing things that catches you up short. Why, before he introduced the idea that love was blameless, Gillian never once stopped to consider she might not be responsible for everything that went wrong. She glances over to gauge Sally's reaction, but Sally is staring at Gary and she has a funny look on her face. It's a look that worries Gillian, because it's totally unlike Sally. Standing there, with her back against the refrigerator, Sally seems much too vulnerable. Where is her armor, where is her guard, where is the logic that can put it all back together again?

"The reason I'm looking for Mr. Hawkins," Gary explains to Gillian, "is that it appears he sold some poisonous plant matter to several college students which has been the cause of three deaths. He offered them LSD, then went and supplied them with the seeds of some highly hallucinogenic, highly toxic weeds."

"Three deaths." Gillian shakes her head. Jimmy told her there'd been two. He told her it wasn't his fault; the kids were greedy and stupid and tried to trick him out of the money he was rightfully due. "Fucking spoiled brats," that's what he'd called them. "College-boy babies." He could lie about anything, as though it were a sport. Gillian feels ill thinking how she automatically believed Jimmy and took his side. *Those kids must have been looking for trouble.* She remembers thinking that. "This is awful," she tells Gary Hallet about the deaths at the university. "It's horrible."

"Your friend has been identified by several witnesses, but he's disappeared."

Gillian is listening to Gary, but she's also thinking about the way things used to be. August in Tucson can bring the desert floor up to 125 degrees. One broiling week, soon after they'd first met, she and Jimmy didn't even leave the house—they just switched on the air conditioner and drank beer and fucked each other every way Jimmy could think of, which mostly had to do with his immediate gratification.

"Let's not call him my friend," Gillian says.

"Fine," Gary agrees. "But we'd like to catch up to him before he sells any more of this garbage. We don't want this to happen again."

Gary stares at Gillian with his dark eyes, which makes it difficult to look away or manage a half-decent fabrication. Maybe this gal knew about the college kids dying, and maybe she didn't, but she certainly knew something. Gary sees that inside her—he can tell by the way she stares at the floor. There is culpability in her expression, but that could be only because she was the one James Hawkins came home to on the night the history major went into convulsions. Maybe it's because she's just realized who it was she was fucking and calling sweetheart all that time.

Gary is waiting for Gillian to declare herself in some way, but Sally is the one who can't keep her mouth shut. She's been trying, she's been telling herself not to talk, to go on following Gillian's lead, but she can't do it. Could it be she's compelled to speak out only because she wants Gary Hallet's attention? Could it be she wants to feel exactly the way she does when he turns to her?

"It won't happen again," Sally tells him.

Gary meets her gaze. "You sound pretty certain of that." But of course, he knows from her letter how sure of herself she can be. *Something's not right there*, she wrote to Gillian. *Leave him. Get your own place, a house that's yours alone. Or just come home. Come home right now.*

"She means Jimmy will never go back to Tucson," Gillian hurries to say. "Believe me, if you're after him, he knows it. He's stupid, but he's not an idiot. He's not going to go on selling drugs in the same town where his clientele have been dying."

Gary takes his card out and hands it to Gillian. "I don't want to scare you, but this is a dangerous person we're dealing with. I'd appreciate it if you'd call me if he tries to contact you."

"He won't contact her," Sally says.

She cannot keep her mouth shut. It's simply impossible. What is wrong with her? That's what Gillian's glare is asking, and that's what Sally is asking herself. It's just that this investigator gets such a worried look when he focuses on something. He's a man of concern, she sees that. He's the kind of man you'd never want to lose once you'd finally found him.

"Jimmy knows we're through," Gillian announces. She goes to pour herself a cup of coffee, and while she's at it she sticks an elbow into Sally's ribs. "What's wrong with you?" she whispers. "Will you just shut up?" She turns back to Gary. "I made it perfectly clear to Jimmy that our relationship was finito. That's why he won't contact me. We're history."

"I'm going to have to have the car impounded," Gary says.

"Naturally," Gillian says graciously. If they're lucky, this guy will be gone in under two minutes. "Go right ahead."

Gary stands and runs his hands through his dark hair. He's supposed to leave now. He knows that. But he's dragging his feet. He wants to go on looking into Sally's eyes, and drown a thousand times a day. Instead, he takes his coffee cup to the sink.

"You don't have to bother with that," Gillian tells him warmly, desperate to be rid of him.

Sally smiles when she sees the way he places the cup and the spoon down so carefully.

"If anything does happen to come up, I'll be in town until tomorrow morning."

"Nothing will happen," Gillian assures him. "Trust me."

Gary reaches for the notebook he keeps to remind himself of details and flips it open. "I'll be at the Hide-A-Way Motel." He looks up and sees nothing but Sally's gray eyes. "Someone at the rental car desk recommended it."

Sally knows the place, a dump on the other side of the Turnpike, near a vegetable stand and a fried-chicken franchise known for its excellent onion rings. She could not care less if he's staying in a lousy motel like that. She doesn't give a damn that he's leaving tomorrow. As a matter of fact, she'll be leaving, too. She and her girls will be out of here in no time. If they wake early, and don't stop for coffee, they can make it to Massachusetts by noon. They can be opening the curtains in the aunts' dark rooms to let in some sunlight just after lunch.

"Thanks for the coffee," Gary says. He spies the half-dead cactus on the window ledge. "This is definitely not representative of the species. It's in sad shape, I'll tell you that."

Last winter, Ed Borelli gave each of the secretaries at the high school a cactus for Christmas. "Plop it on your windowsill and forget about it," Sally had advised when complaints were raised about who on earth would want such a thing, and other than slosh some water onto its saucer now and then, that's exactly what she herself has done. But Gary is paying the cactus a good deal of attention. He's got that worried look, and he's fumbling with something stuck between the saucer the cactus rests on and its pot. When he turns back to face Sally and Gillian, he seems so pained that Sally's first thought is that he's pricked his finger.

"Damn it," Gillian whispers.

It's Jimmy's silver ring Gary is holding on to, and that's what's causing him such pain. They're going to lie to him and he knows it. They're going to tell him they've never seen this ring before, or that they bought it in an antique store, or that it must have dropped from the heavens above.

"Nice ring," Gary says. "Real unusual."

Neither Sally nor Gillian can figure how this can be possible; they know for a fact that ring was on Jimmy's finger, it's buried out back, and yet here it is in the investigator's hand. And he's looking at Sally now; he's waiting for an explanation. Why shouldn't he be; he's read a description of this ring in three depositions: A rattler on one side of it, he remembers that. A coiled snake, which is exactly what he's got now.

Sally feels that heart-attack thing again; it's something wrong in the center of her chest, like a red-hot poker, like a piece of glass, and there's nothing she can do about it. She couldn't lie to this man if her life depended on it—and it does—and that's the reason she doesn't say a word.

"Well, look at that." Gillian is all wonder and sugar. It's so easy for her to do this, she doesn't have to think twice. "That old thing's probably been there for a million years."

Sally's still not talking, but she's leaning all her weight against the refrigerator, as though she needed help to stand up.

"Is that so?" Gary says, still drowning.

"Let me take a look." Gillian goes right up to him and takes the ring out of his hands and studies it as if she's never seen it before. "Cool," she says, giving it back. "You should probably keep it." This is such a nice touch she is truly proud of herself. "It's much too big for any of us."

"Well, great." Gary's head is pounding. Fuck it. Fuck it all. "Thanks."

As he slips the ring into his pocket, he's thinking that Sally's sister is really good at this; she's probably well aware of James Hawkins's whereabouts as of this very second. Sally, however, is another story; maybe she doesn't know anything, maybe she's never seen this ring before. Her sister could have her fooled completely, could be siphoning money, groceries, family heirlooms to Hawkins as he watches TV in some basement apartment in Brooklyn, waiting for the heat to die down.

But Sally isn't looking at him, that's the thing. Her beautiful face is turned away because she knows something. Gary has seen it before, countless times. People who are guilty of something think they can hide it by not looking you in the eye; they presume you can read their shame, that you can see in through their eyes to their very soul, and in a way they're right.

"I guess we're done," Gary says. "Unless there's something you've suddenly thought of that I should know."

Nothing. Gillian grins and shrugs. Sally swallows, hard.

Gary can practically feel how dry her throat is, how the pulse at the base of her neck is throbbing. He's not certain how far he would go to cover for someone. He's never been in the position before, and he doesn't like the feel of it, yet here he is, standing in a stranger's kitchen in New York on a humid summer day, actually wondering if he could look the other way. And then he thinks about his grandfather walking to the courthouse to legally claim him on a day when it was a hundred and twelve in the shade. The air started to sizzle; the mesquite and the Russian thistle burst into flame, but Sonny Hallet had thought to bring a container of cool spring water with him, and he wasn't even tired when he walked inside the courthouse. If you go against what you believe in, you're nothing anyway, so you might as well stick to your guns. Gary's going to fly home tomorrow and hand this case over to Arno. He can't even pretend it will turn out all right: that Hawkins will surrender, and Sally and her sister will be proven innocent of assisting a murder suspect, and Gary himself will start writing to Sally. If he did, perhaps she wouldn't be able to throw away his letters; she'd have to read each one again and again, exactly the way he did when hers was delivered, and before she knew it, she'd be lost, the way he seems to be at this very moment.

Since none of this is going to happen, Gary nods and heads for the door. He has always known when to step aside, and when to sit by the road and just wait for whatever was going to happen next. He saw a mountain lion one afternoon because he decided to sit down on the bumper of his truck and drink some water before changing a blown tire. The mountain lion came padding toward the asphalt, as if it owned the road and everything else, and it took a good look at Gary, who had never before been grateful for a flat tire.

"I'll have the Oldsmobile picked up by Friday," Gary says now, but he doesn't look behind him until he's out on the porch. He doesn't know that Sally might easily have followed him, if her sister hadn't pinched her and whispered for her to stay where she was. He doesn't know how badly this thing inside Sally's chest hurts her, but that's what happens when you're a liar, especially when you're telling the worst of these lies to yourself.

"Thanks a million," Gillian sings out, and by the time Gary turns to look behind him, there's nothing to see but the locked door.

As far as Gillian's concerned, it's all over and done with. "Well, hallelujah," she says when she goes back to the kitchen. "We got rid of him."

Sally is already dealing with the lasagna noodles that have been congealing in the colander. She tries to pry them out with a wooden spoon, but it's too late, they're stuck together. She dumps the whole thing into the trash and then she starts to cry.

"What is your problem?" Gillian asks. It is times like these that provoke perfectly rational people to say what the hell and light up cigarettes. Gillian looks through the junk drawer, hoping to find an old pack, but the best she comes up with is a box of wooden matches. "We got rid of him, didn't we? We seemed totally innocent. In spite of that damn ring. I'll tell you that thing scared the pants off me. That was like looking the devil right in the eye. But honey, we fooled that investigator anyway, and we did a good job of it."

"Oh," Sally says, completely disgusted. "Oh," she cries.

"Well, we did! We pulled it off, and we should be proud of ourselves."

"For lying?" Sally rubs at her leaking eyes and nose. Her cheeks are red and she's snuffling like crazy and she can't get rid of that awful feeling in the dead center of her chest. "Is that what you think we should be proud of?"

"Hey." Gillian shrugs. "You do what you have to." She peers into the trash at the globby noodles. "Now what do we do for dinner?"

That's when Sally throws the colander across the room.

"You are in bad shape," Gillian says. "You'd better call your internist or your gynecologist or somebody and get a tranquilizer."

"I'm not doing this." Sally grabs the pot of tomato sauce, to which she's added onions and mushrooms and sweet red pepper, and pours it into the sink.

"Fine." Gillian is ready to agree to any reasonable plan. "You don't have to cook. We'll get take-out."

"I'm not referring to dinner." Sally has grabbed her car keys and her wallet. "I'm talking about the truth."

"Are you out of your mind?" Gillian goes after Sally, and when Sally keeps heading toward the door, Gillian reaches for her arm.

"Don't you dare pinch me," Sally warns her.

Sally walks out onto the porch, but Gillian is still right behind her. She follows Sally down the driveway.

"You're not going to see that investigator. You can't talk to him."

"He knows anyway," Sally says. "Couldn't you tell? Couldn't you see by the way he was looking at us?"

Just thinking about Gary's gaunt face and all the worry that was there makes her chest feel even worse. She's going to find herself suffering from a stroke or angina or something before this day is through.

"You can't go after that guy," Gillian tells Sally. There's not a bit of nonsense in her tone. "We'll both be sitting in jail if you do. I don't know what would make you even consider this."

"I've already decided," Sally says.

"To do what? Go to his motel? Get down on your knees and beg for mercy?"

"If I have to. Yes."

"You're not going," Gillian says.

Sally looks at her sister, considering. Then she opens the car door.

"No way," Gillian says. "You're not going after him."

"Are you threatening me?"

"Maybe I am." She isn't going to let her sister screw up her future just because Sally feels guilty about something she didn't even do.

"Oh really?" Sally says. "How exactly do you plan to get to me? Do you think you could possibly ruin my life any more than you already have?"

Wounded, Gillian takes a step back.

"Try to understand," Sally says. "I have to set this right. I can't live this way."

A storm has been predicted, and the wind has begun to rise;

strands of Sally's black hair whip across her face. Her eyes are luminous and much darker than usual; her mouth is as red as a rose. Gillian has never seen her sister look so disheveled, so unlike her usual self. At this moment Sally seems to be someone who would rush headlong into a river, when she hasn't yet learned how to swim. She'd jump from the branches of the tallest tree, convinced all she needed for a safe landing were her outstretched arms and a silk shawl to billow out and catch the air as she fell.

"Maybe you should wait." Gillian is trying her sweetest voice, the one that has talked her out of speeding tickets and bad affairs. "We can discuss it. We can decide together."

But Sally has made her decision. She refuses to listen; she gets into her car, and short of jumping behind the Honda to block it, Gillian can't do anything but stand and watch as Sally drives away. She watches for a long time, too long, because, in the end, all Gillian is watching is the empty road, and she's seen that before. She's seen it much too often.

There's a lot to lose when you have something, when you're foolish enough to let yourself care. Well, Gillian has gone ahead and done it by falling in love with Ben Frye, and her fate is now out of her hands. It's riding along, sitting shotgun in that Honda with Sally, and all Gillian can do is pretend that nothing is wrong. When the girls come home, she says that Sally's out running errands, and she orders from the Chinese take-out place on the Turnpike, then phones Ben and asks him to pick up dinner on his way over.

"I thought we were having lasagna," Kylie says as she and Gideon set the table.

"Well, we're not," Gillian informs her. "And can't you use

paper plates and cups so we don't have to mess around with washing dishes?"

When Ben arrives with dinner, Kylie and Antonia suggest they wait for their mom, but Gillian won't hear of it. She starts dishing out shrimp with cashews and pork fried rice, the sort of carnivorous fare Sally would never allow on her table. The food is good, but it's a dreadful dinner anyway. Everyone is out of sorts. Antonia and Kylie are worried, because their mother is never late, especially on a night when there's packing left to do, and they both feel guilty eating shrimp and pork at her table. Gideon isn't helping matters; he's practicing his belching, which is driving everyone but Kylie completely crazy. Scott Morrison is the worst, gloomy as can be at the prospect of a week without Antonia. "What's the point?" is his response to just about everything this evening, including "Would you like an eggroll?" and "Do you want orange soda or Pepsi?" Eventually Antonia bursts into tears and runs from the room when Scott answers the question of whether or not he'll write while she's away with his same old "What's the point?" Kylie and Gideon have to plead Scott's case through Antonia's closed bedroom door, and just when Scott and Antonia have made up and are kissing in the hallway, Gillian decides enough is enough.

By now, Sally has probably spilled her guts to that investigator. For all Gillian knows, Gary Hallet has gone over to the mini-mart on the Turnpike that's open all hours and rented a tape recorder so he can get her confession in her own words. Trapped with no recourse, Gillian has a major migraine, one that Tylenol couldn't begin to cure. Every voice sounds like fingernails against a chalkboard, and she has absolutely no tolerance for even the smallest piece of happiness or joy. She can't stand to see Antonia and Scott kissing, or hear Gideon and Kylie teasing each other. All evening she's been avoiding Ben, because for her Scott Morrison's philosophy really holds true: What *is* the point? Everything is about to be lost, and she can't stop it; she might as well give up and call it a day. She might as well phone for a taxi and climb out the window, with her most important belongings tossed into a pillowcase. She knows for a fact that Kylie has plenty of money saved in her unicorn bank, and if Gillian borrowed some she could get a bus ticket halfway across the country. The only problem is, she can't do that anymore. She has other considerations now; she has, for better or for worse, Ben Frye.

"It's time for everyone to go home," Gillian declares.

Scott and Gideon are sent away with promises of phone calls and postcards (for Scott) and boxes of saltwater taffy (for Gideon). Antonia cries a little as she watches Scott get into his mother's car. Kylie sticks her tongue out at Gideon when he salutes, and she laughs when he takes off running through the damp evening, clomping along in his army boots, waking the squirrels that nest in the trees. Once those boys are gotten rid of, Gillian turns to Ben.

"Same goes for you," she says. She's throwing paper plates in the trash at breakneck speed. She already has the dirty silverware and the glasses soaking in soapy water, which is so unlike her usual messy self that Ben is starting to get suspicious. "Vamoose," she tells Ben. She hates it when he looks at her that way, as though he knew her better than she knew herself. "These girls have to finish packing and be on the road by seven a.m."

"Something is wrong," Ben says.

"Absolutely not." Gillian's pulse rate must be a good two hundred. "Nothing's wrong."

Gillian turns to the sink and gives her attention to the soaking silverware, but Ben puts his hands on her waist and leans against her. He's not so easily convinced, and Lord knows he's stubborn when he wants something.

"Go on," Gillian says, but her hands are soapy and wet and she's having difficulty pushing him away. When Ben kisses her, she lets him. If he's kissing her, he can't ask any questions. Not that it would do any good to try to explain what her life used to be like. He wouldn't understand, and that may be the reason she's in love with him. He couldn't imagine some of the things she's done. And when she's with him, neither can she.

Out in the yard, twilight is casting purple shadows. The evening has turned even more overcast, and the birds have stopped calling. Gillian should be paying attention to Ben's kisses, since they may well be the last they share, but instead she's looking out the kitchen window. She's thinking about how Sally may be telling the investigator what's in her garden, way in the back, where no one goes anymore, and that's where she's looking while Ben kisses her; that's why she finally sees the hedge of thorns. All the while no one was watching, it has been thriving. It has grown nearly two feet since this morning, and, nurtured by spite, it's growing still, coiling into the night sky.

Gillian abruptly pulls away from Ben. "You have to go," she tells him. "Now."

She kisses him deeply and pledges all sorts of things, love promises she won't even remember until the next time they're in bed and he reminds her. She works hard, and at last she wins.

"You're sure about this?" Ben says, confused by how hot-and-cold she is, but wanting more all the same. "You could spend the night at my place."

"Tomorrow," Gillian vows. "And the next night and the night after that."

When at last Ben leaves, when she's watched out the front window to make certain he's really gone, Gillian goes into the yard and stands motionless beneath the murky sky. It is the hour when the crickets first begin to call out a warning, their song quickened by the humidity of the coming storm. At the rear of the yard the hedge of thorns is twisted and dense. Gillian walks closer and sees that two wasps' nests hang from the branches; a constant buzzing resonates, like a warning issued, or a threat. How is it possible for these brambles to have grown unnoticed? How could they have allowed it to happen? They believed him to be gone, they wished it to be so, but some mistakes come back to haunt you again and again, no matter how certain you are that they've finally been put to rest.

As she stands there, a fine drizzle begins, and that's what makes Kylie come after her, the fact that her aunt is standing out there all alone, getting wet without seeming to notice.

"Oh, no," Kylie says when she sees how tall the hedge of thorns has grown since she and Gideon played chess on the lawn.

"We'll just cut them down again," Gillian says. "That's what we'll do."

But Kylie shakes her head. No clippers could get through those thorns, not even an ax would do. "I wish my mom would get home," she says.

Laundry has been left on the line, and if it stays out it will be soaked, but that's not the only problem. The hedge of thorns is giving off something nasty, a mist you can barely see, and the hems of each sheet and shirt have become blotchy and discolored. Kylie may be the only one who can see it, but every stain on their clean laundry is deep and dark. Now she realizes why she hasn't been able to imagine their vacation, why it's all been a blank inside her head.

"We're not going to the aunts'," she says.

The branches of the hedge are black, but anyone who looks carefully will see that the thorns are as red as blood.

Puddles are collecting on the patio by the time Antonia pushes open the back door. "Are you guys crazy?" she calls. When Gillian and Kylie don't answer, she takes a black umbrella from the coat rack and runs out to join them.

A storm with near-hurricane-force winds has been predicted for late tomorrow. Other people in the neighborhood have heard the news and have gone out to buy rolls of masking tape; when the wind arrives to rattle their windows, the glass will be held together with X's of tape. It's the Owens house that's in danger of being blown off its foundation.

"Great way to start a vacation," Antonia says.

"We're not going," Kylie tells her.

"Of course we're going," Antonia insists. "I'm already packed."

In her opinion, it's truly creepy out tonight; it makes no sense to be standing here in the dark. Antonia shivers and considers the overcast sky, but she doesn't look away long enough to miss seeing that her aunt has grabbed Kylie's arm. Gillian holds on tight to Kylie; if she dared to let go she might not be able to stand on her own. Antonia looks to the rear of the yard, and then she understands. There's something under those horrible thornbushes.

"What is it?" Antonia asks.

Kylie and Gillian are breathing a little too quickly; fear is rising off them in waves. It's possible to smell fear like this; it's a little like smoke and ashes, like flesh that's come too close to a fire.

"What?" Antonia says. As soon as she takes a step toward the bushes, Kylie pulls her back. Antonia squints to see through the shadows. Then she laughs. "It's just a boot. That's all it is."

It's snakeskin, one of a pair that cost nearly three hundred dollars. Jimmy would never go to Western Warehouse or any-place like that. He liked more expensive shops; he always preferred items that were one-of-a-kind.

"Don't go over there!" Gillian says when Antonia starts to retrieve the boot.

The rain is coming down hard now; there's a curtain of it, gray as a blanket of tears. In the place where they buried him, the earth looks spongy. If you reached your hand in, you might just be able to pluck out a bone. You might be dragged down yourself, if you weren't careful, deep into the mud, and you'd struggle and you'd try to draw a breath, but it wouldn't do the least bit of good.

"Did either of you find a ring back here?" Gillian asks.

The girls are both shivering now, and the sky is black. You'd think it was midnight. You'd think it was impossible for the heavens to have ever been blue, like ink, or robins' eggs; like the ribbons girls thread through their hair for luck.

"A toad brought one into the house," Kylie says. "I forgot all about it."

"It was his." Gillian's voice doesn't even sound like her. This voice is too thick and sad, and much too distant. "Jimmy's."

"Who's Jimmy?" Antonia says. When no one answers her she looks to the hedge of thorns, and then she knows. "He's back there." Antonia leans against her sister.

If it storms as badly as the meteorologists have predicted and the yard should flood, then what? Gillian and Kylie and Antonia are drenched through and through; the umbrella Antonia holds aloft can't protect them. Their hair is plastered to their heads; their clothes will have to be wrung out in the shower.

The ground near the thornbushes looks indented, as if it were already sinking in upon itself or, worse, sinking in on Jimmy. If he rises to the surface, like his silver ring, like some horrid, wicked fish, it will be over for them.

"I want my mother," Antonia says in a very small voice.

When they finally turn and run for the house, the lawn squishes under their feet. They run even faster; they run as though their nightmares were right behind them on the grass. Once they're inside, Gillian locks the door, then drags a chair over and positions it under the doorknob.

That dark June night when Gillian pulled into the driveway under a circle of light may as well have been a hundred years ago. She isn't the same person she was when she arrived. That woman who tiptoed up to the front door with the sort of urgency only desperation can dispense would have already packed her car and been gone. She would never have stuck around to see what that investigator from Tucson would do with everything Sally told him. She wouldn't have remained in the vicinity, and she wouldn't have left a note behind for Ben Frye, even if she cared for him the way she does tonight. She'd be halfway through Pennsylvania by this time, with the radio on, loud, and a full tank of gas. She wouldn't bother to look in her rearview mirror, not for a minute, not once. And that's the difference, it's simple and it's plain: The person that's here now isn't going anywhere, except into the kitchen to fix her nieces some camomile tea to settle their nerves.

"We're perfectly fine," she tells the girls. Her hair is a disaster and her breathing is ragged; mascara is streaked across her pale skin in wavering lines. Still, she's the one who's here, not Sally, and it's up to her to send the girls to bed and to assure them that she can take care of things. No need to worry, that's what she tells them. They're safe and sound tonight. While the rain pours down, while the wind rises in the east, Gillian will think of a plan, she'll have to, because Sally could no more help her figure out what to do than she could leap from a tree and fly.

No longer balanced by logic, Sally is weightless tonight. She, who has always valued the sensible and the useful above all else, lost her way as soon as she drove down the Turnpike. She couldn't find the Hide-A-Way Motel, though she's passed it a thousand times before. She had to stop at a gas station and ask directions, and then she had her heart-attack thing, which forced her to search out the filthy restroom, where she washed her face with cool water. She looked at her reflection in the smudged mirror above the sink and breathed deeply for several minutes until she was steady once more.

But she soon discovered that she wasn't as steady as she'd thought. She didn't see the brake lights of the car ahead of her after she'd pulled back onto the Turnpike, and there was a minor fender-bender, which was completely her fault. The left headlight of her Honda is now barely attached and is in danger of falling off completely every time she steps on the brake.

By the time she finally pulls up to the Hide-A-Way, her family at home is halfway through dinner, and the parking lot of the fried-chicken franchise diagonally across the Turnpike is packed with customers. But food is the last thing Sally wants. Her stomach is jumpy and she's nervous, she's insanely nervous, which is probably why she brushes her hair twice before she gets out of the car and starts for the motel office. Pools of oil shimmer on the asphalt; one lonely crab apple tree, plopped down in the single plot of earth and surrounded by some red geraniums, shudders when the traffic on the Turnpike zooms by. Only four cars are parked in the lot, and three are real bombs. If she were looking for Gary's car, the one farthest from the office would seem the most likely choice—it's a Ford of some sort and it looks like a rental car. But more than that, it's been left there so neatly and carefully, exactly the way Sally would imagine Gary would park his car.

Thinking about him, and his worried look, and those lines on his face, makes Sally even more nervous. Once she's inside the motel office, she rearranges the strap of her purse over her shoulder; she runs her tongue over her lips. She feels like somebody who's stepped outside her life into a stretch of woods she didn't even know existed, and she doesn't know the pathways or the trails.

The woman behind the desk is on the phone, and it seems

she's in the middle of a conversation that could go on for hours.

"Well, if you didn't tell him, how could he know?" she's saying in a disgusted tone of voice. She reaches for a cigarette and sees Sally.

"I'm looking for Gary Hallet." Once Sally makes this announcement, she thinks she must really be crazy. Why would she be looking for someone whose presence spells calamity? Why would she drive over here on a night when she's so confused? She can't concentrate at all, that much is obvious. She can't even remember the capital of New York State. She no longer recalls which is more caloric, butter or margarine, or whether or not monarch butterflies hibernate in winter.

"He went out," the woman behind the desk tells Sally. "Once a moron, always a moron," she says into the phone. "Of course you know. I know you know. The real question is, Why don't you do something about it?" She stands, pulling the phone behind her, then lifts a key from the rack on the wall, and hands it over. "Room sixteen," she tells Sally.

Sally steps back as if burned. "I'll just wait here."

She takes a seat on the blue plastic couch and reaches for a magazine, but it's *Time* and the cover story is "Crimes of Passion," which is more than Sally can bear at the moment. She tosses the magazine back on the coffee table. She wishes she had thought to change her clothes and wasn't still wearing this old T-shirt and Kylie's shorts. Not that it matters. Not that anyone cares what she looks like. She gets her brush out of her purse and runs it through her hair one last time. She'll just tell him, and that will be that. Her sister's an idiot—is that a federal offense? She was warped by the circumstances of her childhood, then she went out and screwed things up for herself as an adult to ensure that it would all match. Sally thinks about trying to explain this to Gary Hallet while he's staring at her, and that's when she realizes she's hyperventilating, breathing so quickly that the woman behind the desk is keeping an eye on her in case Sally should pass out and she has to dial 911.

"Let me ask you this," the woman behind the desk is saying into the phone. "Why do you ask me for advice if you're not going to listen to it? Why don't you just go ahead, do whatever you want, and leave me out of it?" She gives Sally a look. This is a private conversation, even if half of it is going on in a public place. "You sure you don't want to hang out in his room?"

"Maybe I'll just wait in my car," Sally says.

"Super," the woman says, shelving her phone conversation until she has her privacy back.

"Let me guess." Sally nods to the phone. "Your sister?"

A baby sister out in Port Jefferson, who has needed constant counsel for the past forty-two years. Otherwise, she'd have every single credit card charged to the max and she'd still be married to her first husband, who was a million times worse than the one she's got now.

"She's so self-centered, she drives me nuts. That's what comes from being the youngest and having everyone fuss over you," the woman behind the desk announces. She's slipped her hand over the mouthpiece of the telephone. "They want you to take care of them and solve all their problems and they never give you the least bit of credit for anything."

"You're right," Sally agrees. "Being the baby does it. They never seem to get over it."

"Don't I know," the other woman says.

And what of being the oldest, Sally wonders as she goes outside, stopping at the vending machine beside the office to get herself a diet Coke. She steps over the rainbow-edged pools of oil on her way back to her car. What if you're forever trapped into telling someone else what to do, into being responsible and saying "I told you so" a dozen times a day? Whether she wants to admit it or not, this is what Sally has been doing, and she's been doing it for as long as she can remember.

Right before Gillian had her hair chopped off, and set every girl in town marching into beauty shops, begging for the very same style, her hair had been as long as Sally's, perhaps a bit longer. It was the color of wheat, blinding to look at under the sun and as fine as silk, at least on those rare occasions when Gillian chose to brush it. Now Sally wonders if she was jealous, and if that was why she teased Gillian about what a mess she always looked, with her hair all bunched up and knotted.

And yet on the day Gillian came home with her hair cut short, Sally was shocked. She hadn't even consulted with Sally before she'd gone through with it. "How could you have done this to yourself?" Sally demanded.

"I have my reasons," Gillian said. She was sitting in front of her mirror, applying blush into the hollows of her cheeks. "And they are all spelled C-A-S-H."

Gillian swore that a woman had been following her for several days, and had finally approached her that afternoon. She had offered Gillian two thousand dollars, there, on the spot, if Gillian would accompany her to a salon and have her hair clipped off to the ears so this woman with short, mousy hair could have a false braid to wear to parties.

"Sure," Sally said. "Like anyone in their right mind would ever do that."

"Really?" Gillian said. "You don't think anyone would?"

She reached into the front pocket of her jeans and pulled out a roll of money. The two thousand, in cash. Gillian had a huge smile on her face, and maybe Sally just wanted to wipe it right off.

"Well, you look awful," she said. "You look like a boy."

She said it even though she could see that Gillian had an incredibly pretty neck, so slim and sweet the mere sight of it would make grown men cry.

"Oh, who cares?" Gillian said. "It'll grow back."

But her hair never grew long again—it wouldn't reach past her shoulders. Gillian washed it with rosemary, with violets and rose petals and even ginseng tea—none of it did any good.

"That's what you get," Sally announced. "That's where greed will take you."

But where has being such a good girl and a prig taken Sally? It's brought her to this parking lot on a damp and dreadful night. It's put her in her place, once and for all. Who is she to be so righteous and certain her way is best? If she'd simply called the police when Gillian first arrived, if she hadn't had to take charge and manage it all, if she hadn't believed that everything—both the cause and the effect—was her responsibility, she and Gillian might not be in the fix they're in right now. It's the smoke emanating from the walls of their parents' bungalow. It's the swans in the park. It's the stop sign no one notices, until it's too late.

Sally has spent her whole life being vigilant, and that takes logic and good common sense. If her parents had had her with them she would have smelled the acrid scent of fire, she knows that she would. She would have seen the blue spark that fell onto the rug, the first of many, where it glittered like a star, and then a river of stars, shiny and blue on the shag carpeting just before it all burst into flame. On that day when the teenagers had had too much to drink before they got into one of their daddies' cars, she would have pulled Michael back to the curb. Didn't she save her baby from the swans when they tried to attack her? Hasn't she taken care of everything since—her children and the house, her lawn and her electricity bill, her laundry, which, when it hangs on the line, is even whiter than snow?

From the very start, Sally has been lying to herself, telling herself she can handle anything, and she doesn't want to lie anymore. One more lie and she'll be truly lost. One more and she'll never find her way back through the woods.

Sally gulps her diet Coke; she's dying of thirst. Her throat actually hurts from those lies she told Gary Hallet. She wants to come clean, she wants to tell all, she wants someone to listen to what she has to say and really hear her, the way no one ever has before. When she sees Gary crossing the Turnpike, carrying a tub of fried chicken, she knows she could start her car and get away before he recognizes her. But she stays where she is. As she watches Gary walk in her direction, a line of heat crisscrosses itself beneath her skin. It's invisible, but it's there. That's the way desire is, it ambushes you in a parking lot, it wins every time. The closer Gary gets, the worse it is, until Sally has to slip one hand under her shirt and press down, just to ensure that her heart won't escape from her body.

The world seems gray, and the roads are slick, but Gary doesn't mind the dim and somber night. There have been nothing but blue skies in Tucson for months, and Gary isn't bothered by a little rain. Maybe rain will cure the way he feels inside, and wash away his worries. Maybe he can get on the plane tomorrow at nine twenty-five, smile at the flight attendant, then catch a couple of hours' sleep before he has to report into the office.

In his line of work, Gary is trained to notice things, but he can't quite believe what he's seeing now. Part of the reason for this is that he's been imagining Sally everywhere he goes. He thought he spied her at a crosswalk on the Turnpike as he was driving here, and again in the fried-chicken place, and now here she is in the parking lot. She's probably another illusion, what he wants to see rather than what's right in front of him. Gary walks closer to the Honda and narrows his eyes. That's Sally's car, it is, and that's her, there behind the wheel, honking the horn at him.

Gary opens the car door, gets into the passenger seat, and slams the door shut. His hair and his clothes are damp, and the bucket of chicken he has with him is steamy hot and smells like oil.

"I thought it was you," he says.

He needs to fold his legs up to fit in this car; he balances the bucket of chicken on his lap.

"It was Jimmy's ring," Sally says.

She didn't plan to spill it immediately, but maybe it's just as well. She's staring at Gary for his reaction, but he's simply looking back at her. God, she wishes she smoked or drank or something. The tension is so bad that it feels as though it were at least a hundred and thirty degrees inside the car. Sally is surprised she doesn't just burst into flame.

"Well?" she says finally. "We were lying to you. That ring in my kitchen belonged to James Hawkins."

"I know." Gary sounds even more worried now than before. She's the one, and he knows it. Under certain circumstances, he might be willing to give up everything for Sally Owens. He might be willing to leap headlong into this ravine he feels coming up, without considering how fast he'd be falling or how brutal the moment of impact might be. Gary combs his wet hair back with his fingers and, for a moment, the whole car smells like rain. "Have you had dinner?" He lifts the bucket of chicken. He's also got onion rings and fries.

"I couldn't eat," Sally tells him.

Gary opens the door and sets the bucket outside in the rain. He has definitely lost his appetite for chicken.

"I might pass out," Sally warns him. "I feel like I'm going to have a stroke."

"Is that because you understand I have to ask if you or your sister know where Hawkins is?"

That is not the reason. Sally is hot right down to her fingertips. She takes her hands off the steering wheel so steam doesn't rise from beneath her cuticles, and places both hands in her lap. "I'll tell you where he is." Gary Hallet is looking at her as if the Hide-A-Way Motel and all the rest of the Turnpike didn't even exist. "Dead," Sally says.

Gary thinks this over while the rain taps against the roof of the car. They can't see out the windshield, and the windows are fogged up.

"It was an accident," Sally says now. "Not that he didn't deserve it. Not that he wasn't the biggest pig alive."

"He went to my high school." Gary speaks slowly, with an ache in his voice. "He was always bad news. People say that he shot twelve ponies at a ranch that refused to hire him for a summer job. Shot them in the head, one by one."

"There you go," Sally says. "There you have it."

"You want me to forget about him? Is that what you're asking me to do?"

"He won't hurt anyone anymore," Sally says. "That's the important thing."

The woman who works in the motel office has run outside, wearing a black rain poncho and carrying a broom she'll use to try to unclog the gutters before tomorrow's predicted storm. Sally herself isn't thinking about her gutters. She's not wondering if her girls thought to close the windows, and at this moment she doesn't care if her roof will make it through gale-force winds.

"The only way he'll hurt someone is if you keep looking for him," Sally adds. "Then my sister will get hurt, and I will, too, and it will all be for nothing."

She's got the sort of logic Gary can't argue with. The sky is getting darker, and when Gary looks at Sally he sees only her eyes. What's right and what's wrong have somehow gotten confused. "I don't know what to do," he admits. "In all of this, I seem to have a problem. I'm not impartial. I can pretend to be, but I'm not."

He's staring at her the way he did when she first answered the door. Sally can feel his intentions and his torment both; she's well aware of what he wants.

Gary Hallet is getting leg cramps sitting in the Honda, but he's not going anywhere yet. His grandfather used to tell him that most folks had it all wrong: The truth of the matter was, you could lead a horse to water, and if the water was cool enough, if it was truly clear and sweet, you wouldn't have to force him to drink. Tonight Gary feels a whole lot more like the horse than the rider. He has stumbled into love, and now he's stuck there. He's fairly used to not getting what he wants, and he's dealt with it, yet he can't help but wonder if that's only because he didn't want anything too badly. Well, he does now. He looks out at the parking lot. By afternoon he'll be back where he belongs; his dogs will go crazy when they see him, his mail will be waiting outside his front door, the milk in his refrigerator will still be fresh enough to use in his coffee. The hitch is, he doesn't want to go. He'd rather be here, crammed into this tiny Honda, his stomach growling with hunger, his desire so bad he doesn't know if he could stand up straight. His eyes are burning hot, and he knows he can never stop himself when he's going to cry. He'd better not even try.

"Oh, don't," Sally says. She moves closer to him, pulled by gravity, pulled by forces she couldn't begin to control.

"I just do this," Gary says in that sad, deep voice. He shakes his head, disgusted with himself. This time he'd prefer to do almost anything but cry. "Pay no attention."

But she does. She can't help herself. She shifts toward him, meaning to wipe at his tears, but instead she loops her arms around his neck, and once she does that, he holds her closer.

"Sally," he says.

It's music, it's a sound that is absurdly beautiful in his mouth, but she won't pay attention. She knows from the time she spent on the back stairs of the aunts' house that most things men say are lies. Don't listen, she tells herself. None of it's true and none of it matters, because he's whispering that he's been looking for her forever. She's halfway onto his lap, facing him, and when he touches her, his hands are so hot on her skin she can't believe it. She can't listen to anything he tells her and she certainly can't think, because if she did she might just think she'd better stop.

This is what it must be like to be drunk, Sally finds herself thinking, as Gary presses against her. His hands are on her skin, and she doesn't stop him. They're under her T-shirt, they're into her shorts, and still she doesn't stop him. She wants the heat he's making her feel; she, who can't function without directions and a map, wants to get lost right now. She can feel herself giving in to his kisses; she's ready to do just about anything. This is what it must be like to be crazy, she guesses. Everything she's doing is so unlike her usual self that when Sally catches sight of her image in the cloudy side-view mirror, she's stunned. It's a woman who could fall in love if she let herself, a woman who doesn't stop Gary when he lifts her dark hair away, then presses his mouth to the hollow of her throat.

What good would it do her to get involved with someone like him? She'd have to feel so much, and she's not that kind. She couldn't abide those poor, incoherent women who came to the aunts' back door, and she could not stand to be one of them now, wild with grief, overcome with what some people call love.

She pulls away from Gary, out of breath, her mouth hot, the rest of her burning. She has managed to exist this long without; she can keep on doing it. She can make herself go cold, from the inside out. The drizzle is letting up, but the sky has become as dark as a pot of ink. In the east, thunder sounds as the storm moves in from the sea.

"Maybe I'm letting you do this so you'll stop the investigation," Sally says. "Did you ever think of that? Maybe I'm so desperate I'd fuck anyone, including you."

Her mouth tastes bitter and cruel, but she doesn't care. She wants to see that wounded look on his face. She wants to stop this before that option is no longer hers. Before what she feels takes hold and she's trapped, like those women at the aunts' back door.

"Sally," Gary says. "You're not like that."

"Oh, really?" Sally says. "You don't know me. You just think you do."

"That's right. I think I do," he says, which is about as much of an argument as Sally's going to get.

"Get out," she tells Gary. "Get out of the car."

At this moment, Gary wishes he could grab her and force her, at least until she gave in. He'd like to make love to her right here, he'd like to do it all night and not give a damn about anything else, and not listen if she told him no. But he's not that kind of man, and he never will be. He's seen too many lives go wrong when a man allows himself to be led around by his dick. It's like giving in to drugs or alcohol or the fast cash you've just got to have, no questions asked. Gary has always understood why people give in and do as they please with no thought of anyone else. Their minds shut off, and he's not going to do that, even if it means he won't get what he really wants.

"Sally," he says, and his voice causes her more anguish than she would ever have imagined possible. It's the kindness that undoes her, it's the mercy in spite of everything that's happened and is happening still.

"I want you to get out," Sally says. "This is a mistake. It's all wrong."

"It isn't." But Gary opens the door and gets out. He leans back down, and Sally makes herself look straight ahead, at the windshield. She doesn't dare look at him.

"Close it," Sally says. Her voice sounds fragile, a shattered, undependable thing. "I mean it."

He closes the car door, but he stands there watching. Even if she doesn't look, Sally knows he hasn't walked away. This is the way it has to be. She'll be removed forever, distant as stars, unhurt and untouched, forever and ever. Sally steps on the gas, knowing that if she turned to see, she'd find he was still standing in the parking lot. But she doesn't look back, because if she did she'd also discover how much she wants him, for all the good it will ever do her.

Gary does watch her drive away, and he's watching still when the first bit of lightning cracks across the sky. He's there when the crab apple on the far side of the parking lot turns white with heat; he's close enough to feel the charge, and he'll feel it all the way home, as he's high above them in the sky, headed west. With a close call like that, it makes perfect sense that he'll be shaking as he turns the key in his own front door. As Gary understands it, the greatest portion of grief is the one you dish out for yourself, and he and Sally have both served themselves from the same table tonight, the only difference being that he knows what he's missing, and she has no idea of what's causing her to cry as she drives down the Turnpike.

When Sally gets home, her dark hair loose, her mouth bruised by kisses, Gillian is waiting up for her. She's sitting in the kitchen, drinking tea and listening to the thunder.

"Did you fuck him?" Gillian says.

The question is both completely startling and totally commonplace, since it's Gillian who's asking. Sally actually laughs. "No."

"Too bad," Gillian says. "I thought you would. I thought you were hooked. You had that look in your eye."

"You were wrong," Sally says.

"Did he at least make you a deal? Did he tell you we're not suspects? Will he let it slide?"

"He has to think it over." Sally sits down at the table. She feels the way she would if someone had smacked her. The weight of never seeing Gary again descends like a cloak made of ashes. She thinks about his kisses and the way he touched her, and she gets turned inside out all over again. "He has a conscience."

"Just our luck. And it only gets worse."

Tonight the wind will continue to rise, until there's not a single trashcan left standing on the street. The clouds will be as tall as black mountains. In the backyard, beneath the hedge of thorns, the earth will turn to mud, and then to water, a pool of deception and regret.

"Jimmy's not staying buried. First the ring, then a boot. I'm afraid to guess what's going to come up next. I start to think about it, and I just kind of black out. I listened to the news, and the storm that's coming is going to be bad."

Sally moves her chair closer to Gillian's. Their knees touch. Their pulse rate is exactly the same, the way it always was during a thunderstorm. "What do we do?" Sally whispers.

It's the first time she's ever asked for Gillian's opinion or advice, and Gillian follows her example. It's actually true, what they say about asking for help. Take a deep breath and it hurts a whole lot less to admit it out loud.

"Call the aunts," Gillian tells Sally. "Do it now."

ON the eighth day of the eighth month the aunts arrive on a Greyhound bus. The minute the driver hops down, he makes certain to get their black suitcases from the luggage compartment first thing, even though the larger of their suitcases is so heavy he has to use all his strength just to budge it and he nearly tears a ligament when he lifts it out.

"Hold your horses," he advises the other passengers, who are all complaining that they're the ones who must have their suitcases now in order to catch a connecting bus or run to meet a husband or a friend. The driver just ignores them and goes about his business. "I wouldn't want you ladies to wait," he tells the aunts.

The aunts are so old it's impossible to tell their age. Their hair is white and their spines are crooked. They wear long black skirts and laced leather boots. Though they haven't left Massachusetts in more than forty years, they're certainly not intimidated by travel. Or by anything else, for that matter. They know what they want and they're not afraid to be outspoken, which is why they pay no attention to the other passengers' complaints, and continue to direct the driver on how to place the larger suitcase on the curb carefully.

"What have you got in here?" the driver jokes. "A ton of bricks?"

The aunts don't bother to answer; they have very little tolerance for dim-witted humor, and they're not interested in making polite conversation. They stand on the corner near the bus station and whistle for a taxi; as soon as one pulls over, they tell the driver exactly where to go—along the Turnpike for seven miles, past the mall and the shopping centers, past the Chinese restaurant and the deli and the ice cream shop where Antonia has worked this summer. The aunts smell like lavender and sulfur, a disquieting mixture, and maybe that's the reason the taxi driver holds the door open for them when they arrive at Sally's house, even though they didn't bother to tip him. The aunts don't believe in tips, and they never have. They believe in earning your worth and doing the job right. And, when you come right down to it, that's what they're here for.

Sally offered to pick them up at the bus station, but the aunts would have none of that. They can get around just fine on their own. They prefer to come to a place slowly, and that's what they're doing now. The lawns are wet, and the air is motionless and thick, the way it always is before a storm. A haze hangs over the houses and the chimney tops. The aunts stand in Sally's driveway, between the Honda and Jimmy's Oldsmobile, their black suitcases set down beside them. They close their eyes, to get a sense of this place. In the poplar trees, the sparrows watch with interest. The spiders stop spinning their webs. The rain will begin after midnight, on this the aunts agree. It will fall in sheets, like rivers of glass. It will fall until the whole world seems silver and turned upside down. You can feel such things when you have rheumatism, or when you've lived as long as the aunts have.

Inside the house, Gillian feels twitchy, the way people do before lightning is about to strike. She's wearing old blue jeans and a black cotton shirt, and her hair's uncombed. She's like a kid who refuses to dress up for company. But the company's arrived anyway; Gillian can feel their presence. The air is as dense as chocolate cake, the good kind, made without flour. The ceiling light in the living room has begun to sway; its metal chain makes a clackety sound, as if somewhere a top had been spun too fast. Gillian yanks the curtains back and takes a look.

"Oh, my god," she says. "The aunts are in the driveway."

Outside, the air is turning even thicker, like soup, and it has a yellow, sulfury odor, which some people find rather pleasant and others experience as so revolting they slam their windows shut, then turn their air conditioners on high. By evening, the wind will be strong enough to carry off small dogs and toss children from their swing sets, but for now it's just a slight breeze. Linda Bennett has pulled into her driveway next door; when she gets out of her car, she has a bag of groceries balanced on her hip and she waves to the aunts with her free hand. Sally mentioned that some elderly relatives might arrive for a visit.

"They're a bit odd," Sally warned her next-door neighbor, but to Linda they look like sweet little old ladies.

Linda's daughter, who used to be Jessie and now calls herself Isabella, slides out of the passenger seat and wrinkles her nose—through which she has taken to wearing three silver rings—as if she smells something rotten. She looks over and sees the aunts studying Sally's house.

"Who are those old bats?" the so-called Isabella asks her mother.

Her words are carried across the lawn, each nasty syllable falling into Sally's driveway with a clatter. The aunts turn and look at Isabella with their clear gray eyes, and when they do she feels something absolutely weird in her fingers and her toes, a sensation so threatening and strange that she runs into the house, gets into bed, and pulls the covers over her head. It will be weeks before this girl mouths off to her mother, or anyone else, and even then she'll think twice, she'll reconsider, then rephrase, with a "Please" or a "Thank you" thrown in.

"Let me know if you need anything during your visit," Linda calls to Sally's aunts, and all at once she feels better than she has in years.

Sally has come to stand beside her sister, and she taps on the window to get the aunts' attention. The aunts look up and blink; and when they spy Sally and Gillian on the other side of the glass, they wave, just as they did when the girls first arrived at the airport in Boston. For Sally to see the aunts in her own driveway, however, is like seeing two worlds collide. It would be no less unusual for a meteorite to have landed beside the Oldsmobile, or for shooting stars to drift across the lawn, than it is to have the aunts here at last.

"Come on," Sally says, tugging on Gillian's sleeve, but Gillian just shakes her head no.

Gillian hasn't seen the aunts for eighteen years, and although they haven't aged as much as she, she never quite took notice of how old they were. She always thought of them together, a unit, and now she sees that Aunt Frances is nearly six inches taller than her sister, and that Aunt Bridget, whom they always called Aunt Jet, is actually cheerful and plump, like a little hen dressed up in black skirts and boots.

"I need time to process this," Gillian says.

"Two minutes had better be enough," Sally informs her, as she goes outside to welcome their guests.

"The aunts!" Kylie shouts when she sees they've arrived. She calls upstairs to Antonia, who rushes to join her, taking two steps at a time. The sisters make a dash for the open door, then realize that Gillian is still at the window.

"Come with us," Kylie says to her.

"Go on," Gillian advises the girls. "I'll be right here."

Kylie and Antonia hurry to the driveway and throw themselves at the aunts. They hoot and holler and dance the aunts around until they are all flushed and out of breath. When Sally phoned and explained about the problem in the yard, the aunts listened carefully, then assured her they'd be on the bus to New York as soon as they set out food for the last remaining cat, old Magpie. The aunts always kept their promises, and they still do. They believe that every problem has a solution, although it may not be the outcome that was originally hoped for or expected.

For instance, the aunts had never expected their own lives to be so completely altered by a single phone call in the middle of the night those many years ago. It was October and cold, and the big house was drafty; the sky outside was so gloomy it pushed down on anyone who dared to walk beneath it. The aunts had their schedule, to which they kept no matter what. They took their walk in the morning, then read and wrote in their journals, then had lunch—the same lunch every day—mashed parsnips and potatoes, noodle pudding, and apple tart for dessert. They napped in the afternoon and did their business at twilight, should anyone come to the back door. They always had their supper in the kitchen—beans and toast, soup and crackers—and they kept the lights turned low, to save on electricity. Every night they faced the dark, since they could never sleep.

Their hearts had been broken on the night those two brothers ran across the town green; they'd been broken so hard and so suddenly that the aunts never again allowed themselves to be taken by surprise, not by lightning, and certainly not by love. They believed in their schedules and very little else. Occasionally they would attend a town meeting, where their stern presence could easily sway a vote, or they'd visit the library, where the sight of their black skirts and boots induced silence in even the rowdiest book borrowers.

The aunts assumed they knew their life and all that it would bring. They were well acquainted with their own fates, or so they believed. They were quite convinced nothing could come between their present and their own quiet deaths, in bed, of course, from pneumonia and complications of the flu at the ages of ninety-two and ninety-four. But they must have missed something, or perhaps it's simply that one can never predict one's own fortune. The aunts never imagined that a small and serious voice would phone in the middle of the night, demanding to be taken in, disrupting everything. That was the end of parsnips and potatoes at lunch. Instead, the aunts got used to peanut butter and jelly, graham crackers and alphabet soup, Mallomar cookies and handfuls of M&M's. How odd that they would be grateful to have had to deal with sore throats and nightmares. Without those two girls, they would never have had to run down the hall in their bare feet in the middle of the night to see which one had a stomach virus and which one was sleeping tight.

Frances comes to the porch to better assess her niece's house. "Modern, but very nice," she announces.

Sally feels the sting of pride. It's as high a compliment as Aunt Frances would ever give; it means that Sally's done it all on her own, and done well. Sally's grateful for any kind words or deeds; she can use them. She was awake all night because every time she closed her eyes she'd see Gary so clearly it was as if he were there beside her at the kitchen table, in the easy chair, in her bed. She has a tape that keeps playing inside her head, over and over, and she can't seem to stop it. Gary Hallet is touching her right now, he has his hands on her as she leans to grab her aunt's suitcase. When she tries to lift this piece of luggage, Sally is shocked to discover she hasn't the strength to do it alone. Something inside rattles like beads, or bricks, or perhaps even bones.

"For the problem in the yard," Aunt Frances explains.

"Ah," Sally says.

Aunt Jet comes over and links her arm through Sally's. During the summer that Jet turned sixteen, two local boys killed themselves for her love. One tied iron bars to his ankles and drowned himself in a quarry. The other was done in on the train tracks outside of town by the 10:02 to Boston. Of all the Owens women, Jet Owens was the most beautiful, and she never even noticed. She preferred cats to human beings and turned down every offer from the men who fell in love with her. The only one she ever cared for was that boy who was hit by lightning when he and his brother went tearing off across the town green to prove how brave and daring they were. Sometimes, late at night, Jet and Frances both hear the sound of those boys laughing as they run through the rain, then stumble into the darkness. Their voices are still young and filled with expectation, exactly as they sounded at the moment they were struck down.

Lately, Aunt Jet has to carry a black cane that has a carved raven's head; she's bent over with arthritis, but she never complains about the way her back feels when she unlaces her boots at the end of the day. Each morning she washes with the black soap she and Frances mix up twice a year, and her complexion is close to perfect. She works in her garden and can remember the Latin name of every plant that grows there. But not a day goes by that she doesn't think about the boy she loved. Not a moment passes that she doesn't wish that time were a movable entity and that she could go backward and kiss that boy again.

"We're so glad to be here," Jet announces.

Sally smiles a beautiful sad smile. "I should have invited you a long time ago. I didn't think either of you would like it."

"That just goes to show that you never can tell about a person by guessing," Frances informs her niece. "That's why language was invented. Otherwise, we'd all be like dogs, sniffing each other to find out where we stood."

"You're absolutely right," Sally agrees.

The suitcases are lugged inside, which is no easy job. Antonia and Kylie shout, "Heave ho!" and work together, under the aunts' watchful eyes. Waiting by the window, Gillian has considered escaping through the back door so she won't have to face the aunts' critique on how she's messed up her life. But when Kylie and Antonia lead the aunts inside, Gillian is standing in the very same spot, her pale hair electrified.

Some things, when they change, never do return to the way they once were. Butterflies, for instance, and women who've been in love with the wrong man too often. The aunts cluck their tongues as soon as they see this grown woman who once was their little girl. They may not have had regular dinnertimes or made certain that clean clothes were folded in the bureaus, but they were there. They were the ones Gillian turned to that first year, when the other children at nursery school pulled her hair and called her the witch-girl. Gillian never told Sally how awful it was, how they persecuted her, and she was just three years old. It was embarrassing, that much she knew even then. It was something you didn't admit to.

Every day Gillian came home and swore to Sally that she'd had a lovely afternoon, she'd played with blocks and paints, and fed the bunny that eyed the children sadly from a cage near the coat closet. But Gillian couldn't lie to the aunts when they came to fetch her. At the end of each day her hair was in tangles and her face and legs were scratched red. The aunts advised her to ignore the other children—to read her books and play her games by herself and march over to inform the teacher if anyone was nasty or rude. Even then, Gillian believed she was worthy of the awful treatment she got, and she never did go running to the teacher and tattle. She tried her best to keep it inside.

The aunts, however, could tell what was happening from the sorry slope of Gillian's shoulders as she pulled her sweater on and because she couldn't sleep at night. Most of the children eventually tired of teasing Gillian, but several continued to torment her—whispering "witch" every time she was near, spilling grape juice on her new shoes, grabbing fistfuls of her hair and pulling with all their might—and they did so until the Christmas party.

All the children's parents attended the party, bringing cookies or cakes or bowls of eggnog sprinkled with nutmeg. The aunts came late, wearing their black coats. Gillian had hoped they would remember to bring a box of chocolate chip cookies, or perhaps a Sara Lee cake, but the aunts weren't interested in desserts. They went directly to the worst of the children, the boys who pulled hair, the girls who called names. The aunts didn't have to use curses or herbs, or vow any sort of punishment. They merely stood beside the snack table, and every child who'd been mean to Gillian was immediately sick to his or her stomach. These children ran to their parents and begged to be taken home, then stayed in bed for days, shivering beneath wool blankets, so queasy and filled with remorse that their complexions took on a faint greenish tinge, and their skins gave off the sour scent that always accompanies a guilty conscience.

After the Christmas party, the aunts took Gillian home and sat her down on the sofa in the parlor, the velvet one with the wooden lion's feet whose claws terrified Gillian. They told her how sticks and stones could break bones, but taunting and name-calling were only for fools. Gillian heard them, but she didn't really listen. She put too much worth in what other people thought and not enough in her own opinion. The aunts have always known that Gillian sometimes needs extra help defending herself. As they study her, their gray eyes are bright and sharp. They see the lines on her face that someone else might not notice; they can tell what she's been through.

"I look awful, right?" Gillian says. There's a catch in her voice. A minute ago she was eighteen and climbing out her bedroom window, and now here she is, all used up.

The aunts cluck louder and come to embrace Gillian. It is so unlike their usual cool style that a sob escapes from Gillian's throat. To their credit, the aunts have learned a thing or two since they were snagged into raising two little girls. They've watched *Oprah;* they know what can happen when you hide your love away. As far as they're concerned, Gillian is more attractive than ever, but then the Owens women have always been known for their beauty, as well as the foolish choices they make when they're young. In the twenties, their cousin Jinx, whose watercolors can be found in the Museum of Fine Arts, was too headstrong to listen to a word anyone else said; she got drunk on cold champagne, threw her satin shoes over a high stone wall, then danced on broken glass until dawn and never walked again. The most beloved of the great-aunts, Barbara Owens, married a man with a skull as thick as a mule's who refused to have electricity or plumbing put into their house, insisting such things were fads. Their favorite cousin, April Owens, lived in the Mojave Desert for twelve years, collecting spiders in jars filled with formaldehyde. A decade or two on the rocks gives a person character. Although she'd never believe it, those lines in Gillian's face are the most beautiful part about her. They reveal what she's gone through and what she's survived and who exactly she is, deep inside.

"Well," Gillian says when she's done crying. She wipes at

her eyes with her hands. "Who would have thought I'd get so emotional?"

The aunts settle in, and then Sally pours them each a small glass of gin and bitters, which they always appreciate, and which they particularly like to get them started when there's work to be done.

"Let's talk about the fellow in the backyard," Frances says. "Jimmy."

"Do we have to?" Gillian groans.

"We do," Aunt Jet is sorry to say. "Just little things about him. For instance—how did he die?"

Antonia and Kylie are gulping diet Cokes and listening like crazy. The hair on their arms is standing on end; this could get really interesting.

Sally has brought a pot of mint tea to the table, along with a chipped cup her daughters gave her one Mother's Day, which has always been her favorite. Sally can't drink coffee anymore; the scent of it conjures Gary up so completely she could have sworn he was sitting at the table when Gillian was pouring water through the filter this morning. She tells herself it's the lack of caffeine that's been making her lethargic, but that's not what's wrong. She's been unusually quiet today, moody enough to make Antonia and Kylie take notice. She seems so different. The girls have had the feeling that the woman who was once their mother is gone forever. It's not only that her black hair is loose, instead of being pulled away from her face; it's how sad she looks, how far away.

"I don't think we should discuss this in front of the children," Sally says.

But the children are riveted; they'll die if they don't hear what happened next; they simply won't be able to stand it.

"Mother!" they cry.

They're almost women. And there's not a thing Sally can do about it. So she shrugs and nods to Gillian, giving her the okay.

"Well," Gillian says, "I guess I killed him."

The aunts exchange a look. In their opinion this is one thing Gillian is not capable of. "How?" they ask. This is the girl who would scream if she stepped on a spider in her bare feet. If she pricked her finger and drew blood she'd announce she was ready to faint and then proceed to fall on the floor.

Gillian admits she used nightshade, a plant she always had contempt for when she was a child, pretending it was ragweed so she could give it a good pull when the aunts asked her to clear out the garden. When the aunts ask for the dosage she used and Gillian tells them, the aunts nod, pleased. Exactly as they thought. If the aunts know anything, they know nightshade. Such a dosage wouldn't kill a fox terrier, let alone a six-foot-tall man.

"But he's dead," Gillian says, stunned to hear that her remedy could not have killed him. She turns to Sally. "I know he was dead."

"Definitely dead," Sally agrees.

"Not by your hand." Frances could not be more certain of it. "Not unless he was a chipmunk."

Gillian throws her arms around the aunts. Aunt Frances's announcement has filled her with hope. It's a silly and ridiculous thing to possess at her age, particularly on this awful night, but Gillian doesn't give a damn. Better late than never, that's the way she sees it.

"I'm innocent," Gillian cries.

Sally and the aunts exchange a look; they don't know about that.

"In this case," Gillian adds when she sees their expressions.

"What killed him?" Sally asks the aunts.

"It could have been anything." Jet shrugs.

"Alcohol," Kylie proposes. "Years of it."

"His heart," Antonia suggests.

Frances announces that they may as well stop this guessing game; they'll never know what killed him, but they're still left with a body in the yard, and that is why the aunts have brought along their recipe for getting rid of the many nasty things one can find in a garden—slugs or aphids, the bloody remains of a crow, torn apart by his rivals, or the sort of weeds that are so poisonous it's impossible to pull them by hand, even when wearing thick leather gloves. The aunts know precisely how much lye to add to the lime, much more than they include when they boil up their black soap, which is especially beneficial to a woman's skin if she washes with it every night. Bars of the aunts' soap, wrapped in clear cellophane, can be found in health-food stores in Cambridge and in several specialty shops along Newbury Street, and this has bought not only a new roof for their old house but a state-of-the-art septic system as well.

At home the aunts always use the big cast-iron cauldron, which has been in the kitchen since Maria Owens first built the house, but here Sally's largest pasta pot will have to do. They'll have to boil the ingredients for three and a half hours, so even though Kylie is always nervous that someone down at Del Vecchio's will recognize her voice as the one belonging to the wiseacre who had all those pizzas delivered to Mr. Frye's house a while back, she phones in and asks for two large pies to be delivered, one with anchovies, for the aunts, the other cheese and mushroom with extra sauce.

The mixture on the back burner starts to bubble, and by the time the delivery boy arrives, the sky has grown stormy and dark, although beneath the thick layers of clouds is a perfect white moon. The delivery boy knocks three times and hopes that Antonia Owens, whom he once sat next to in algebra, will appear. Instead, it's Aunt Frances who yanks open the door. The cuffs of her sleeves are smoky, from all the lye she's been measuring, and her eyes are as cold as iron.

"What?" she demands of the boy, who has already clutched the pizzas tightly to his chest simply because of the sight of her.

"Pizza delivery," he manages to say.

"This is your job?" Frances wants to know. "Delivering food?"

"That's right," the boy says. He thinks he can see Antonia in the house; there's somebody beautiful with red hair, at any rate. Frances is glaring at him. "That's right, ma'am," he amends.

Frances reaches into her skirt pocket for her change purse and counts out eighteen dollars and thirty-three cents, which she considers highway robbery.

"Well, if it's your job, don't expect a tip," she tells the boy.

"Hey, Josh," Antonia calls as she comes to collect the pizzas. She's wearing an old smock over her black T-shirt and leggings. Her hair has turned to ringlets in all this humidity and her pale skin looks creamy and cool. The delivery boy is unable to speak in her presence, although when he gets back to the restaurant he'll talk about her for a good hour before the kitchen staff tells him to shut up. Antonia laughs as she closes the door. She's gotten back some of whatever she'd lost. Attraction, she now understands, is a state of mind.

"Pizza," Antonia announces, and they all sit down to dinner in spite of the awful smell coming from the aunts' mixture boiling on the rear burner of the stove. The storm is rattling the windowpanes and the thunder is so near it can shake the ground. One big flash of lightning, and half the neighborhood has lost its electricity; in houses all along the street, people are searching for flashlights and hurricane candles, or just giving up and going to sleep.

"That's good luck," Aunt Jet says when their electricity goes as well. "We'll be the light in the darkness."

"Find a candle," Sally suggests.

Kylie gets a candle from the shelf near the sink. When she passes the stove she holds her nose closed with her fingers.

"Boy, does that stink," she says of the aunts' mixture.

"It's supposed to," Jet says, pleased.

"It always does," her sister agrees.

Kylie returns and places the candle in the center of the table, then lights it so they can go on with their supper, which is interrupted by the doorbell.

"It better not be that delivery boy back for more," Frances says now. "I'll give him a real piece of my mind."

"I'll get it." Gillian goes to the door and swings it open.

Ben Frye is on the porch, wearing a yellow rain slicker; he's holding a box of white hurricane candles and a lantern. Just seeing him makes a chill go down Gillian's spine. From the first, she's been figuring that Ben was taking his life in his hands each time he was with her. With her luck and her history, anything that could go wrong would. She'd been sure she'd bring disaster to whoever loved her, but that was back when she was a woman who killed her boyfriend in an Oldsmobile, now she's someone else. She leans out the front door and kisses Ben on the mouth. She kisses him in a way that proves that if he was ever thinking of getting out of this, he'd better stop thinking right now.

"Who invited you here?" Gillian says, but she has her arms around him; she's got that sugary smell anyone who gets too close to her can't help but notice.

"I was worried about you," Ben says. "They can call this thing a storm, but it's really a hurricane."

Tonight, Ben has left Buddy alone to bring the candles over, even though he knows how anxious thunder makes the rabbit. That's what happens when Ben wants to see Gillian, he has to go on and do it, no matter what the consequences. Still, he's so unused to being spontaneous that whenever he does something like this he has a slight ringing in his ears, not that he cares. When Ben returns to his house he's bound to find a telephone book shredded or the soles chewed off his favorite running shoes, but it's worth it to be with Gillian.

"Get out while the going's good," Gillian tells him. "My aunts are here from Massachusetts."

"Great," Ben says, and before Gillian can stop him he's inside the house. Gillian tugs at the sleeve of his rain slicker, but he's on his way to greet their guests. The aunts have serious business ahead of them; they'll flip their lids if Ben careens into the kitchen assuming he's about to meet two dear old ladies. They'll rise from their chairs and stomp their feet and turn their cold gray eyes in his direction.

"They arrived this afternoon and they're exhausted," Gillian says. "This is not a good idea. They don't like company. Plus, they're ancient."

Ben Frye pays no attention, and why should he? The aunts are Gillian's family, and that's all he needs to know. He lopes right into the kitchen, where Antonia and Kylie and Sally stop eating the minute they see him; quickly they turn to see the aunts' reaction. Ben doesn't catch on to their anxiety any more than he notices the fiery scent rising from the pot on the stove. He must presume the smell emanates from some special cleaning fluid or detergent, or perhaps some small creature, a baby squirrel or an old toad, has curled up to die underneath the back doorstep.

Ben goes over to the aunts, reaches into the sleeve of his rain slicker, and pulls out a bunch of roses. Aunt Jet accepts them with pleasure. "Lovely," she says.

Aunt Frances runs a petal between her thumb and forefinger to verify that the roses are real. They are, but that doesn't mean Frances is so easily impressed.

"Any more tricks?" she says in a voice that can turn a man's blood to ice.

Ben smiles his beautiful smile, the one that made Gillian weak in the knees from the start and that now reminds the aunts of the boys they once knew. He reaches behind Aunt Frances's head, and before they know it, he has pulled from thin air a chiffon scarf the color of sapphires, which he proudly presents.

"I couldn't accept this," Frances says, but her tone isn't quite so cool as before, and when no one's looking, she loops the scarf around her neck. The color is perfect for her; her eyes look like lake water, clear and gray-blue. Ben makes himself comfortable, grabs a piece of pizza, and begins to ask Jet about their trip down from Massachusetts. That's when Frances signals to Gillian to come close.

"Don't screw this one up," she tells her niece.

"I don't intend to," Gillian assures her.

Ben stays until eleven. He fixes instant chocolate pudding for dessert, then teaches Kylie and Antonia and Aunt Jet how to build a house of cards and how to make it fall down with a single puff of air.

"You got lucky this time," Sally tells her sister.

"You think it was luck?" Gillian grins.

"Yeah," Sally says.

"No way," Gillian says. "It took years of practice."

Just then the aunts both tilt their heads at the very same time and make a very little noise low in their throats, a kind of click so close to silence that anyone who wasn't listening carefully might mistake it for the faint call of a cricket or the sigh of a mouse beneath the floorboards.

"It's time," Aunt Frances says.

"We have family business to discuss," Jet tells Ben as she leads him to the door.

Aunt Jet's voice is always sweet, yet the tone isn't one someone would dare to disobey. Ben grabs his rain slicker and waves to Gillian.

"I'll call you in the morning," he declares. "I'll come over for breakfast."

"Don't screw this one up," Aunt Jet tells Gillian after she's closed the door behind Ben.

"I won't," Gillian assures her as well. She goes to the window and takes a look at the backyard. "It's awful tonight."

The wind is tearing shingles from the roofs, and every cat in the neighborhood has demanded to be let in or has taken refuge in a window well, to shiver and yowl.

"Maybe we should wait," Sally ventures.

"Bring the pot around back," Aunt Jet tells Kylie and Antonia.

The candle in the center of the table casts a circle of wavery light. Aunt Jet takes Gillian's hand in her own. "We have to see to this now. You don't put off dealing with a ghost."

"What do you mean, a ghost?" Gillian says. "We want to make certain the body stays buried."

"Fine," Aunt Frances says. "If that's how you want to look at it."

Gillian wishes she'd had a gin and bitters herself when the aunts did. Instead, she finishes the last of her cold coffee, which has been sitting in a cup on the counter since late afternoon. By tomorrow morning the creek behind the high school will be deep as a river; toads will have to scramble for higher ground; children won't think twice about diving into the warm, murky water, even if they're dressed in their Sunday clothes and wearing their best pair of shoes.

"Okay," Gillian says. She knows her aunts are talking about more than a body; it's the spirit of the man, that's what's haunting them. "Fine," she tells the aunts, and she swings open the back door.

Antonia and Kylie carry the pot out to the yard. The rain is quite near; they can taste it in the air. The aunts have already had the girls bring their suitcase over to the hedge of thorns. They stand close together, and when the wind rustles their skirts the fabric makes a moaning sound.

"This dissolves what once was flesh," Aunt Frances says. She signals to Gillian.

"Me?" Gillian takes a step backward, but there's no place to go. Sally is right behind her.

"Go on," Sally tells her.

Antonia and Kylie are holding on to the heavy pot; the wind is so strong that the hedge of thorns whips out, as if trying to cut them. The wasps' nests sway back and forth. It is definitely time.

"Oh, brother," Gillian whispers to Sally. "I don't know if I can do this."

Antonia's fingers are turning white with the effort she needs not to drop the pot. "This is really heavy," she says in a shaky voice.

"Believe me," Sally tells Gillian. "You can."

If there's one thing Sally is now certain of, it's how you can amaze yourself by the things you're willing to do. Those are her daughters, the girls she wanted to lead normal lives, and she's allowing them to stand over a pile of bones with a spaghetti pot filled mostly with lye. What has happened to her? What has snapped? Where is that logical woman, the one people could depend on, day after day? She can't stop thinking about Gary, no matter how hard she tries. She actually called the Hide-A-Way to ask if he'd checked out, and he has. He's gone, and here she is, thinking about him. Last night, she dreamed of the desert. She dreamed the aunts had sent her a cutting from an apple tree in their yard and that it bloomed without water. And in her dream the horses that ate apples from that tree ran faster than all the others, and any man who took a bite from a pie Sally fixed with these apples was bound to be hers, for life.

Sally and Gillian take the pot from the girls, although Gillian keeps her eyes closed as they turn it over and pour out the lye. The damp earth sizzles and is hot; as the mixture seeps deeper into the ground, a mist appears. It's the color of regret, it's the color of heartbreak, the gray of doves and early morning.

"Step back," the aunts tell them, for the earth has begun to bubble. The roots of the thornbushes are being dissolved by the mixture, as are stones and beetles, leather and bones. They can't move away fast enough, but still something is happening beneath Kylie's feet.

"Damn it," Sally cries.

Right under Kylie's feet the earth is shifting, falling in on itself, like a landslide, going down. Kylie feels it, she knows it, yet she freezes. She's falling into a hole, she's falling fast, but Antonia reaches to grab the back of her shirt and then pulls. She wrenches Kylie back so hard and so fast that Antonia can hear her own elbow pop.

The girls stand there, out of breath and terrified. Without realizing it, Gillian has latched on to Sally's arm; she's holding on so tight that Sally will have the marks of her sister's fingers on her skin for days afterward. Now they all step back. They do it quickly. They do it without having to be told. A thread of blood-red vapor is rising from the place where Jimmy's heart would have been, a small tornado of spite that disappears as it meets the air.

"That was him," Kylie says of the red vapor, and sure enough, they can smell beer and boot polish, they can feel the air grow as hot as embers in an ashtray. And then nothing. Nothing at all. Gillian can't be sure if she's crying, or if the rain has begun. "He's really gone," Kylie tells her.

But the aunts are taking no chances. They've carried along twenty blue stones inside their largest suitcase, stones Maria Owens had brought to the house on Magnolia Street more than two hundred years ago. Stones such as these form the path in the aunts' garden, but there were extras stored beside the potting shed, enough to fashion a small patio in the spot where the lilacs once grew. Now that the hedge of thorns is nothing but ashes, it's easy for the Owens women to put down a circle of stones. The patio won't be fancy, but it will be wide enough for a small wrought-iron table and four chairs. Some of the little girls in the neighborhood will beg to have tea parties out here, and when their mothers laugh and ask why this patio is better than their own, the little girls will insist the blue stones are lucky.

There's no such thing as luck, their mothers will tell them. Drink your orange juice, have your cakes, keep your party in your own backyard. And yet, every time their mothers' backs are turned, the little girls will drag their dolls and teddy bears and china tea sets over to the Owens patio. "Good luck," they'll whisper as they clink their cups together in a toast. "Good luck," they'll say as the stars rise above them in the sky.

Some people believe that every question has a logical answer; there's an order to everything, which is neat and based purely on empirical evidence. But really, what could it be but luck that the rain doesn't begin in earnest until their work is done. The Owens women have mud under their fingernails, and their arms ache from carting those heavy stones. Antonia and Kylie will sleep well tonight, as will the aunts, who have been plagued by insomnia from time to time. They will sleep the whole night through, even though lightning will strike in twelve separate places on Long Island before the storm is over. A house in East Meadow will be burned to the ground. A surfer in Long Beach who always longed for hurricanes and big waves will be fried. A maple tree that has grown in the Y field for three hundred years will be split in two and will have to be taken down with chain saws to make certain it won't collapse on top of the Little League team.

Only Sally and Gillian are awake to watch when the worst of the storm arrives. They're not worried by weather reports. Tomorrow there will be branches strewn across the lawn, and the trashcans will roll down the street, but the air will be fragrant and mild. They can have their breakfast and coffee outside, if they wish. They can listen for the song of sparrows who've come to beg for crumbs.

"The aunts didn't seem as disappointed as I thought they'd be," Gillian says. "In me."

The rain is coming down hard; it's washing those blue stones out in the yard clean as new.

"They'd be stupid if they were disappointed," Sally says. She loops her arm through her sister's. She thinks she may actually mean what she's just said. "And the aunts are definitely not stupid."

Tonight Sally and Gillian will concentrate on the rain, and tomorrow on the blue sky. They will do the best they can, but they will always be the girls they once were, dressed in their black coats, walking home through the fallen leaves to a house where no one could see into the windows, and no one could see out. At twilight they will always think of those women who would do anything for love. And in spite of everything, they will discover that this, above all others, is their favorite time of day. It's the hour when they remember everything the aunts taught them. It's the hour they're most grateful for.

ON the outskirts of the city the fields have turned red and the trees are all twisted and black. There is frost covering the meadows and smoke rising from the chimneys. In the park, in the very center of town, the swans rest their heads beneath their wings for comfort and warmth. The gardens have been put to bed, except for the one in the Owens yard. Cabbages are growing there, although some of them will be plucked from the rows this morning, and cooked with bouillon. Potatoes have already been dug up, boiled, and mashed, and are currently being flavored with salt, pepper, and sprigs from the rosemary that grows beside the gate. The willowware serving bowl has been rinsed clean and is drying on the rack.

"You're using too much pepper," Gillian tells her sister.

"I think I can manage to make mashed potatoes." Sally has fixed them at every Thanksgiving dinner she's cooked since she first left the aunts' house. She is completely sure of what she's doing, even though the kitchen utensils are old-fashioned and a bit rusty. But of course, since Gillian is such a changed woman she gives advice freely, even when she doesn't know what she's talking about.

"I know about pepper," Gillian insists. "That's too much."

"Well, I know potatoes," Sally says, and as far as she's concerned, that had better be that, especially if they want to serve dinner at three.

They arrived late last night; Ben and Gillian are staying in the attic, Kylie and Antonia are sharing what used to be a sitting room, and Sally is in the chilly little alcove up near the back stairs on a fold-out cot. The heat's on the fritz, so they've dragged out all the old feather quilts and built a fire in every fireplace, and they've called the boiler man, Mr. Jenkins, to come repair whatever's wrong. Even though it's Thanksgiving morning and Mr. Jenkins doesn't want to leave the comfort of his easy chair, when Frances got on the phone with him they all knew he'd be there by noon.

The aunts keep complaining that too much fuss is being made, but they smile when Kylie and Antonia grab them and kiss their cheeks and tell them how much they love them and insist they always will. The aunts are advised that they mustn't be concerned that Scott Morrison is taking the bus up from Cambridge, since he'll bring a sleeping bag and will camp out on the living room floor; they'll barely even be aware of his presence, and that goes for the two roommates he's bringing along as well.

The only cat left is Magpie, who is so ancient he gets up only in order to get to his food bowl. The rest of the time he's curled onto a special silk cushion on a kitchen chair. One of Magpie's eyes doesn't open at all anymore, but his good eye is fixed on the turkey, which is cooling on an earthenware platter in the center of the wooden table. Buddy is being kept in the attic—Ben is there with him, feeding him the last of the carrots from the aunts' garden—since Magpie has been known to catch baby bunnies who cower between the rows of cabbage. He's been known to eat them whole.

"Don't even think about it," Gillian tells the cat when she sees him eyeing the turkey, but as soon as her back is turned,

Sally takes a bit of white meat, which she herself would never eat, and feeds old Magpie by hand.

The aunts usually have a broiled chicken delivered from the market on Thanksgiving Day. One year they made do with frozen turkey dinners, and another year they said to hell with the whole silly holiday and had a nice pot roast. They were thinking of doing up another roast this year when the girls all insisted on coming to visit for the holiday.

"Oh, let them cook," Jet tells her sister, who can't stand the clinking and clanking of pots and pans. "They're having fun."

Sally stands at the sink, rinsing off the potato masher, the very same one she used as a child when she insisted on making nutritious suppers. She can see through the window to the yard, where Antonia and Kylie are running back and forth, chasing away the squirrels. Antonia wears one of Scott Morrison's old sweaters, which she has dyed black, and it's so big that when she waves her arms at the squirrels she looks as if she had long woolen hands. Kylie is laughing so hard she has to sit down on the ground. She points to one squirrel who refuses to move, a mean granddaddy who's screaming at Antonia, since he considers this to be his garden; the cabbages they've been gathering he's been watching all summer and fall.

"Those girls are pretty cute," Gillian says when she comes to stand beside Sally. She meant to argue some more about the pepper, but she drops the subject when she sees the look on her sister's face.

"They're all grown up," Sally says in her matter-of-fact voice.

"Yeah, right," Gillian sputters. The girls are chasing the granddaddy squirrel around in a circle. They shriek and throw their arms around each other when he suddenly jumps onto the garden gate and glares down at them. "They look real mature."

In the beginning of October, Gillian finally received word from the attorney general's office in Tucson. For more than two months the sisters had been waiting to see what Gary would do with the information Sally had given him; they'd been moody and distant from everyone except each other. Then, at last, a letter came, registered mail, from someone named Arno Williams. James Hawkins, he wrote, was dead. The body had been found out in the desert, where he must have been holed up for months, and in some kind of drunken stupor he'd rolled into his campfire and been burned beyond recognition. The only way they'd been able to identify him after he'd been brought down to the morgue was through his silver ring, which had melted somewhat and which was now being sent to Gillian, along with a certified check for eight hundred dollars from the sale of the Oldsmobile they'd impounded, since Jimmy had listed her as his only next of kin down at the Department of Motor Vehicles, which, in a way, was more or less the truth.

"Gary Hallet," Gillian said right away. "He slipped that ring to some dead guy who couldn't be identified. You know what this means, don't you?"

"He just wanted to see that justice was done, and it has been."

"He's completely hooked." Gillian couldn't seem to let this go. "And so are you."

"Will you please shut up?" Sally had said.

She refused to think about Gary. She really did. She rubbed at the center of her chest with two fingers, then grabbed her left wrist between the thumb and forefinger of her right hand to check her pulse rate. She didn't care what Gillian said; something was definitely wrong with her. Her heart did actual flip-flops; it beat too fast and then too slow, and if that didn't mean she had some sort of condition, she didn't know what did.

Gillian shook her head and groaned; that's how pathetic Sally had looked. "You really don't know. That heart-attack thing you've been having? It's love," she crowed. "That's what it feels like."

"You're nuts," Sally had said. "Don't think you know everything, because let me tell you, you don't."

But there was one thing Gillian did know for sure, and that was why, the very next Saturday, she and Ben Frye got married. It was a small ceremony at the town hall, and they didn't exchange wedding rings, but they kissed for so long at the counter in the hall of records that they were asked to leave. Being married feels different this time to Gillian.

"Fourth time's the charm," she says to people who ask her what the secret of a happy marriage is, but that's not the way she feels about it. She knows now that when you don't lose yourself in the bargain, you find you have double the love you started with, and that's one recipe that can't be tampered with.

Sally goes to the refrigerator for some milk to add to the mashed potatoes, although she's sure Gillian will tell her to add water instead, since she's such a know-it-all lately. Sally has to push several covered dishes around and as she does a lid falls off a shallow pot.

"Look here," she calls to Gillian. "They're still at it."

In the pot is the heart of a dove, pierced by seven pins.

Gillian comes to stand beside her sister. "Somebody's getting spelled, that's for sure."

Sally carefully puts the lid back in place. "I wonder what ever happened to her."

Gillian knows she's talking about the drugstore girl. "I used to think about her whenever things went wrong," Gillian admits. "I wanted to write to her, to let her know I was sorry I said all those things to her that day."

"She probably jumped out a window," Sally guesses. "Or she drowned herself in the bathtub."

"Let's go find out," Gillian says. She puts the turkey on top of the refrigerator, where Magpie can't reach it, and quickly shoves the mashed potatoes in the oven to keep them warm, along with a pan of chestnut stuffing.

"No," Sally says, "we're too old to snoop." But she lets herself be pulled along, first to the coat closet, where they each grab an old parka, and then out the front door.

They hurry down Magnolia Street and turn onto Peabody. They pass the park, and the town green, where lightning always strikes, and head straight for the drugstore. They pass several closed shops—the butcher, and the baker, and the dry cleaner's.

"It's going to be closed," Sally says.

"No way," Gillian tells her.

But when they get there, the drugstore is dark. They stare through the window at the rows of shampoos, at the rack of magazines, at the counter where they drank so many vanilla Cokes. Everything in town is closed today, but as they turn to go they see Mr. Watts, whose family has owned the drugstore forever and who lives in the apartment above. He's following his wife and carrying the two sweet potato pies they're taking to their daughter's over in Marblehead.

"The Owens girls," he says when he spies Sally and Gillian.

"Check." Gillian grins.

"You're closed today," Sally says. They trail Mr. Watts, though his wife is waiting at the car, signaling for him to hurry. "What happened to that girl? The one who stopped talking?"

"Irene?" he says. "She's in Florida. She moved there about a week after her husband died last spring. I think I heard she's already remarried."

"Are you sure we're talking about the same person?" Sally asks.

"Irene," Mr. Watts assures them. "She's got a coffee shop down in Highland Beach."

Gillian and Sally run all the way home. They're laughing as they run, so they have to stop every now and then to catch their breath. The sky is gray, the air is raw, yet it doesn't bother them in the least. All the same, when they reach the black gate, Sally suddenly stops.

"What?" Gillian says.

It can't be what Sally thinks. What she thinks she sees is Gary Hallet out in the garden, crouching down, digging at the cabbages, and that just cannot be.

"Well, look who's here," Gillian says, pleased.

"They did it," Sally says. "With the dove's heart."

As soon as he sees Sally, Gary stands, a scarecrow in a black coat who doesn't know whether or not he should wave.

"They did not," Gillian says to Sally. "They didn't have anything to do with it."

But Sally doesn't care if Gillian phoned Gary last week and

asked what on earth he was waiting for. It doesn't matter if he's had the aunts' address folded into his coat pocket ever since that phone call. By the time she runs down the bluestone path, it doesn't make a bit of difference what people think or what they believe. There are some things, after all, that Sally Owens knows for certain: Always throw spilled salt over your left shoulder. Keep rosemary by your garden gate. Add pepper to your mashed potatoes. Plant roses and lavender, for luck. Fall in love whenever you can.

ABOUT THE AUTHOR

ALICE HOFFMAN is the author of more than thirty works of fiction, including *The World That We Knew, The Rules of Magic, Practical Magic, The Marriage of Opposites, The Red Garden*, the Oprah's Book Club selection *Here on Earth, The Museum of Extraordinary Things*, and *The Dovekeepers*. She lives near Boston.